Also by Philip Ross
published by Tor Books

Blue Heron

Choice of Evils

A Good Death

Hovey's Deception

The Kreuzeck Coordinates

Talley's Truth

True Lies

PHILIP ROSS
WHITE FLOWER

TOR

A TOM DOHERTY ASSOCIATES BOOK
NEW YORK

"Stopping by Woods on a Snowy Evening" from *The Poetry of Robert Frost*, edited by Edward Connery Lathem, copyright 1923 by Robert Frost. Reprinted by permission of Henry Holt and Company, Inc.

This is a work of fiction. All the characters and events portrayed in this book are fictitious, and any resemblance to real people or events is purely coincidental.

WHITE FLOWER

A TOR BOOK
Published by Tom Doherty Associates, Inc.
49 West 24 Street
New York, NY 10010

Library of Congress Cataloging-in-Publication Data
Ross, Philip
    White flower / Philip Ross.—1st ed.
        p.   cm.
    "A Tom Doherty Associates book."
    ISBN 0-312-93143-3 : $16.95
    I. Title.
    PS3568.O8439W47   1989
    813'.54—dc19   88-29166

First edition: February 1989
0   9   8   7   6   5   4   3   2   1

With thanks to Lars for technical help and for all his other gifts of friendship.

CHAPTER 1

Marley paused where the roads diverged, to take his bearing. To his left, at the height of a short, steep rise, the meeting house of what a plaque proclaimed to be The First Religious Society in Carlisle stood foursquare, clear-shaped, and sharp. Its clapboards repeated, "straight and narrow," tier upon tier. White with certainty, it raised an admonishment of steeple against the February sky's mottled-gray equivocation.

A Mercedes sedan came toward him on the road to his right, up to the stop sign. It had been meant to be maroon and elegant. Marley's Subaru was supposed to be silver and sleek. Splashed and spattered, encrusted with slush and sand, salt-rimed, halted there between the chunky heaps of snow plowed to the sides of the roads, the cars looked like hulks that had been locked in a frozen sea for decades.

When Marley didn't move, the other driver pulled through the intersection and passed him. Then Marley went on his way, along the numbered route for half a mile, turning right onto a dirt road. He crawled in first gear, jolting, trying to keep from bottoming, over the ice-caked surface. On either side black tree trunks stood as bars between him and the nondescript fields that—not under cultivation nor as yet developed into house lots—had been let go to barren scrub and old snow. He came at last to the drive where an oval sign hanging out from a tree said, "Detweiller," and turned.

Since the Detweillers were his friends, Marley had always lied to them, pretending to like their house. Redwood siding, a plan that wasn't based on right angles and well-defined rooms, a hodgepodge of pitches to the roofs—that sort of thing might be well and good in California, but Marley always felt that Russ and Joanna had done something . . . improper . . . in bringing the style with them to New England.

He pulled up beside Joanna's Volvo wagon, which had been left outside the garage. Through the windows in the garage doors he could see Russ's red Porsche. He went to the family entrance, the glass door into the passageway between garage and house. Joanna was already there. She opened the door for him.

"Hello, James. How are you?" Bright smile, bright eyes. Her eyes were too bright (Marley saw that instantly). The tears were right there, ready, glittering like the icicles at either side of the door. But she looked good. The small, pointed collar of her mauve silk blouse was turned up at her neck, perking above a variegated blue and purple coarse-knit sweater; blue jeans. Everything casual, but color-coordinated, of course. The jeans old, not the skintight stretch kind—nothing so flagrant—but tight enough to show the good shape of her belly and bottom and thighs. Her auburn hair was short and swept back, that mannish cut that can emphasize so simply but effectively that the wearer is a good-looking woman.

Yes, Joanna was looking good, Marley thought; she was looking god-awful. Had she put those obvious smudges on her cheekbones, drawn black rings around her eyelids, held her orange lipstick in her fist like a child and smeared half the tube of it back and forth across her mouth without realizing what she was doing? Had she meant to hide behind her makeup, or had she used only the usual amount: the tightness, the white waxiness of her skin making it seem slathered on?

"I'm fine, Joanna." Marley put his hand over hers and held it tightly. "How are *you*?"

Her tears welled, but she forced her smile wider. "I'm fine, James." She tried to look him in the eye to prove it; couldn't; tried again; gave it up and turned away, freeing her hand. "Come on into the house."

"Right." Marley looked for a peg for his sheepskin coat.

"Just put it over something else," Joanna said.

Pegs projected from the wall at different levels so family members of all sizes could reach them and hang up their own clothes. On the upper row were Joanna's and Russ's— among them the sheepskin coat that Russ had bought after seeing Marley's—and a stocking cap and muffler that must be thirteen-year-old Timothy's. Marley hung his coat over that one.

"Can I get you a drink, James?"

"No, thanks."

"Please. I know it's only two o'clock in the afternoon, but I'd like one, and I'm not letting myself drink alone. One carefully measured martini before supper while the kids and I are setting the table. But I would like one now. It does help."

"Okay, Joanna. A small one. Thanks."

"Scotch and soda, no ice."

"Right."

Joanna crossed to the counter that separated the "living area" from the "kitchen space." She took bottles and glasses from a cabinet in its face, put them on the counter. "Here, help yourself. My father always used to say, 'It's a mean man pours another man's whiskey.'"

"Thank you." Marley poured three-eighths of an inch of whiskey into one of the Waterford glasses.

Joanna went to the refrigerator with her glass, for ice. She returned, bringing a bottle of soda water for Marley. "The kids are being very good," she said. "It used to be a rotating assignment for them to help me with last-minute things and the table. The other two would be in their rooms watching TV until I called them to eat. Now they all help; or just sit around and tell me about school." She measured vodka carefully into a one-ounce glass, turned it into the other one. There was no vermouth anywhere in sight. "I have my martini, they have fruit juice. We keep close together. I guess it must reassure us that we're still a family . . . It's very nice. I'm going to miss them—February break starts tomorrow: They're all going away. Tim's been invited to go up to Vermont tonight with a friend, skiing; and I'm sending the girls to my folks tomorrow. It'll be good for them to be away." She took a quick sip of her drink.

Marley raised his glass then sipped.

"I'm sorry," she said, "I didn't say 'Cheers' first. Cheers." She held out her glass, and after an instant Marley clinked his to it.

"Cheers, Joanna."

"Why not?" she asked. "Life goes on, doesn't it?"

Coming around the counter, she said, "Let's sit down." She set off toward the distant end of the living room where a fire burned in an open-doored Vermont Castings woodstove. The flames failed to make the room cheery. Only people could do that. Joanna had chosen neutral colors— beige, off-white, black, straw, and mud—to be background for the flash and dash of the people who would come to all the parties she and Russ had imagined having. And perhaps she'd seen the room as it would have looked, vibrant with California sunshine; it didn't feel so severe, Marley knew, in the summer. Now the dull sky and dingy snow outside seemed not to be giving light, but to be drawing it through the tall windows and out of the house like heat.

A couch faced the fire, a bentwood rocker sat at one side, an Eames chair on the other. Joanna went to the rocker. Marley went around the other side, passing the chair, and sat on the couch.

"The kids really are giving me a lot of support," she said; and then after a moment, "You really should adopt Melissa, and have her live with you all the time, James. It'd be the best thing in the world for you."

"Oh, I don't think so, Joanna. It wouldn't be right for either of us—even if her uncle would agree, which I'm sure he wouldn't. She comes and stays with me most school holidays—she'll be home next week. But given the kind of work I do . . . the traveling . . . If she really lived with me she'd be alone most of the time."

"Not if you married Elaine."

"Joanna, I've told you . . ."

"Well, I think you do love her, even if you're not *in* love. I mean, you have her come stay in your house whenever Melissa's there; you date her when you're in Boston: Obviously you like her."

"She's a friend. She is a wonderful person, and I do like her—very much. But it's just platonic."

"Oh, I know that: watching you two do the minuet around each other . . . But it doesn't have to be; if you two actually ever *touched* each other, I'll bet the sparks would light up the sky for miles around."

"Elaine . . . Elaine is not that kind of woman."

"What kind of woman?"

"She's not . . ."

"What?"

"All right—she's just not very *sexy*."

"You mean she doesn't hang it out."

"I mean I don't think she . . . Look, Joanna, this isn't what I came here to talk about, okay?"

Sitting tipped forward in her rocker, Joanna seemed for another moment to be locked on target unevadably. But then she must have remembered what Marley *had* come about.

"Yes." She sat back. "That's right. Thank you for coming, James."

"I would have anyway; but since I was going to be passing through Boston . . ."

"You could have gone directly. You didn't have to get off the interstate and drive over all these back roads."

"Easy driving—the roads are clear."

"It was nice of you to come."

Marley shrugged and sipped his drink.

"Don't shrug it off." Joanna rocked forward again, the ice clinking in her glass. "It was a nice thing to do. You're a nice man, James. I may be particularly prejudiced at the moment, but I think a nice man nowadays is hard to find. It's quite an accomplishment to be one, and you ought to let yourself glory in it. And you should let me thank you. I'm very grateful for kindnesses these days." She let herself rock back again. She stared at her glass, holding it with both hands, as if by looking hard enough she'd discover it wasn't already half empty. "For expressions of affection." A tear ran from each eye. After a moment she wiped them with the back of one hand.

"Are you all right?"

"Oh, yes. They're right there, all the time. Sometimes they just start flowing, but it doesn't matter. Things get a little blurry, but it doesn't matter. I'm fine. Just fine." She took a drink, returned the glass to her lap. "Just fine."

"Everything is under control," she said, emphasizing every syllable. "Up in the morning; kids off to school—lunches made, teeth brushed. Plan the menu. Go to the office, make sure the crew are all at their stations, check correspondence. Shop on the way home. Clean the house—this house has never been so clean. No house has ever been so clean. Pay bills. Make phone calls, write letters. I've got a list—naturally, I would make a list. People who have to be told, by category. Close friends who get all the gory details. Not so close friends who get just the fact. Russ's business friends, customers—"

Abruptly, Joanna rocked forward again. "Do you know that son of a bitch didn't tell *anyone*! Not Bill Wright, his assistant; none of the people in his office . . . our secretary. Do you know, he left it for *me*! *I* had to call *his* secretary. I had to call the principal at the high school—Russ was head of a PTA committee that was advising on software for the remedial reading program—*I* had to call them and tell them Russ wouldn't be fulfilling his commitments, because he'd walked out on me with a hot-twat China doll who obviously must give him satisfactions he couldn't get at home!

"I hope she is hot! I hope she burns his goddamned prick right off!"

Marley sat very still, looking down at his glass.

Joanna sank back again. "I'm sorry," she said. She drank. She wiped her cheeks with the back of her hand again. "I guess I am just a little upset." Then cheerily, singing it, "But fine!" and, separating the words, "Just fine."

Marley drank. "I'm glad to hear it, Joanna," he said then. "But if—just maybe—there are any moments when you're not, and you need some help, somebody to talk to, I hope you'll let me know. How about practical matters? Money?"

"That really is fine. Russ says he's giving me the house, the cars, half the savings account—he withdrew his half be-

fore he left. Our investment accounts require both sig-
natures. He says he'll give me half, but we'll deal with it
officially in the settlement. Child support, alimony, income
from the business—we'll deal with them all in the settlement. He says he intends to be generous. Peach of a guy,
isn't he?"

"You're in touch with him."

"No. I'm in touch with a lawyer, who's going to be in
touch with Russ's—assuming Russ ever gets his face out of
Lotus Blossom's crotch long enough to call one. He left me
a letter. You want to see it?"

Joanna was out of her chair before Marley nodded.
While she trekked to a rolltop desk and back he stared at
the fire.

"Here," she said, handing a folded paper to him over the
back of the couch.

Marley opened the letter, looked up at Joanna.

"That's right," she said, moving toward the end of the
couch. "Printout. He wrote it on his processor, printed it
out. At least he set the printer for near-letter-quality instead of draft mode."

Marley began to read the letter to himself, but Joanna
recited for him. "'Dear Joanna, I'm leaving you.' Right-to-
the-point Russell. Made a fortune with that mind. 'I'm
sorry.' A man of feeling, too, of course."

Marley looked up at her. She turned away. She stood at
the end of the couch for a moment. She clinked the ice in
her glass. She sat in the rocker again, sipped her drink.
Marley went back to the letter. He finished reading, laid it
to one side. "Did you have any idea this was going to happen?"

"No . . . Well, I suspected. Not that he would leave
me—I never imagined he'd do that. I suspected he was
having an affair. He'd met this girl—there was a software
trade show in Boston back at the beginning of January. We

were at a party. I saw him talking with this girl. She was oriental. There were a lot of oriental people there: Japanese, Chinese—from Hong Kong, Singapore, and American-Chinese, too, of course. Russ said the girl was Bill Wright's girlfriend—Bill is Russ's assistant. Bill wasn't with them when I saw them talking. After a while, after I'd vice-presidented up to everybody I knew, or who I thought knowing might do us some good, I looked around for him, and he was still talking to little Miss Moon-of-my-delight. So I went over, and that was when he introduced her as Bill's girlfriend. Only Bill still wasn't anywhere around. I mean, he was probably in the room. I know he was at the party. But he seemed to be finding people more interesting to be with than Jasmineflower. Lily. Her name really is Lily.

"Which is more than Russ had been able to do. Those parties are absolutely awful, James. I don't know if you've ever been to one, but as a thing to do for fun they come in behind a two-hour meeting of the town library committee. The only point of them is to make contacts, pick up gossip, for business. Well, the only picking up that Russ seemed to be doing was this obvious . . . what do they call them? Joy-joy girl? In a skintight jade-green Chinese dress slit up the side to her hipbone . . . She's young enough to be his daughter, James! She . . ."

Joanna's voice faltered, but her body held its tension. She sat on the edge of her chair, tipped forward, leaning, her arm stretched toward him. Then she looked at the glass in her hand, seemed to realize she'd finished her drink. She shook the ice in the glass, peering into it as if to make sure, then got up, going around behind the chair and facing the kitchen as though thinking of pouring another. She stopped, turned back to Marley.

"Oh, I understand about these things, James. Russ was forty-three last November. It's time for his midlife crisis."

Turning away from Marley, she went to put the glass down on a little table standing against the wall beyond her chair. She spoke again looking down at it. "And the girl is very attractive. Shiny, straight black hair halfway down to her waist. That ivory-gold complexion. The big, heavy-lidded, seductive, slanty eyes—the whole exotic, love slave, harem girl dream."

She looked up and into an oval mirror on the wall above the table. "And I'll be forty next month." With fingertips she touched the outer corner of her eye.

Marley said, "Good. That's the age at which a woman starts to become really interesting."

Joanna twisted just her head to look at him. After a moment she said, "What a lovely man you are, James." After another, "It's very kind of you to say that to try to make me feel better."

"I hope it does make you feel better, Joanna; but I wasn't just saying it."

"No. I'm sure you weren't." Joanna continued to look at Marley, then turned back to the mirror for an equal time.

"I'm going to be seeing him," Marley said.

"You are?"

"Yes. That's why I'm going through Boston. Logan. I . . . Russ is my friend, too. I don't like this—what he's done. But I want to see him—that's *why* I want to see him: to find out what the hell is going on with him."

"I think it's fairly obvious, James. Middle-aged men get tired of their wives, and run off—or at least have affairs—with pretty young girls all the time. I know of three right here in Carlisle within the past two years."

"It may be common, but I don't think it's required. And maybe this is just a fling—not that that would excuse it, but maybe Russ'll come to his senses . . . I don't know if you'd take him back; that's up to you. But for myself, I'd just like to talk to him, and try . . . And David wants me to go, too."

"David Cheyney? Ah, of course." Joanna sat back against the table, crossing her arms. "Russ did run out on Mr. Cheyney, too. I guess nobody gets away with that. What are you going to do, James? Tell Russ he has to keep on working for Mr. Cheyney or you'll break his arms? I mean, you are Mr. Cheyney's enforcer, aren't you?"

For a moment Marley examined his glass as if reading a message in the incisions. "When David called me he spent about the first ten minutes talking about you and the kids, and what an irresponsible and stupid asshole Russ is being. 'Asshole' wasn't David's word, of course. David really likes you—all of you: you, Russ, the kids: the family. I know you've only met him a couple times, but . . . if you ever want to make your kids *really* rich, just have them call David 'Uncle David' instead of 'Mr. Cheyney.' He'll put them in his will. As a matter of fact, I wouldn't be surprised if he's already done it. He called you, didn't he?"

"Yes. I'd put in a call to him—to his office. Russ left that for me, too."

"And he called you back, personally. Asked if you needed any help? Any money?"

"Yes."

"Okay. Well, sure, David is concerned about Russ's work. He's got a big stake—personal as well as financial—in the thing Russ is working on. Maybe more personal than financial. So of course he wants Russ to come back and finish it. And I'm supposed to try to get him to do that. But don't be cynical about David: He's sending me down there as much for your sake as for the program."

Joanna uncrossed her arms. "I'm sorry," she said. "I guess I'm not very trusting right now." She pushed herself away from the table. "When you talk to Mr. Cheyney again—you probably will before I do—thank him for his concern. Tell him I'm very grateful. I am.

"I hope you're successful in getting Russ back to work," she said, coming over to her chair. She paused behind it, her hand on its back, looking at Marley. Then her glance shifted to the Eames chair. "But as far as taking him back goes . . ." She turned, lifting her hand, walking around behind the couch. Her empty chair rocked slightly. "I don't know. For the sake of the kids . . . maybe . . . I don't know."

She drifted on, past Marley, and then to a stop before one of the floor-to-ceiling windows. "As you may have noticed, James, I'm angry. I'm very angry." Her voice was like the black bones of the trees raised against the grimy sky. Colorless light through the window coated her with a thin layer of ice. She crossed her arms and clutched her shoulders.

"God, I hate this place. The cold . . . I'm always cold. The darkness. The snow." She turned slightly, to look over her shoulder at Marley, but didn't move toward him or the small comfort of the fire.

"The first year, we thought the snow was going to be so much fun. Bought snowsuits for Meagan and Page, ski outfits for Russ and Tim and me. Cross-country skis—the whole outfit. Thought that was going to be such fun. Sleds. None of the kids had ever been sledding. Oh, we were going to be just like a postcard, just like a calendar picture, having fun in the snow in New England. Only what you never think about when you see those pictures, what we never thought about, is that snow is cold; so goddamned cold! You put on all those clothes—you can't just walk out the door, you have to allow fifteen minutes to get dressed, dress the kids, put on all those clothes so you're *encased* . . . I hate clothes I can't move in! And then you go out, and you're cold anyway. Your face is cold, your nose is cold; the kids have runny noses. And snow is wet. And even with snowsuits and those boots your feet get wet. The kids' feet are always wet. Everybody has colds. I hate it!"

She spun completely to confront Marley. "Oh, I know you like it. The cold, the winter. You think it builds character. You old New England Yankee Puritans. Well, I don't want my character built. I want to be where winter means you have to wear a pullover on your way to play tennis!"

Joanna turned to the window again. "Oh, God damn him! God damn that son of a bitch! Dragging me here, and then leaving me in this . . . this *arctic wasteland* because he . . . with the kids and all the responsibility—because he wants to run away to a tropical island . . . because he doesn't want . . . because he's got the hots for . . . because I'm getting old, and I don't turn him on anymore, and . . ." She broke. Hands to her face she leaned—almost toppled—forward, her forehead against the cold windowpane, sobbing.

Marley came to her, stood behind her, putting his hands on her shoulders. With gentle pressure he tried to pull her away from the window. "Joanna, Joanna . . ."

Joanna twisted, coming to him, her face buried against his chest. Marley enclosed her within his arms. "There, there," he said. He tried to think of something more to say. "There, there."

She shifted position slightly, and he started to open his embrace. "Don't," she said. "Please. Could I just stand here for a minute, James? Would you just"—her voice broke—"hold me?"

Marley clasped her again, and she began to cry, shaking, with her face to his shoulder. Quickly, he fished out a handkerchief and fumbled it into her hands. Then he held her until enough of her pain had been cried out so that she could be quiet again.

"Thank you," she said at last, but didn't move away from him. "Could we stay this way for another minute?"

"Sure. Are you okay now?"

"Better. As my grandmother used to say, 'Not bad, for an old lady.'"

"Joanna, you're not an old lady. I'm not an old man, and I'm nearly ten years older than you, so you can't be an old lady."

"Women get older sooner than men."

"I don't know if that's true; but in your case, you don't have to worry for quite a while. You're a very attractive woman."

"Thank you. I needed that." She had been cuddled against him, her hands clutching each other under her chin. Shifting, she put her arms around him. "It's nice to be held."

"Yes."

She opened her fists, pressing her palms against his back. Then she slid one hand up until her fingertips touched the back of his neck. Marley stiffened.

Joanna twisted and broke away from him. "I'm sorry," she said softly, not looking at him. She walked back toward the couch.

"Joanna . . ."

"It's all right. I'm sorry, James. I'm sorry."

"You don't have to be . . . Joanna, you *are* attractive, and . . ."

"But I don't turn you on. I understand. Yes, I understand very well."

"Joanna, you do turn me on. As close as you were standing . . . you should know that. You're a beautiful, desirable, sexy woman. But we're *friends*. We like each other, but we're not going to—"

"I wasn't asking you to marry me, James. Adopt my kids. I was just— I wasn't asking you for anything, consciously. I wasn't thinking. I just must have wanted affection and reassurance. And you were there. And we *are* friends. And I'm sorry. If I had been thinking, I'd have known you're much too nice a man ever to take advantage of a woman's emotional distress and go to bed with her, even if going to bed with somebody might be the thing that would do her the most good at the moment."

Joanna had reached the couch and wheeled to face Marley. She stood with her head up, staring him in the eye. He gestured vaguely with both hands.

"Oh, James, you are a dear man." She laughed ruefully. "Now you're trying to decide whether you ought to go to bed with me out of friendship. Well, don't do me any favors. And the moment's passed, anyway."

"No, that's not what I was doing, Joanna. What I was doing was feeling—I'm not going to say 'sorry' for you. Feeling bad, hurting, for you. And hoping I can get across to that stupid idiot, your husband, what he's losing here. And get him back before it's too late for him."

"It may be too late already."

"Is it?"

"I told you, I don't know. Fifteen years . . . After fifteen years of living with somebody, maybe you don't know anymore whether it's love or just habit. I thought it was love. I thought I loved him. Right now I'm not feeling much love for him.

"But you think I should take him back—if he'll come back—don't you? That's the way it should be. He should come back to his faithful wife who's waiting for him faithfully. You want me to wait for him, because that's the right thing for me to do; and he should come back because that's the right thing for him. And the best thing for him. After all, he is your friend, too. And you're much too honorable a man to fuck a friend's wife, aren't you?"

Marley met her glare for a moment. Then he put his hands in his pockets and shrugged. "I guess so. I never thought of it as a fault."

She sighed a deep, long sigh, and turned from him. "I'm sorry. I'm really sorry for all of this."

"I am, too. For all of it. But if you mean this last part . . . I think it's pretty understandable, and I don't think we should worry much about it."

She nodded without speaking. Then she said, "Thank you. Thank you for coming. I think it's made me feel . . . despite . . . I think it's made me feel better. But I think I'd like you to go now. I'm sorry, I invited you for supper, but . . . We *won't* worry much about 'this last part,' but I think it would be better if you didn't stay just now. Another time."

"Certainly. I'll call you as soon as I get back from Montserrat."

"Come by, if you'd like. Come for supper then. Please."

"I will."

Joanna started toward Marley, and he took a step to meet her. Putting one hand on his arm, she leaned up and kissed him lightly on the cheek. He gripped her upper arms and squeezed. "Hang on, kid."

"I will. Thank you."

Marley's car had cooled, so he put on his sheepskin coat before driving away. Since the coat had been hanging in the unheated vestibule it was cold, too.

The first flakes of an approaching snowstorm began to drift down sullenly. They were wet, and clung to his windshield. He passed a flat expanse of white without bushes. It must have been a bog, now snow-covered. Dead cattail stalks stuck up out of it, their color a desiccated yellow, like the spears of an army that had been sucked down and frozen over. A little farther on, a lone crow flew toward him, its wing feathers spread, ragged-looking, as it rowed slowly across the sky.

CHAPTER 2

Even from a distance the island seemed feminine, rising from the sea violet and haze-veiled, mysterious with possibilities of danger, of delight. As the airplane approached the mountains their single silhouette resolved into roundnesses and ridges, separate ranges; yet the more they seemed to be revealed, the more secrets they hid on the far sides of their slopes, in their valleys. Closer still, the planes and points of the island's skeleton were clear; yet lush vegetation covered them like the fur of a lithe but fat-layered feline. An unkempt fur: thick and deep-textured forest, scrubby brush, scars of roads, patches where fields had been scraped, scraggly palm groves. Lush vegetation, but wild even in the cultivated places, wanton.

Marley had removed his sweater and put it into his carry-on during the brief stopover at San Juan; he'd packed away his windbreaker while changing at Antigua from the jet to the island-hopper. But because of the air-conditioning on the jet and the breeze sweeping the Antigua airport, he hadn't felt the full envelopment of tropical air until he reached Montserrat. Coming down the two steps from the little plane was like sinking into a warm bath.

Fewer than twenty people had come to the island with him. They all lined up to have their papers checked by the immigration officer. For the first time in years, Marley found himself in an airport that had a sense of place. The small room opened fully toward the landing strip and the sea beyond. Its floor was cement, its walls some cheap sheathing with chipping paint. Hand-drawn advertisements for local restaurants were taped to them.

"You're on holiday?" an officer asked Marley, looking at his passport and the brief form he'd filled out on the plane.

"That's right. I'm visiting a friend."

"And how long will you be with us?" The man spoke with the lilting rhythm of Caribbean English.

"Just overnight."

"Sorry you can't be here longer. Do enjoy your visit on Montserrat." He gave Marley the passport and a wide smile as though welcoming a personal friend.

"Anything to declare?" a second man asked when Marley lifted his carry-on onto the table. "Any cigarettes, spirits? Any gifts?"

"Nothing." Marley smiled, as he always did when going through customs.

The man smiled back, as no other customs official Marley'd met had ever done. "Have a pleasant stay on Montserrat," he said, and with no more ado nodded Marley on through a doorway into the airport's main room.

"James! Hey, good to see you, man! How are you?" Russ Detweiller seized Marley's hand and pumped his arm. There was no doubt about the sincerity of his greeting— Russ could never pretend even to like a Christmas necktie—and for a moment Marley feared that under the influ-

ence of the tropic air he might revert to California behavior
and actually hug another man in an excess of good fellowship. Although he was wearing sandals, purple shorts,
and a red-and-yellow-splotched shirt, he seemed to have
retained enough sense of propriety to avoid that outrage, at
least. Or perhaps he was too embarrassed. He kept looking
up to meet Marley's eyes, then not meeting them. He
might have been blushing, but it was impossible to tell.

"I'm fine, Russ. And I guess you are, too: You're looking good, getting some sun." Russ's chubby legs, arms,
neck, and cherub cheeks were rose-pink. His nose and
brow (his "brow" extended well over the curve of his forehead, and back through the wispy tendrils of his peach-
colored hair) looked like raw veal.

"Can't help it, it's right up there all the time, every place
I go," Russ said, reaching for Marley's bag.

"It's okay. I've got it." Marley saw Russ's face change,
and thought of a pug-nosed dog told he can't go along for a
ride, and said, "Thanks, it's not heavy," smiling.

"Well, the car's just outside."

Russ asked about Marley's flight as they walked to the
car. Marley told him it had been fine.

"What was the weather like in Boston?"

"Miserable. Raw, windy. It snowed a little last night and
then stopped for a while; but the report said it was coming
back this morning as sleet." Marley paused at the car to
look around—out at a sea the sun's heat had flat-ironed
smooth, up at the green it had drawn out of the island's
rock.

"Yeah," Russ said.

"Yeah."

"You'll have to tell me some more about it, James.
We've only been here a week, but already I've forgotten
what it's like to be cold. I just, you know, can't imagine it."

"It's fading away from me, too. By the second."

"Come on. Let's get to the house. Get you a swim, and put you in a lounge chair by the pool with a planter's punch in your hand—we'll just delete your whole 'winter' file."

When they came to the end of the drive leading from the airport to the main road, Russ slowed, but ignored the stop sign. He could see clearly in both directions; no one was coming. Although the car had automatic transmission, he shifted manually from "drive" down to "2," pulling the wheel hard over to the right, powering them around the corner and away. He made a smooth shift into "drive" again, accelerating until they were up to forty-five. On the two-lane, slightly bumpy road, that speed felt fast. "I tried to get a stick shift," he said, "but all they had for rent were automatics. But even so, if you use it right, the Honda's a pretty snappy car." He had put on his silver-coated, aviator-frame sunglasses, so Marley couldn't see his eyes. From the casual, greased-steel tone he tried to give his tenor voice, though, they must have been squinted just like Jackie Icyxx's assaying an approaching chicane.

Marley moved a little to put himself squarely against the seat back, with both legs stretched out. Calmly, he laid his hand on the grip on the door beside him.

"Yes," he said, "seems to have more pickup than you really need for these roads."

"Yeah. I haven't found anyplace on the whole island I can open it up all the way and see what the limit might be. But on the other hand"—the road made a shallow "S" that Russ negotiated in a nearly straight line by drifting from one side to the other and back again—"you don't ever want to reach the limit, do you? I mean, if you're using everything there is, then you've got nothing to call up if you need more. Isn't that what you told me?"

"Right."

The road was rising steadily, the coast sweeping closer on the right; their lines would be one above the other just ahead at a bend to the left. Marley's fingers tightened on the hand-grip.

Russ roared up toward the corner. Marley sensed they weren't really going too fast to make the turn on a clean, dry road. He forced himself not to think about loose sand or pebbles.

Russ touched the brake, dropped into "2," steered and accelerated again, bringing them tightly around the bend as though they were tethered to its center with a steel cable.

"Did I do that all right, James?"

"Just fine."

"You think I hit the brake maybe just a fraction early?"

"Russ, why ask me? You felt it, it was a perfect turn."

Russ nodded twice, not taking his eyes from the road, accepting Marley's professional assessment professionally. "I might have gone into it just a hair faster; but I thought, 'Why?'"

"Right." Marley could see the road running straight for a distance, but there was another bend ahead. "You're right, Russ," he said in a philosophical tone. "Why take every curve at ten-tenths just because you can? Slow down and enjoy the view."

"You're absolutely right, James!" Russ may have taken Marley's meaning literally—he eased up on the accelerator—but he responded vehemently to the metaphorical sense. "That's exactly what I'm doing, why I'm here! I mean, I'd been working sixty-, eighty-hour weeks—I'd been working eighty-hour weeks for—Jesus!—fifteen years . . . For what? For my house? When was I ever in it, except to grab a meal and sleep? I could've gone to the Marriott—it's closer to my office, I wouldn't have had to drive as much—and gotten the same thing cheaper. My car? A Porsche turbo to drive seven miles back and forth to work? Half the way in third? My family? Who were they? Now I'll have a chance . . . After things settle down I'll bring the kids down here . . . vacations . . . really be able to spend some time—"

"Russ!" Marley broke in emphatically but without apparent alarm, gesturing at the car in the oncoming lane into which they'd drifted.

Russ swerved. "Sorry. I never could do two things at once."

"If you want to talk now . . ."

"No. I'm sorry. I know you didn't come down here just to grab some sun and surf, James. I know you've probably got some things you want to say; and *I've* got some things *I* want to say. But I would like to think it's a friendly visit, too, and I didn't mean to start . . . I'm sorry. We'll talk later, okay?"

"Sure. I think that'd be better." Marley glanced from side to side. "This certainly is a lovely place!" They had turned inland and were winding between lines of hills: those to the north, on their right, lower, open or with scrubby bushes; those to the south higher, lifting beyond cultivated fields to thick, dark rain forest. Wildflowers teemed along the ragged shoulders of the roadway. Sheep and goats grazed, tethered. As the car went by, some of them regarded it with the supercilious smiles and opaque eyes of those who know everything. There were cattle as well, here and there; and white egrets among them. "How did you find it?"

"Basically, research. You know me, James. Read all the guidebooks. Three travel agents. All said the same thing: not touristy, but developed enough so it's not 'primitive.' Friendly people—they really are, the blacks: smile and greet you, anybody you pass when you're walking. And the white people—that's the main tourist business, not really tourists at all: People have houses, stay all winter. A lot of British. You know, people with some real class."

"Have you made friends already?"

"Not yet. Just introduced ourselves, said hello, to the neighbors. But we will."

"Sounds great, Russ."

"It really is. Just shows you, James, you can still find unspoiled places if you take the trouble to look."

"You must have had this in mind for some time, then."

"Yeah. Since October. Even before the first time it snowed. We had that cold week—you remember? Last week in October? Didn't snow, just sat there like we were in a poured-concrete tunnel with mercury-vapor lamps. Dark and cold when I went to work, dark and cold when I came home. Still October, for God's sake! The whole fucking winter to go through—it's not bad enough winter doesn't get over until May in that ridiculous part of the world, it's got to start in October!" Russ shook his head, banishing the ghastly vision. Late afternoon: The sky near the horizon had become a translucent pearly blue; overhead was turquoise. Slanting sunlight pressed yellow like gold leaf onto the hillsides. Russ gazed through the windshield as though letting the view permeate his whole being.

"Naturally, I thought about L.A.—the contrast. But California didn't do it. I guess it wasn't just wanting to be warm. Anyway, I started fantasizing about tropical islands. And then I started doing some actual research. I had a couple places in mind—here, Nevis, or St. Kitts."

"Back last year," Marley said without any particular expression.

"Oh, yeah. This was building up for a long time, James." Then Russ said quickly, "Before I met Lily. I didn't meet her until about a month ago. This wasn't . . . I wasn't planning something . . . you know, like I was secretly planning to leave, and hiding it. It was just that when I did meet Lily . . . She knew about Montserrat, too. Has a friend who's been here, said she'd always wanted to come. So, everything just came together, like it was part of a plan not

that I was making but that was being made . . . Like it was
fate." Russ snapped an apprehensive glance at Marley.
"Do you believe in fate?"

Marley shrugged. "I think people have destinies. Their
character, or their will, makes them put themselves in certain situations: They *make* certain kinds of things happen.
But people can change, too—or at least modify what they
are, which changes the kinds of things that seem to *happen*
to them. There's no outside power that relieves anyone of
responsibility for his own life."

For several minutes they drove on in silence, Russ keeping his eyes on the road. They had turned south now, winding through the hills on the opposite side of the island from
the airport.

"You'll really like Lily," Russ said at last.

Marley wasn't sure whether that was a new topic for conversation or part of the old one. "I'm sure I will, Russ,
since you do."

"She's wonderful. She's so . . . loving. I don't mean only
sex . . . although—just to say it—she's fantastic. I mean,
she's like . . . just *loving*. I mean, Joanna . . . For example, Joanna—when I would come home for supper Joanna
would have it ready. One of the kids would've set the table.
Everything organized so there was nothing for me to do but
sit back in my chair by the fire, drink my martini—already
mixed and in the freezer, of course. I mean, great: What
could I complain about, right? I was out there in the salt
mines all day, bringing home the bread; that was my job.
When I got home, I should be pampered; that was her job.
Super. But, I mean, it was her *job*.

"I felt . . . Ten years ago I loved my work. I mean, it
wasn't *work*. And I sure wasn't getting any money for it. I
hoped I would, but I was doing it—twelve hours, fourteen
hours a day—because it was *fun*. Well, like I told you, it
got to be not fun anymore. It was a job. And taking care of

me, and the kids, and the house, was Joanna's job. Only
I'm not sure it ever was fun for her.

"I mean, when we got married, we were supposed to be
equal partners, you know? We both had jobs, took turns
doing the dishes and stuff at home. Then when Timmy happened, and then I started working on *Find-it* and we could
see it could make a pile for us, and we decided to have
Meagan and Page . . . Well, things worked out different
than we'd thought they would. But we were still equal partners; we just divided the labor differently. Do you see what
I mean? She wasn't doing all that because she wanted to,
for *me,* in a loving way. Do you see? Do you understand,
James?"

Russ had turned his head to Marley. Marley could see
himself in the mirror lenses as Russ must see him: atten-
tive, concerned, considering, judging, silent. He turned to
look out the windshield, feeling that at least one of them
ought to. "Russ . . ." he said, with a nod.

Russ looked and saw the three people who had been
walking along his side of the road and now were drawn
back on the narrow shoulder, staring with stereotypical ap-
prehension—white eyes wide in their black faces—at the
car bearing directly on them. He swerved, whishing past
them, giving them a wave. "Great people," he said. "Always nod hello or wave when you pass them."

Marley glanced over his shoulder and saw the people still
standing in the weeds at the side of the road, staring after
the car.

"I'm sorry," Russ said. "I got going again—talking."

"We'll have plenty of time for that."

"Yeah. You know, I really want to try to do something
for the people here. I'll only be able to employ a couple,
myself—after I start working again. But I've been trying to
think of something, some aspect of the software business
. . . or even hardware—I mean, like computer furniture:

printer stands, whatever. They really are fine people, but they need some industry . . . I really hope I can do something for them."

"I hope you can. But I hope if they do get some kind of industry here it doesn't spoil what they have now. This is gorgeous. And the climate! February! Does it get really hot in the summer?"

"They tell me it gets hotter than now, but never unbearable—there's always a breeze."

"Rainy season?"

"I guess there is, but never just rains all day, day after day."

"Paradise."

"I think it is, James. Right here—it's been here all along. You just have to get off—step out of the squirrel cage, and here it is."

"I am glad to be here, Russ. And grateful for your inviting me to stay with you. I could easily have gone to a hotel."

"No way."

"Well, you and . . . Lily"—Marley hesitated just an instant in saying her name for the first time, aware that in saying it, in saying "you *and* Lily" he was pronouncing them conjoined—"it's only been a week. I certainly didn't think you'd want a house guest just yet."

"You aren't a guest. You're a friend."

"Thanks. But still . . ."

"I told you when you called: If you're a friend, coming to see Lily and me for a friendly visit, you stay with us. If you're not coming as a friend, then we didn't want to see you." Russ's ever-gentle voice was firm, for once, and this time he didn't turn to see how Marley reacted.

"I appreciate that. I appreciate your invitation. I'm glad to be here."

*   *   *

If Russ had been the race-car driver before, now he was the realtor. Once they had turned from the main road, he cruised slowly so that Marley could see the houses along the winding side streets and appreciate that he was in a classy section of town.

Although here and there stood a small, neat bungalow (like a family of modest means but breeding good enough to be accepted socially among the well-to-do), most of the houses were large. They sprawled winged, terraced, balconied, two or—built into the hillside—three stories looking out at the sea. Thick-walled, deep-roofed, stuccoed, painted cream, white, beige, peach, pink; set about with shrubs and vines, hedges along their fences: bougainvillaea, hibiscus, English roses imported and gone native with wild abandon.

"Nice neighborhood," Marley said.

"Yeah. The place we're renting is one of the smaller ones, but it's still got four bedrooms. I got a terrific deal, though. I guess normally it would sit empty for at least half the year. By taking it for a year I got a great price."

"You're really settling in."

"Yeah. This is going to last, James. This isn't just a quickie."

Russ turned into a short drive, past an open wrought-iron gate. "Here we are."

Russ reached the screen door shouting, "Lily! We're here!" clearly so eager to rush right in to her that Marley thought he would and came close behind; but Russ wanted to be the gracious host, too, and backed again to open the door and stand aside, nearly bumping into Marley, half stumbling over his own feet, half hopping to regain his bal-

ance and get out of the way, weaving, bobbing, almost gig-
gling with embarrassment and excitement, waving Marley
on, saying, "Come on in, James! Welcome! Meet the family!"

Setting in place his all-purpose smile, Marley went in to
meet the marriage-breaker, home-wrecker, the siren se-
ducer of middle-aged soon-to-be millionaires.

Lily was crossing the living room to meet him. She was as
advertised: young, small, slender—bones like the ribs of
butterflies' wings; exquisitely doll-faced; the long, straight,
gleaming, raven hair; yes, yes, all the clichés: the peony
complexion, the dark almond eyes that see into secrets and
know what Western men have always suspected but never
dared to believe could be true. Oh, Marley knew her, knew
her type, long before she reached him.

But she wasn't wearing a sarong. She had on a pale blue
T-shirt silk-screened with Snoopy dancing, over a short,
white cotton skirt sprinkled like a May meadow with yellow
and orange and pink daisies. She wore little, neat, flat-
heeled, round-pointed open-work shoes, and although
Marley only glimpsed them as he looked her quickly up and
down, a line from the Song of Solomon (which he had been
inspired to memorize when he was thirteen) came to him:
How graceful are thy feet in sandals, O queenly maiden!

"Lily, this is James Marley!"

"Hi, James! Gee, I'm really glad to meet you! Russ talks
about you all the time." Her voice was little bells and bam-
boo flutes and bunches of multicolored balloons set loose.

"James, this is Lily."

With all the frankness of a puppy Lily stuck out her hand
to him, and when he took it she squeezed his fingers.

Marley said, "I'm very pleased to meet you, Lily," which
was only what one says. But Lily—impulsively yet grace-
fully—leaned up on her tiptoes and quickly kissed his
cheek. He caught her scent. It wasn't Opium, as he'd expected. It was, he realized, Ivory soap.

"I'm *real* glad you could come to see us!" she said; and Marley replied without thinking, "I am, too!"

For a moment Marley and Lily smiled at one another, and Russ beamed at both of them. "Well, come on!" he said, bouncing. "Let me show you your room, and you put on your suit and take that swim!" He turned to Lily. "I'm going to go in again, too. Come in with us."

"Oh, no. I have to finish fixing supper."

"You can do it after. While James and I are having a drink. We won't be in the pool long."

"I don't want to get my hair wet again."

"Oh, come on! It dries right away. Come on, be sociable!"

When Marley came out he found Russ floating on an air cushion in the small pool set into the ground at the back of the house. Feeling naked in his winter fish-belly whiteness, Marley dove quickly into the water and swam twice from end to end. Then he stood where only his head showed above the surface.

"Sure gets the kinks from traveling out, doesn't it?" Russ called to him.

"Sure does. And it's warm!"

"Yeah. Sun's been on it all day. Shadow of the hill must have come over just about twenty minutes ago. But it's warm enough, and the air's warm enough, you can swim all night long—anytime you want."

Marley pushed off with his toes and backstroked slowly from end to end another time. When he stopped and stood again Russ said, "Man, I can sure tell you just got here: all that energy. I see you were already slowing down, though. A couple days here, you'd be able to accept what a pool's for: holds your bones up so your muscles don't have to exert themselves."

"Maybe so, but right now—"

"Hi, love!" Russ called out.

Marley turned to see Lily come to the edge of the pool.
A lifetime—nearly fifty years—of control kept his jaw from
dropping, but his eyes did bug, and then he knew he was
blushing.

Lily was wearing (if the word could be used) the leastest
bikini Marley had ever seen. She sat on the edge, put her
feet into the water, pushed forward supporting herself on
stiffened arms, then slid straight down. Every movement
was simple and natural, nothing brazen, nothing coy. She
seemed to regard both men staring at her as normal, to be
expected and accepted without requiring anything from
her.

Your rounded thighs are like jewels . . .

Your navel is a rounded bowl . . .

Your belly is a heap of wheat, encircled with lilies . . .

Marley ducked under the water, then thrust upward and
swam back and forth once more, briskly, keeping well away
from where Lily paddled, trying not to think, "Oh that my
left hand were under her head, and that my right hand embraced her!"

Faintly, from the kitchen, came a comforting, soft chop-
chop-chop, then the rapidly ringing tinks of stirring. Russ
and Marley heard without listening those pleasant sounds
of Lily preparing their supper for them. They lay back side
by side on lounge chairs by the pool, Marley a white wolf,
Russ a pink baby walrus—unaccountably friends at ease
with one another—sipping planter's punches, looking out
over the sea, watching the sun's evening alchemy. Miraculous transmutations: azure sky into yellow and green, veri-
dian sea into silver and violet. The island sloping up in a
long sweep from shore to peaks on their left: Before it had
seemed as lush as the skin of some fully ripened fruit; now
it was the rich and juicy flesh revealed.

"Yeah," Marley said.

"Yeah. You think you might get to like this, James? I mean, if you really worked at it?"

"If I buckled down, concentrated, used all my willpower? Possibly. In time."

"Yeah."

Marley took a sip of the round, sweet drink. He sighed. *"But I have promises to keep, and miles to go before I sleep."*

"That's Robert Frost, right."

"Yes. 'Stopping by Woods on a Snowy Evening'—*The woods are lovely, dark and deep. But I have promises to keep, and miles to go before I sleep, and miles to go before I sleep.*"

"Yeah. I remember. He says the last line twice."

"Yes."

"Doesn't want you to miss the point."

"I guess not."

"I get the point."

"Sorry. You know I didn't come down here just for the sunset."

"Yeah. I know." Russ sipped his drink. "I really don't want to spoil this by talking about Joanna."

"Okay. Tomorrow?"

"I really don't want to talk about her at all." Russ started to raise his glass again, then put it down. "No, that's not true. As a matter of fact, James, I've got a lot I'd like to say. But not now, okay?"

Marley shrugged. "Your sunset." After a moment he asked, "How do you feel about talking about David Cheyney, your work?"

"Okay. I already told him—left word—the project will get done. I just need a little break. I brought my lap-top PC and my Bernoulli. I'll be able to work just as well by the pool here as frozen inside a block of ice back in Massachusetts. I've only got—probably—less than a week's work on the program: only three more subroutines. Then another week checking the source codes—debugging—then it'll be complete and ready for alpha testing."

"When do you see that as happening—starting work on it again?"

"A couple weeks, a month—no, say two months. I really do not want any more pressure, James, any more deadlines on my back. Now I'm telling you . . . I appreciate you're trying to be cool, you're just asking me, you're not leaning on me . . . but *don't*. I mean, lean. The way I feel . . . any kind of pressure will be definitely counterproductive."

Russ sat forward, his chubby forearm on the arm of his chair, the palm stretched open toward Marley. "Do you understand, James? I'm not just trying to give you a hard time. I am burned out."

"Sure, Russ. But you're so close to the end. And David is really interested in this project."

"Well, tell him not to worry. It'll get finished, and he'll have some more millions to try to find something to do with."

"It's not just the money, Russ, and you know that. David considers software piracy to be a moral evil. Every illegal copy that's made is an outrage. Every day that goes by without an effective use-protection program is a lost battle for the forces of decency."

Russ snorted. "Every month that goes by without protection for the programs put out by David's companies is a lost couple million dollars for him."

"Every year is a lost hundred million for the industry—for guys like you who spent ten years in their basements working fourteen hours a day, as well as for the people like David who bought into the business. Sure, he's mad about his own losses. David's anger about cheating is immense, just on principle. When it's *him* who's been cheated, his wrath is truly phenomenal. Okay. For both reasons he wants to stop it; and you have almost developed what he tells me is the best, simplest, most foolproof system for doing that that anybody has thought of. So, naturally—and not at all unreasonably, Russ—he wants you to get the damn thing done."

"It'll get done. So maybe the pirates'll make an extra hundred mil before we market it; well, that won't break any of us."

"And what if somebody else comes out with a program like yours first, and copyrights it? And all your work, and all David's backing, is just washed away?"

"Nobody is working on anything like my program."

"How do you know? The secrecy all you guys work under . . ."

"Everybody hides his codes, sure, James. You don't let *anybody* know *how* you're doing it, what it's going to look like. But *what* you're doing . . . Word goes around. People talk. Hell, that's how you get investors. It's how you get people to maybe wait a few months for your program instead of buying into a similar one that comes out first that's not going to be as good. So I know a lot of people are working on protection: copy protection, use protection, software, hardware; but nothing suggests that anybody is doing it my way. So you tell David to just give me a little time to catch my breath and get my shit together again, and he'll have his program."

Fish that had been simmered with vegetables in a thick brown sauce, exotically spiced, peppery: "Lily's Chinese-Indian-Creole cuisine," Russ identified it proudly in response to Marley's compliments. "I don't know how she does it—the 'supermarkets' here are not exactly what you'd call well stocked. But every night she throws some things together in the frying pan, and *voilà! Gastronomie!*"

Lily giggled, a tinkling little laugh, and ducked her head:
so pleased but so embarrassed by praise. Leaning forward
conspiratorially, she stage-whispered her secret to Marley,
her friend and confidant: "Pepper sauce. I think if I put
pepper sauce on an old shoe, Russ'd eat it and say it's deli-
cious."

"I sure would if it was your shoe, Sugar Toes."

Marley might have winced; he smiled.

The rectangular table by the glass wall had been set with
Russ's place at one end, Marley to his right, Lily on the
opposite side, her back to the windows. But Lily had put
herself so close to Russ that she might as well have been
around the corner on a bench beside him. She did move to
him as soon as she'd cleared the table after they finished
eating. She'd drawn her chair close, and sat down with her
shoulder snuggled to Russ's, in the same movement lightly
laying her hand high on his thigh, sliding her palm around
it just below his crotch—exactly the way the Saigon bar-
girls did. While Russ and Marley were nearly finished with
their second beers she had barely sipped halfway down her
first; yet she giggled and bobbed, sometimes touching her
head to Russ's neck, like a little innocent becoming tipsy
and in danger of losing all her inhibitions.

And Russ lord-of-the-manored back in his chair, with his
arm proclaimed across Lily's shoulders, sometimes idly
stroking her hair or—yes, he did! right there in front of
Marley!—fondling her earlobe or running his fingers down
inside the neck of her T-shirt while discoursing about snor-
keling and wind-surfing. And he—Russ Detweiller, who
might use his generation's all-purpose modifier in front of
any noun but never told an off-color joke, or listened to
one without blushing—would unknot the hawsers and let
loose elephantine double entendres: "Oh, Lily knows what
I like; she makes things hot all the time for me." Or—in
response to Marley's comment on the quiet of the night—

"Yeah, you can really sleep; but it seems like I'm getting up at all hours, too."

Marley should have disapproved. While he'd have laughed if anyone called him a prude, there *are*, after all, times and places . . . Except that the effervescent delight Russ and Lily took in titillating one another bubbled over him and lifted him completely free of stodge. They seemed so childlike, charming—they were Adam and Eve before the sinful knowledge of sin. Marley beamed at them; not merely his carefully measured mouth-smile, but one from a warm spring somewhere down inside the granite.

Sometime in the soft deep of the night Marley came awake. Gently, not startled; but something had brought him to consciousness. Perhaps only the moonlight, he thought. His room had been dark when he'd gone to bed, and all the world outside, too, despite the dense spatter of stars across the sky, the scatter of lamps that was the distant town. Sky and sea and land had been equally black, a closed-eye blackness with neither flatness nor depth.

The moon must have risen from behind the mountains. Marley could see every detail of his room: the dresser squatting against the far wall, the print of a pale bird suspended mid-wing-beat above it; he even imagined he could see the colors in the ghostly bouquet of the flower-print chair.

Or perhaps it had been some sound. There were sounds. For several moments Marley lay listening; not with any sense of alarm; simply aware of the trilling of toads and peeper frogs. Peepers! That sleigh-bell peal of spring come at long last to New England, heard then and no other time—here in February! Marley lay, half covered by a sheet only, listening, joy-filled. And, by concentrating, he could hear the rush of shallow waves on the shore a quarter mile away.

And then there was something else: faint but close, an animal or human sound. He tensed but didn't move, focusing all attention. Silence for a moment, then a voice, a barely vocalized whisper giving some curt, urgent instruction.

Marley rolled free of the sheet and out of bed, fluidly, low, and crept to the window, peering through at a bottom corner.

The moon shone almost straight downward. No light came directly through the window to strike his face; reflection from the screen would probably mask it. As long as he made no abrupt movements, Marley felt sure he wouldn't be seen from outside.

But he could see clearly, himself. That overhead light revealed the lawn all the way down to the vine-covered wall. In one glance Marley swept it, took in the shimmering swimming pool, the terrace, and saw the strange shape there.

It was a living thing, a creature; he recognized that instantly; but he couldn't identify it. Pale-fleshed but with a wide, dark patch; asymmetrical, grotesquely humped, both angular and sinuous . . . For a second, half-formed images presented themselves: a sea monster, starfishlike; a huge iguana; two iguanas; and then he knew.

Russ lay on the tipped-back lounge chair, his arms up, elbows bent, clutching the top of the cushion above his head. Lily knelt on the grass beside him, her back toward Marley, leaning over Russ, her hair spreading across her shoulders, across his chest. She moved like a sea anemone swaying in softly eddying currents, her head slowly drifting up and down over his torso, her arm undulating out and back as she caressed his thighs.

Marley stood for an instant amazed, aware he was watching, knowing he shouldn't. Each time Lily swayed, her head moved lower, her fingertips higher. She paused, hand and head together, then Russ gasped.

The surge of Russ's ecstasy flashed through Marley, too, with a force that shocked him free. He stepped back from the window so he couldn't see them any longer. Yet he stood looking out at the sky, flooded with lust. *Oh that you would kiss me with the kisses of your mouth! Draw me after you, let us make haste!* He felt some disgust with himself, and with Russ for doing that out there where he might see.

Suddenly he realized they knew he *would* see. Russ insisting that Lily swim with them, fondling her, all the innuendoes at supper: showing her off. He was showing her off to Marley, showing how desirable a woman she was—*his* woman, the desirable woman who desired *him*.

Marley made himself breathe again, and moved to look at an angle through the window—not at *them* but toward the mountains, the shore and sea. The land lay still under the moonlight, dark, solid; the sea flat, a shining surface. But despite their placid, material density, both seemed permeated, vibrant with the energy descending upon them. A waft of air flowed over him—like a liquid, cool and warm at once—and was gone, taking the sear of his passion, leaving its glow.

For some time he stared at the night, was with the night. He heard a little splash, and another. After a moment he stepped forward and looked through the window again at what he knew he would see.

Russ stood in the pool, at the shallow end, where the water came only to his waist. Lily lay on the air cushion, her hair spread, floating. The moon shone full on her face, on its black halo, gleamed from the fine-spun silkiness of Russ's hair, glowed in slowly fluttering filaments in the water around them. His arms were stretched downward, his hands over her little breasts. Her legs were clamped around his hips. She tightened and relaxed them, and he moved her, so she drifted gently to and away from him.

Marley looked; he didn't watch. He did look for one moment. It seemed right. They wanted him to; and it seemed—not for them, but for himself—that he should see them. Adam and Eve before the fall. The act of love: not a euphemism, but like a sacred rite from which the veil had been lifted only for an instant so he might know its mystery's truth. Marley looked for that moment, awestruck, then lay down on his bed again and in a little peaceful while drifted into sleep.

CHAPTER 3

"Hi, James! You have a good sleep?" Lily was busy behind the counter that separated kitchen from living area when Marley came from his bedroom.

"Yes, I did."

"Sit down. Have some breakfast."

Marley went to the place already set for him facing the sea. The glass doors had been slid back. Air moved with the faintest feather touch, cool but not chill, wafting flower scents and the smell of coffee. He sat indoors and outside at the same time, it seemed, as in a dream able to combine contradictions and be in two places at once. He had slept well, awakened fully refreshed. Yet so gently, effortlessly, had the flowering day begun to open its petals that he felt as incorporeal as though still asleep.

"I hope you like grapefruit. It's right off a tree from our own yard here! Would you like some eggs?"

"No, thank you. Yes, I do like grapefruit. One right off a tree will be a real treat."

"Cereal? Toast?"

"Just a piece of toast would be fine. Thanks."

"So that's how you keep yourself so nice and thin, James."

Lily was wearing her Snoopy T-shirt again, and no bra; the points of her barely-a-palmful breasts poked it as she moved. As ever, she seemed fresh from a shower, scrubbed and toweled; and Marley was reminded that the girl who's most exciting seen naked is the one next door. He forced himself not to think about seeing Lily naked. Indeed, it was hard to believe he had seen her. Looking out at the flowers in the garden, the pastel houses polka-dotting the nearby slopes, the shining mountains and ever-new sea, he could think the pale and pitch-blue monochrome of moonlit passion had been a fantasy of his own lascivious imagination.

Lily clicked a slice of bread down in the toaster and called out, "Coffee now?"

"Please."

"Strong enough you can stand your spoon up in it, right? That's what Russ said."

"Right. Thanks." Marley ate a section of the succulent, tart-sweet fruit. "Where is Russ?"

"He's out jogging. You have to get out early if you want to jog. Pretty soon it'll be too hot."

"Russ has taken up jogging?"

"Yeah. We usually go together."

"Well. I've never known Russ to do anything that strenuous. I know Joanna always was after him to exercise more."

"Yes. He told me," Lily said, coming to Marley and setting a mug of coffee on the table for him. "Sugar's there. Can I get you some milk?"

"No, thanks." Marley looked directly up at her. "How did you get him to do it?" he asked lightly, with his pleasant smile, as though admiring, not appraising.

Lily's smile was just as fun-filled, her eyes just as sharp. "I told him I loved his body. I told him I love it when a man keeps himself in shape. I asked him if he'd like to run with me when I went out in the morning. I asked him not to go too fast for me. I asked him to turn around and come back before *I* got too tired. I said when we come back we should take a shower together because the exercise makes me horny, and even if we don't go all the way and shoot the morning it's nice to feel each other up."

"Are you going to have some coffee with me?"

"No. I had mine."

"Well, then, sit down."

"I'll just get your toast."

Marley returned to his grapefruit. "How long is Russ going to stay away?"

"Till about ten o'clock."

"That should give us plenty of time."

"He thought so."

"His idea?"

"Yes. But I thought it was a good one. You did come down here to find out about us. Russ really likes you, James. He wants you to like me. So it seemed like a good idea for you and I to be able to talk."

"Yes." Marley ate the last of the grapefruit, looking over the scarlet hibiscus blossoming along the wall below, out at the sparkling cerulean sea. The toast popped up. Lily brought it to him on a little pansied plate. "Thanks."

Lily sat at the end of the table, to his left, where Russ had been the evening before. She had her hair pulled back and knotted so that it hung away from her neck and shoulders; cooler that way, probably. Worn like that, the shape more severe, it should have made her look older. It didn't; her face, her whole body, had the smooth, tight, full-of-life fleshiness of blooming youth. Yet she was old, too, Marley realized: an old, knowing, ancient child like those he'd seen in Nam, standing outside the hootches, watching, waiting to see what he and his men would do, having already seen it all before.

She moved the butter dish close to him, and he began buttering the toast. "Thank you. So, what did you and Russ think you and I should talk about?"

"Russ thought we should just talk, and you'd find out what a nice person I am." Her little voice was brooklike and bright as always; it didn't change as she continued. "But I wanted to talk because I knew you'd find out for yourself that I'm not a nice person. Sugar?" She lifted the sugar bowl with both hands and set it next to Marley's cup.

"Thanks."

"I know—from Russ—that you're kind of like a private detective: a private private detective for Mr. Cheyney."

Marley was about to recite his standard I'm-not-a-detective disclaimer, but she went on.

"I know you're not, really; but you do find out things, and do things, for him—just like you're finding out right now. So I knew you'd find out about me. So I thought I'd better just tell you. Will you have some jelly?"

"Please."

Lily moved the jar of strawberry jam close to his plate. "Thank you."

"I was born here—I mean, in Boston—so I'm American. And we lived in Alston, not in Chinatown, so I went to school—grade school and high school—with mostly Anglo kids; and watched TV: so me no speakee Chinee pidgin-talkee, you likee? But my father and mother came over from Taiwan—he cooked for Joyce Chen for a while, and then opened his own place. On borrowed money. So we spoke Chinese at home. And I was brought up the way a Chinese girl is supposed to be, to be like a *girl* is 'supposed' to be.

"And then my father died, and we—we never had much

money anyway—and then we had even less. The men who'd loaned my father the money for his restaurant, they took care of my mother and me—a job as a stitcher in one of the sweatshops for her, and a job as a waitress for me. And I learned that the way I'd been brought up was good career training. You smile, you please people—that is, men—you'll do all right. You let men use you, and that's how you use them.

"That's what you think I'm doing with Russ, isn't it?"

Marley knew how he could come across to people: how that jaw, and the dark eyebrows, and the gray hair at the sides made him look. So he smiled and modulated his voice so as not to seem like a *hanging* judge, at least. "I'm trying not to think anything, Lily. I'm here because I'm trying to find out." Lily continued looking him steadily in the eye, and he added, "But, sure: A young woman runs off with a much older, well-to-do—about to be very wealthy—man: sure, there's bound to be a suspicion. I guess, to be honest, a presumption . . . a prejudice. I have been trying to keep an open mind; and I'll say you aren't what I expected."

"Well, then, you're not so sharp like you're supposed to be, James. 'Cause I am what you expected. I started out being a waitress, when I was thirteen. By seventeen I was a 'hostess.' If I hadn't been so pretty and smart I'd still be doing hand-jobs under the table in the Combat Zone. But I'm too good-quality for that, and the guy I worked for saw it. So I moved up to being an 'escort.' For VIPs, when they came to town—from San Francisco, L.A., Hong Kong, Taipei.

"Then I met Russ, and just like you think, James, I thought, 'Here's my winning ticket for the Super Sweeps!' Middle-aged guy, had it with his wife, so much money in his pockets he's walking on his knees, wants to *fl-yyy*.

"My mark. My man, oh, yeah." Then, for the first time, Lily's marble-hard eyes left Marley's and looked at something not there in that room. "Oh, yeah," she repeated softly.

"Do you know, James," she said, turning back to him, those eyes no longer glinting, but glowing. "Would you believe he took me to the Aquarium? The first time he took me out, it was in the *afternoon,* and he took me to the *Aquarium,* to look at the *turtles* and the *dolphins.* And we had lunch on the pier. *And he never touched me!*

"I was all over *him.* I mean, I started to be; but then I could see he didn't want it. Oh, of course he did. He was so stiff for me he could hardly walk. But he didn't want it. Not right away. He wanted to do it right—do it nice, get to know each other, let me know he wasn't interested in me just for *that.*

"When we did do it, the first time—would you believe not until the *seventh* date? Well, now was my chance: get his weenie out of his wife's icebox and into my microwave, he'd never go back. I was still thinking like that, making it ha-ha and dirty. He was being—he'd been—so nice, so respectful to me, so thoughtful . . . kind . . . so sweet. But I wasn't gonna fall for him. I mean, who the fuck d'you think I am? Betsy-Barbie Pinkpussy?

"Of course, I pretended like I was in love with him. When I . . . I don't need to go into all the details . . . when I did a couple of my special tricks I put a little extra spin on them. I pretended—I told myself I was just pretending—I was crazy in love with him.

"You know what happened? What he did? That jerk. He said it was so wonderful and he never knew it could be like that! Can you believe it? *'He never knew it could be like that!'* Like one of those paperback books you get in the supermarket. And there were . . . there were tears in his eyes."

And Lily's own eyes were full. "And then . . ." She swallowed. "And then he said . . . He didn't say, 'Nice action, baby; here's an extra hundred.' He said, 'Now you be still and let me love *you.' Love* you."

Lily took a very deep breath, and let it out slowly, and then she and Marley sat in a silence broken only by the song of some bird.

"I used to read those romances, sometimes," she said. "I never believed it. I never believed that sex could be love, even though that's what people call it. But that's what Russ did—he loved me.

"And I love him, James. That wasn't how it started. It started just the way you thought. But that's how it is now. And I'd do anything in the world for him. There isn't much I can do for him—I don't think there's much: I don't have much education; but he says he doesn't really care about that anyway . . . But I can cook for him, and keep house, and make him feel good about himself, and make him laugh, and love him—do that. That, I can do. Did you see us—last night?"

"Yes."

"It was Russ's idea. When he said it, I didn't want to—at first. But then I did. I wanted you to see, I'm glad you did, because now you'll know."

"Now I know."

"Hi, James, how ya doin'?" Russ called, and then, "Oh. Sorry. Were you asleep?"

"I guess I was," Marley said, blinking, astonished. Asleep: He actually had been; at ten o'clock of a bright, sunshiny morning, after a good night's sleep. He'd sat back in one of the lounge chairs, his feet up, to wait for Russ, to think about Lily. Sat out of the sun but feeling heat building into the day. Sat staring at the ever-changing, constant sea curving itself into an arm of the solid, erodable island;

the sea embraced by the island, the island surrounded, contained within the sea . . . "I must have drifted right away."

"You really ought to spend about a week here. A month. I mean, James, now exactly what is it you have to do back there in igloo land?"

"I don't know. It seems to me there was something, but it is slipping. You have a good run?"

"Yeah. Drove down to Fox's Bay and ran back and forth along the beach. You have a nice time talking with Lily?"

"Yes."

"She said you dried the dishes. She must like you; I only get to do that with her when I've been really nice. She said you walked around the yard, and she showed you where she wants to plant flowers. And you're going to send her a book?"

"Yes."

"That'll be great, James. Lily never had a garden—just some plants in her apartment. Thank you. I guess you like her."

"Yes, I do."

"Yeah. She's really terrific." Russ sat on the other lounge chair, facing Marley but not looking at him. Pink, a roll of flesh bulging over the waistband of his bathing suit. But a fish-and-low-starch diet, and running, burning up energy in plenty of sex, helping Lily garden, and the other kinds of exercise she'd see he got without him realizing, would trim him, Marley thought. He'd never have Marley's cable-leanness, but she'd get the flab off him.

"James . . . I know I said we'd talk about Joanna today, but I really don't want to. I mean, you see Lily; you see what she's like, why I feel the way I do about her . . . I mean, let's leave it at that. I don't want to have to bad-mouth Joanna to explain . . . Joanna's okay. She's a super person, in her way. We had some good years together. We're just not . . . I'm not saying it's anybody's fault, but we're not just right for each other anymore. You understand?"

"I hear you, Russ. I like Lily, and I understand why you feel the way you do about her. But what about how Joanna feels about you? About your leaving her? What about Tim, and Meagan, and Page? You have responsibilities, Russ. You took them on, you *made* them."

"I'm taking care of my responsibilities. I'm giving Joanna the house, the cars, half the bank accounts; I'm going to pay child support—not just support, like *she* has to take care of them, and I'm just going to *help*. I mean, medical bills, college, whatever: I'll take care of it totally. I'm going to bring the kids down here—vacations: the whole summer, if they want to. I am taking care of my responsibilities, James. But I think I've got a responsibility to myself, too. What about that one? When you think about a person's responsibilities, do you ever think about that one?"

Marley thought about Russ's letter to Joanna, and about his leaving it to her to tell people, and about . . . and about . . . "I think it's awfully easy to call what feels good, and what's easy, 'having a responsibility to yourself.'"

"Yeah. Well, I guess I knew I could count on you to set me straight about the straight-and-narrow."

"You asked me, Russ."

"Yeah. I did."

A bone-dull wind blew out of the blackness that was Boston Harbor, through the open sides of the parking garage at Logan. Cold would lurk in the concrete there even in July. The place was a citadel of winter, which now held and laid waste the whole city.

Marley shivered in spite of his stoical self-control while hurriedly mantling himself into his sheepskin coat.

After thirty-six hours in the trunk of his car, the coat absorbed his body heat instead of making him warmer. Entering the car itself was like sitting down in a walk-in freezer.

And he was already heart-chilled.

He'd called David Cheyney's office as soon as his flight got in. David expected prompt reports; there were people on duty in New York at every hour to receive or transmit them. Marley had meant to say only, "I've seen Russell. He's not coming back. He will finish the program, but he won't be rushed. I'll call tomorrow and talk with you personally." That—he'd thought—would end the assignment. But there had been a message for him. "Mr. Cheyney has discovered that someone on the West Coast is working on a software program that seems to be nearly identical to Mr. Detweiller's. Please call Mr. Cheyney at seven-thirty tomorrow morning."

"Bad luck," Marley tried to tell himself. "Luck. Coincidence. Bad news, but only a coincidence." For a few moments he had blown on the coal, trying to convince himself there was heat in it. Then he started through the frigid night toward Carlisle.

When he'd arrived at Logan he'd been planning to spend the night in a hotel in Boston, call Joanna, and arrange to see her in the morning on his way home to Vermont. Now he knew he wasn't going home; his work wasn't finished, it was only beginning, and he'd have to start it with her. He'd called her and asked if he could stay at her house.

"Maybe I'm jumping to a conclusion," he said to her when they were seated by the fire. "But . . . David's message was terse, but he chooses his words carefully. He said someone was working on a program that seemed to be 'nearly identical' with Russ's. That just can't be a coincidence. 'Similar' might be a coincidence: A lot of people must be working on protection programs, and there are probably a limited number of logical approaches. But *identical* . . . Somebody must have stolen Russ's work."

"Who! How!"

"That's what I'll have to try to find out. Not that it really matters—not in the way it might seem. Everything's already clear; or, at least, I think it is. Unless Russ has been carrying around printouts of his work and leaving them in men's rooms, or doodling on tablecloths in restaurants, his codes were stolen from his office: either literally stolen—a burglary, something like that—or one of his employees sold him out."

"I can't believe that! They're all Russ's friends. Our friends."

"Well, then, we'll hope it was a burglary. I'll have to try to find out, but that's a secondary issue. Necessary to know, but secondary. The primary issue is Lily."

"You think she's involved."

"Frankly, I've been trying not to think that. I liked Lily, Joanna. I was going to have to tell you that; and I will tell you all about it—about what I thought after seeing her: her and Russ, together. But . . . the point here is not simply that Russ's work has been stolen. His work isn't finished. Presumably he could finish it sooner than whoever's got it as it is so far. He'd bring it to copyright—even if the other person came in in a nearly dead heat, Russ could establish precedence.

"But Russ isn't working. He's run away to a tropical island, and he's having—forgive me—a honeymoon. Maybe that's just a coincidence, Joanna. Maybe my evil mind is making me see plots, and jumping to really despicable conclusions. Well, if so, then I'll owe Lily an abject apology. But I just can't see Russ's meeting her exactly at this time as coincidence."

"We've got to call him, tell him!"

"Sure. I will call him in the morning, after I've talked with David. To tell him about somebody else working on his program. That ought to get him back to work himself. But I am not going to say a word about Lily. Not until— unless—I have some kind of proof. If I—or you, which would be even worse—make any kind of unsubstantiated accusation about her . . . I think that would be, in the term that Russ used to me, 'counterproductive.'

"If Lily is part of a plot, then Russ has to know— for *him:* because we care about *him;* never mind the program. But we're going to have to be able to prove it to him."

For a moment Joanna continued to focus on Marley the high drive of her full attention. Then she slumped back. As before, they had taken rocker and couch in front of the open fire. The chocolate-colored draperies had already been drawn across the windows when Marley arrived. The lamps at each end of the couch imitated candlelight. Marley was fully warm at last—in flesh, at least. He could pretend he didn't know what was all around them.

"That bastard," Joanna said quietly. "That poor, inno- cent baby bastard son of a bitch!" Her long, strong, know- ing-how fingers knotted together. "Leaving me for a . . . a Mata Hari, a . . . After all I've done . . . A cheap little obvious gold digger that he's too blind, too shallow to see the difference— She'll twist him and jerk him around and tear out his heart, and the poor, sweet baby won't be able . . . too sincere himself to see through her, and too *stupid,* too . . . and she'll just *kill* him, and he won't know what . . . the poor, dear, pitiful, stupid, ungrateful, goddamned son of a bitch bastard!"

She ended angled forward again, clutching the arms of her chair, staring at Marley—who was as still as a rabbit pretending to be a rock.

"I'm sorry," she said.

"Don't be. You're right—all of it."

The anger seemed to leave her and let her lean back again, even her head, against the woven cane. She rocked herself slightly once, and twice.

"You were going to tell me about them," she said.

"Yes." Marley had already worked out what he would say. "Strong sexuality, but genuinely loving . . ." He spared her explicit description. "Russ is crazy about her, and she gives him reason to be: pampers him, builds his ego . . ."

"Just what you men like."

"Doesn't everybody? He gives her what she wants, too. Or, at least what she *told* me she wants. Apparently, she's had a hard time . . ." He glossed over Lily's background: ". . . strict upbringing . . . father died . . . waitressing . . . She says—and I believed her—that she's never really had anyone love her, care about her, before. So she's happy to do what she does for Russ."

Hurling one leg across the other, flinging arm over arm, Joanna slung herself into the corner of her chair in a parody of nonchalant repose. "Well, isn't that just lovely? What an ideal relationship—a boy and his dog. Just what every man dreams of. I can see *you* think it's lovely. I'm surprised you didn't ask her if there're any more at home like her."

Marley really was a boulder for several moments until she seemed to tire of trying to drill into him. "I don't think their relationship is ideal. I wouldn't like that sort of thing myself. And I don't approve. But it seems to be what *they* want, and they're consenting adults. They seemed to be happy. I thought they *both* were. Russ certainly is; and no matter how this turns out . . . I guess what I have to tell you, Joanna, is that I don't think Russ is going to come back to you. I think that's a rotten thing, but it's a fact. I'm sorry."

She dropped her stare, and some—only some—of the stiffness went out of her shoulders like an overstrained cable beginning to part strand by strand but still holding. "Well," she said, her voice also trying and failing to keep its bite, "maybe it's for the best. With Meagan and Tim and Page—I really don't need a fourth child to take care of." She seemed to be trying to draw strength from the square-cornered order of overlapped magazines on the coffee table in front of Marley. She must have been sitting too far away from them; she sagged, and put her palm across her eyes. "Maybe now I can find someone to take care of me."

Marley decided that saying, "I'm sure you will," was fatuous, but he said it anyway.

"Do you really think so? I mean, *truly*? That it's possible . . . I don't want someone to take care of me as though I were a baby. I'm strong, James; but I'm . . . If I was *too* strong, if I babied Russ, it's because I *had* to. He . . ."

"Never mind. But I am strong. But am I desirable? Do all men really want someone like that girl? Tell me, James. If there is such a thing as a grown-up man, you're it. Am I desirable?"

Marley suddenly had that Vietnam feeling, when you sense there are trip wires everywhere. He tried to think very quickly what he would say very carefully.

Joanna caught it. "Oh, I'm not . . . I didn't mean . . . Not *us*! I just wanted . . . a professional opinion."

Marley breathed again and smiled. "You are desirable, Joanna. You are not only a very handsome woman, but—I think precisely because you are strong—a man who doesn't want babying either way would find you *extremely* desirable."

For an instant, Joanna hugged herself, smiling. Then she opened her arms toward Marley. "God, you are a wonderful man, James! If you would *only* take an interest in serious things like money and power and social status we could be a dynamite couple."

Marley rocked back, laughing. The two of them grinned at one another.

"Well," Joanna said, serious again, "what do we do now?"

"Basically, shock treatment. I'm going to have to move very fast. Russ said he only had another week's work on the program, and he hasn't been working for at least a week, as it is. Whoever's got the part of program that was stolen surely hasn't been on vacation, too. We're going against a clock, and there's no telling how little time's left on it.

"And there's another thing . . . The way this seems to be happening . . . Russ's codes stolen and being worked on by somebody clear across the country, and if Lily *is* involved: It all would suggest a scale of plotting, of organization and resources . . . People who operate on that level and are unscrupulous enough to steal things tend to be dangerous."

Joanna's eyes went wide.

"Not to you," Marley assured her quickly. "I'm thinking of Russ. Now, if they want to beat him—you and him, your company—to copyrighting the program, they wouldn't—as a first move—do something to harm *him*. If they did—no matter what that meant to you personally—you and David would immediately hire someone else to complete Russ's work. Obviously, the design is far enough along so that somebody can do that. The trick would be to keep Russ designing it in theory, but not actually working. That's why his meeting Lily is . . . suspect. But if he starts working again, and it becomes a flat-out, out-in-the-open race . . ."

"Yes, I understand. But, then, wouldn't it be better to tell Russ what's going on, get him back to work, without letting anybody know we know about the theft?"

"Sure. But we can't do that. If Lily is part of a plot, she'll know if he goes back to work. She can inform. She could sabotage him. I don't think she'd do something that would stop him or hurt him instantly, so I will try to put him in motion. But very soon afterward . . . He'll have to know about her. We're back to where we started: We have to tell him about her; and to do that we have to have proof."

"We've got to do something to protect him!"

"Right. The first thing in the morning, before we do anything else, I'll talk with David. I'll have him fly down a squad of security people to keep an eye on Russ without his even knowing it."

"Who? What kind of people? Is it really true that David Cheyney has his own private army?"

"Well, not exactly. David's just your ordinary, everyday billionaire—he owns a few things he wants protected. And then his companies: the high-tech ones . . . even the low-tech ones . . . Being the businessman he is, he decided that instead of paying somebody else's security service for guards, he'd form his own company. Some of the people who work for it—a few I've met—have military experience. But that's typical in that business."

"People say he does things for the CIA."

"Some people say he *is* the CIA, but it's not true."

"Isn't that where you met him? In Vietnam?"

"I met him in Vietnam after I'd left the army. When I went back there to work with the refugees. We were both involved with the Friends Service Committee—at different levels, of course. Despite what you and Russ fantasize about me, I never was in the CIA."

"I don't believe it. The things you've done since then—I

mean, just the few I know about: Where else would you learn how to do them?"

"No matter what I tell you, you won't believe me. To get back to the point, I'll have some men go down to the island and watch over Russ. But I never would count absolutely on something like that. The only real security will be in finding what evidence we can so that we can get him away from Lily and to a place that we control."

CHAPTER 4

Marley only looked for confirmation. As he'd discussed the case further with Joanna he became more certain that there wasn't much mystery. Bill Wright was Russ's assistant, the person with greatest access to Russ's work, and he had introduced Russ to Lily. Marley felt he wasn't going to have to do much detecting.

He stared steadily at Bill Wright across the round, white plastic table, not smiling. He hadn't smiled at anyone, merely glanced and nodded as Joanna introduced each of the staff: "This is Ardeen Marks, who keeps the books and helps me with advertising and marketing. Bill Wright, Russ's assistant; he's a programmer—he's working on an update of *Swiftkick* right now—and handles customer support. And Irene Rich, our office manager—who, of course, is the brains of the outfit."

They'd all smiled at Marley. They'd all looked apprehensive, of course: Joanna and Marley sweeping in at twenty

past nine, interrupting them just as they were settling into
the morning's work, calling them together in the confer-
ence and lunchroom cubicle. They'd all looked alarmed
when Joanna introduced, "James Marley, from David
Cheyney's organization. He's investigating some unusual
circumstances in connection with Russ's leaving."

But they'd all smiled their Pleased-to-meet-you's, expecting Marley to show likewise he'd come in peace. Marley
almost always tried to give that impression. Not today. A
curt nod at each of the women, just long enough to show
he'd recorded their features and would know them in a file
of mug shots. Then he locked on to Bill Wright.

The young man didn't seem to notice, and his initial mis-
givings seemed to disappear. Nice-looking man, big. Might
have played football, wrestled. No awkwardness about his
bulk. He had that ease that goes with good upbringing, fine
physical coordination, and the certainty that no one was
going to give him any trouble. Informally dressed—jeans, a
turtleneck, an M.I.T. sweatshirt, Reeboks. He seemed relaxed. His smile didn't fade completely until Joanna explained that David Cheyney had evidence that Russ's
program had been stolen. Then Bill Wright came up in his
chair, eyes wide, incredulous, horrified. The two women
looked that way, too: stunned, mystified, not able—and
then not willing—to believe. But they, as soon as the initial
shock had swept over them, darted glances at Marley: ner-
vously, guiltily looking to see whether he might think them
guilty.

But Bill Wright, who worked most closely with Russ,
going in and out of Russ's cubicle all day, looking over
Russ's shoulder while he was working, being Russ's
bounce-board; Bill—with his own key to the office—who
could, and often did, work alone there at night: Bill Wright
was a new little lambkin. Marley's steady stare—the master
hangman judging exactly how much slack to put in the

rope—didn't disconcert him at all. No one could think *him* guilty; at least, no one could think so because *he* thought so.

Irene Rich got directly to the point. "How . . . how could that happen, Joanna?"

"That's exactly what I want to ask all of you," Marley broke in. "According to Mrs. Detweiller, Mr. Detweiller was designing the program on his own. I've been told he talked through some of the problems with you, Bill, but that you never actually worked on it—or even saw the codes. Is that true?"

"No, sir, never." Not a trace of defensiveness in Bill's bewildered voice. "The only thing I can think of . . ."

"Yes?"

"Russ was working on the program using a Bernoulli. He kept it in the safe at night. And his backups, too. Anybody—"

"What's a Bernoulli?" Marley snapped. He knew perfectly well, of course; but his tone said nobody was going to flim-flam him with fancy lingo.

Bill Wright's purity admitted no imputation. What a pleasure to explain his craft to a layman! "It's an extra drive. You plug it into your computer, it gives you virtually infinite capacity."

Marley wanted Bill to be worried, but to feel superior—over-confident—too. He played dumb. "The program's in it?"

"The program's on a diskette that you put in and take out."

Marley seemed appalled. "One of those flimsy little—what do you call 'em—floppies? You put your thumb in the wrong place, you've wiped out sixty peoples' records?"

"Yes, sir. I mean, no sir. They're not really floppy any more. The actual disk is inside a plastic case. They're not flimsy. And the window for the drive-head to read the disk is covered by a metal shutter that slides over it when you take it out of the machine. I mean, they're not air-tight, but there's no danger of harming what's inside by ordinary handling."

"And the whole program is on one of those?"

"Yes, sir."

"How big is it?"

"Russ was using a five-and-a-quarter inch diskette."

Marley framed a square of space that size with his hands. "The whole program?"

"Yes, sir."

Marley shook his head as though dubious, and then disapproving. "So somebody could just slip it in his pocket and walk out."

"Russ was very security-conscious, sir. He always kept it in the safe when he wasn't working with it."

"In the safe?"

"Yes, sir."

"Where is the safe?" Marley might have asked Joanna, or Irene, or the room at large. But he asked Bill. His tone said he didn't need to ask at all.

If Bill suspected Marley'd been leading him into a trap, he didn't show it. "In Russ's office, sir."

"Who has access to it?"

"Anybody who could get into the building, sir. The safe's not hidden—it's a free-standing one in the corner of Russ's office. If somebody got in here at night, cracked it . . . If they had their own Bernoulli, the program could be copied in about five minutes."

"Has there been a break-in?" Marley did turn to Joanna, as to a rebuttal witness.

"No. Not that we know of."

"Isn't there a security system?"

"Of course."

Marley trained on Bill Wright again, said nothing as though nothing needed to be said.

Bill sat perfectly still: no fidgeting, no twitching fingers, no shifting eyes. He couldn't, though, control completely his inner reflexes. His normally ruddy cheeks had become blotchy red, and sweat sheened on his forehead.

Clearly, he recognized the problem; he tried earnestly to help solve it. "I don't know, sir, but I'd think that anybody who was going to break in here to steal a program would know what he was doing. I mean, I guess—from what you see in the movies—professionals can get around any system."

Marley continued to stare at Bill Wright—not as though he'd heard and didn't believe—but as though Bill hadn't spoken at all. All five of them sat and stared: Marley and Joanna at Bill, Bill at Marley, Irene back and forth at the two men, Ardeen at her hands folded in front of her on the table.

When silence finally reached some thousand pounds per square inch, Marley spoke—not caring who overheard, but only to Bill, "Well. Mr. Cheyney's investigators on the West Coast will report by this afternoon. Then we'll have all the pieces together and we can call in the police."

Bill Wright's innocence would not be outraged. He nodded with grave but happy expectation.

Marley jerked his head abruptly. "Okay, Mrs. Detweiller. I've got all I need here for now." He rose. "Thank you all for your cooperation," he said like a taped message, and stalked from the room without looking at any of them.

"Yes, I saw, James; but I still don't believe it. Bill is Russ's friend. My friend, too: He's a sweet guy."

"He's a sweet guy who's been bought, Joanna. Somehow, by somebody. Nobody who doesn't have a guilty conscience works that hard to prove he's innocent."

"Maybe he's just tranquil. Maybe he meditates, and he's so at peace with himself he *doesn't* assume he's guilty of anything anybody thinks he might be."

"My gut feeling about him, Joanna, is that he's the kind of real sweet, polite, squeaky-clean, all-American boy who one day takes his arsenal up to the roof and mows down passersby. At one time I was a little like that myself; I recognize the symptoms. But we'll find out for sure about him—in this case—soon. I put a time on coming back after him—this afternoon. I think he'll do something to beat it. If he doesn't, then I'll go back and push him some more. If I'm wrong . . . okay. That's something that happens from time to time, so I know how to make a complete and very sincere apology. But it doesn't happen often."

Marley and Joanna were sitting in her car in the parking lot of a convenience store and launderette. "Now," Marley continued, "you watch from here. Call me if he leaves." Joanna's car was equipped with a telephone. "Follow him—but keep back, don't let him see you; that's more important than possibly losing him. If you can see that he *is* heading for home, let me know that. Then drop away, go back to your house, and wait to hear from me."

"This is what you do, James? This is what your work is like—breaking into people's apartments?"

"Sometimes. Not regularly. Most of the time it's things like meeting you and Russ to give David an opinion on Russ's prospects. Or going down this week to find out about him."

"Well, you seem to be pretty expert about this part."

"I've had some experience."

"But it's illegal. What if. . . ?"

"Fortunately, David can afford a good lawyer."

No more patches of sunlight, pale as flushes on the face of a moribund old man, fleeted across the snow-covered, ash-colored fields. The layer of high cloud stretched evenly. No sun, no portent of snowstorm; by eleven o'clock the day had slipped into coma.

Marley had the directions Joanna'd written for him lying on the passenger seat, but didn't refer to them. They were easy to remember. Four miles on the numbered route, left at the first crossroad. That formerly bumpkin lane through apple country had been made mannerly when the orchards were torn out for split-level manors and clusters of rural townhouse condos. The quirky bends along the course of a now icebound brook had been smoothed and widened, and here and there a guardrail showed in the ridge of unwanted snow shoved to the edges of its shoulders.

After perhaps a mile, past Ladyslipper Lane and Cowslip Crescent and their ilk, Marley reached Cider Hills Condominiums. He cruised slowly along the semicircular drive looking for Bill Wright's number. The buildings were sided with imitation barn-boards; chimneys stood up through their sharp-slanted roofs like stumps in a logged-over forest. Units in each section were attached to one another as though children's blocks had been sprawled at random and the arrangement replicated with obsessive compulsiveness: an illusion of free will in a world predetermined.

He pulled up in front of Bill Wright's unit and looked carefully from side to side. The sense of separateness had been well achieved. None of the immediate neighbors could see Bill's doorway directly and watch his comings and goings. Those in distant sections around the curve might; but no one seemed to be at home in them. All of the residents must be like Bill—young professionals off at work, moving upward. The development felt like some ancient monumental city constructed according to an esoteric geometry, then unaccountably abandoned.

Although he wouldn't be seen tampering with the lock, Marley would never have considered breaking in without advance intelligence. He'd have assumed that an electronics freak like Bill would have a security system. Without the countermeasures of the new-age housebreaker he wouldn't have known what kind or been able to disarm it. But Bill Wright had betrayed his *friends*—people he'd entertained in his home, to whom he'd shown off all his gadgets. So Marley didn't have to worry. He didn't even have to break in.

He pulled ahead and parked in front of the next unit, walked back to Bill's. Going directly to the door, he punched four numbers on a keypad mounted on the casing. The lock clicked open, and he went inside. He strode quickly through the living room, opened the closet next to the entrance from the garage, pushed a hanging dustpan aside, and flipped the switch to disarm the alarm box. He returned to the living room.

Workbench, Scandinavian Design. Stereo system with standard and CD players, tape deck, VCR. TV with a giant screen. Backward-elbow drafting-table lamps for lighting. Dirty dishes—probably from last night's supper—on the coffee table in front of the couch facing the TV. Stack of computer magazines, copies of *Road and Track, Car and Driver.* Over the couch a poster-size, framed, arty photograph of a Ferrari racer at full bore.

Marley glanced into the kitchen—more dirty dishes stacked on an essentially clean counter, waiting to be put into the washer—and went to the bedroom. He wasn't searching, not looking for anything in particular, just looking. On a shelf facing the foot of the bed, another TV, another VCR, another tape deck.

Framed photos on the dresser. Mom—hair curly and every one in order, bright eyes looking right at you, sweet smile and set jaw. Dad—handsome, pleasant: "At ease, men; I used to be an enlisted man myself." Three of a grinning dog. Marley pulled out the dresser drawers, starting with the lowest, felt beneath the clothes without mussing them.

A handmade quilt had been pulled up over the bed, dirty clothes dumped on the quilt. The boy had left his mom's home and didn't have to keep his things picked up, but anything that wasn't in its place clearly had one, and the room was clean.

On the bedside table a paperback novel: On its cover a bare-chested warrior with a sword stood in front of a rocket ship. Marley pulled out the table's drawer. This month's copies of *Playboy, Penthouse, Hustler.* Bill lived alone and felt free to leave his dirty laundry in plain sight, but not his naked women.

On the floor of the open-doored closet stood four pairs of what looked to be hand-tooled cowboy boots. A work-table supported by low file cabinets ran along one wall. Bill's personal computer was on it. Marley guessed Bill would keep his checkbook balance and budget records on spreadsheet files, wished he had time to try to get into them, was sure he already knew what he would find. He pulled open the file drawers.

A telephone—one of those that let you call anyone in the world just by pressing a button—and an answering machine were at the end of the table. The machine's message-indicator light was blinking.

The telephone rang. Marley picked it up. "Yes?"

"James? He's on his way! I've been calling every three minutes!"

"I got in just about that long ago. He's coming already?"

"Yes. He came rushing out of the office not five minutes after you left. He went to the booth at the gas station and made a call, and now he's on his way. He'll be there any minute!"

"Where are you?"

"I'm at the crossroad. I was afraid if I followed him any farther—"

"Right. Okay, go home."

"James—"

"No time. Go home. I'll be in touch."

Bill Wright spun his golden Corvette into his parking place, stopped there, and jumped out, not opening the garage. He rushed through the front entrance and to the burglar alarm, opened the panel door, and reached for the toggle without actually halting. Then he stopped instantly despite his momentum, like a basketball player, on balance, ready.

Marley hadn't reset the alarm.

Bill was wearing a bright red, waist-length ski jacket. He unzipped it to give his arms freedom, brought his hands up to "on guard." He flexed his big shoulders to loosen them. Then he began to prowl forward. Marley might be as tall as he, but had to be fifty pounds lighter. And twenty-five years older. And—although maybe in reasonable shape for an old guy—didn't look like he ran every day and went to a club three times a week like Bill did.

Bill glanced into the kitchen, then again, coming closer to see over the counter in case Marley crouched behind it. He crept along the short hallway, making not a single sound. He paused before passing the bathroom. The door stood partially ajar. He pushed the door open, deliberated, then went on toward the bedroom, walking turned half sideways, checking back so he'd see at least peripherally anyone coming from the bath. As he approached the bedroom doorway he leaned from side to side to see into the corners.

He stepped into the room. "Okay, fuckhead!" He had the words ready to say when he saw Marley. But Marley wasn't there.

Bill glided to the center of the room, so he could see into

the closet, see Marley's legs showing under the clothes hanging on the rack.

"I see you, fuckhead. Come out." But Marley wasn't there.

The bed was too low to hide under. Bill nodded once to himself, turned, and went back to the bathroom. Standing balanced, braced, he edged to the shower stall. That's where they always hide, of course. In the movies. The last place they're looked for; should be the first because that's where they always hide. He waited, then said it.

"Okay, fuckhead, come the fuck out of there!"

No response. He whipped the curtain back.

Marley wasn't there.

For a moment Bill stood stunned with the anticlimax, for another wondering where else Marley could be hiding. But there wasn't anyplace else. He paused, figuring the situation. Obviously, Marley had been there, hadn't found anything (nothing for him to find), left again. He must be assuming Bill still was at work. There was time to get away.

Bill whirled and strode into the bedroom. From his closet he pulled out a soft gym bag, threw it onto the bed, opened it. From one of the file cabinets he snatched out his checkbook and some papers and the key to his safe-deposit box. He grabbed them and three plastic diskette storage boxes, spun back to place them in the suitcase. Then he stood for a moment, as though thinking what else of everything to pack. Maybe he was regretting all the things he couldn't take. Maybe fright was beginning to get down inside him. He was sweating, and his hands started to quiver.

The doorbell rang. He jerked upright as though the bell wire were connected to his tailbone.

After counting ten seconds, Marley pushed the button again, holding it for three. Ten again, and then three. Ten and three. Six times until Bill evidently accepted that Marley wasn't going to leave, and decided what to do about that. He opened the door.

"What do you want?"

Marley caught it all: Bill's surprise, his shocked unbalance because he hadn't figured it right; the abruptness, the angry tone: his attempting to be in control; the fear, the opening with a question, giving away command despite the tone.

Marley had been a soldier, an officer. Once, he'd thought he'd make the army his career—until Vietnam changed his mind. He knew about command. He stood at full height, and—although no taller—bored down into Bill's eyes.

"I want information," he snapped. He leaned like the first quarter inch of a locomotive starting to move, and Bill swayed back. "Your choice, buddy: Talk to me or the police."

Bill faded back a step, and Marley breasted in after him, not letting him get farther away. Without turning he closed the door of Bill's house behind him.

"You stole Russ's program. You introduced him to Lily so that—"

"No . . ."

"Don't you fucking 'no' me, boy! I *know* you did. I just want to know who you're working for."

"Who the fuck're you, Mr. Marley! You've got no right—! You were in here. That's breaking and entering. That's a crime. Maybe *you* want to talk to the police about *that!*"

The lion tamer works by intimidating the beast, moving in, pressing it. But he has to know when to back off. Without actually relaxing, Marley shrugged, softened his tone. "You're right. You could bring charges."

He allowed Bill a moment of thinking he didn't have to lash out to protect himself. Then he said, "Why don't you call them? You can tell them about me, and I can tell them about you, and we can all go down to the station house and talk it over." Then he raised the hoop again. "Tell *me* all about it, and maybe you won't have to talk to the police at all."

"I can't."

Marley had proved what he wanted to then. Bill hadn't denied. All Marley needed was detail. He moved in. "You fucking well better! If you're afraid of anybody, boy, you'd better be *terrified* of me!"

Bill Wright cringed. Big boy, always big, strong; footballer, wrestler, worked out, took some karate. But Marley'd caught those *"Sirs,"* the need to please, the neatness of the well-brought-up; he'd seen Bill's mom and dad many times before that morning.

"If you're afraid of somebody, I'll protect you. But if you don't tell me what I want to know, buddy-boy"—Marley moved on Bill, not shouting but loud, voice hard, words like whip snaps—"I can squeeze your balls until you're screaming"—moved on him physically, making him cower.

Even the best tamer makes mistakes. Bill struck, his arm swinging fast as a big cat's slash, hitting Marley side-of-the-head, staggering him against the coffee table, toppling him. He fell sideways over the table, onto the couch.

Marley was stunned for the barest instant; fully aware again even as he fell; rolling, coming up at once. But in that moment Bill bolted for the door.

His Corvette stood where he'd parked it. Thirty thousand dollars' worth of high-powered road machine, with a twenty-thousand-dollar Callaway upgrade on top. Zero to sixty in four-point-six seconds, one seventy-eight top speed. Only a Ferrari Testarossa might catch it, and neither the police nor Marley had one.

But Marley had moved the lesser car he did have tight against the Corvette's rear bumper.

Bill saw that in one dismayed glance, then sprinted past the two cars and along the drive.

At the doorway, Marley stared after him. Did the kid really think he could *run* away?

At another season he might have, Marley recognized. Bill might have dashed down the drive and out of the condominium grounds, then cut into the woods. Beyond the condo grounds, Marley knew from his map, was a wilderness preserve: trees, underbrush, two ponds, part of the local water supply. Bill might have run in there, outrun older Marley. Now the woodland lay under two feet—three feet—of snow. Where did the boy think he could run to?

Somewhere. He must have been thinking something— he'd slowed his pace from the first panicked sprint to one he probably could keep up for five miles if he had to.

Marley moved in the same way—quickly but with deliberation. He went around his car, got in, started the engine, backed out—all movements precise. He began following Bill just at the bottom of second gear.

He wasn't trying to run Bill down; didn't want to catch him then: corner him and have to fight him. Marley could fight. Bill might be big, younger, strong; but Marley had fought for his life; he probably knew more tricks. But why fight? Let the kid run. Let him exhaust himself—run out his energy, his strength, his panic, his hope of escape.

Then switch tactics. Marley'd bulldozed to break through denial; now he could come on soft and sympathetic. "I want to help you, Bill. I'm not out to jail you. We don't have to tell the police at all." Work on the boy's guilt, but be understanding. Judgmental, as Bill would expect—as he'd want—but then forgiving. Marley'd been brought up strictly, too. He felt for the kid despite what he'd done. Marley planned it as he cruised sixty feet or so behind the running man.

Marley glided in his silver, salt-smeared car that— although moving—seemed a part of the sterile landscape. Snow stretching unbroken to the arctic, winding scar of charcoal asphalt, trees stiff, fossilized like gray coral, Marley's spearhead-shaped machine: Only Bill Wright with his human fear lived. His red jacket—cherry-red, blood-red—

was the only vital color. Each leg lifted, bending, stretching, driving; his arms reached in turn and pulled as though drawing him through air solid with cold.

Where did he think he was running to?

Away, Marley decided. Just *away*. At first he must have thought that Marley wouldn't follow, or could be outdistanced on the road. Marley saw Bill snap a look over his shoulder and know the truth. By then he had run two hundred yards and was where the road passed through the protected area. Beyond the road's shoulders, on either side, was a chain link fence. At fifty-foot intervals large signs said "NO" and listed forbidden activities as if the law might deter anyone whom the fence did not.

Bill looked back again and saw Marley still there. Suddenly he veered, leaped over the ridge of plowed snow, and—wading up to his knees, twisting as though swimming—floundered to the fence. He seized it, got a toe in, climbed, climbed another toehold, then—looking up— seemed at last to realize that strands of barbed wire ran at an angle back above his head.

Marley slowed and stopped and waited.

Bill hung on the fence, his torso lifting and falling with his heavy breathing, a scarlet moth. Except for that, nothing moved. The almost inaudible rumble of Marley's car's motor only emphasized a profound silence; yet the tension of the young man's clinging on the wire was like a single high note impossibly sustained.

Marley waited. Bill hung. He looked at Marley's car, up at the barbed wire, then for a long moment through the fence. Then he climbed down again. He kept his eyes on Marley, obviously expecting him to come on. But Marley waited, letting him stagger to the road.

Bill stood at the roadside, but when Marley—hoping the chase was over—eased the car forward, Bill whirled and began running once more.

"Let him run just a little farther," Marley thought. Where could he go? "Then pull up beside him slowly and try to talk sense to him from inside the car."

The road had been curving gradually to the left. It bent more sharply. Bill rounded the corner. Marley came inexorably behind him and saw an open space appearing ahead. The road map he'd studied flashed into his mind. The back road he and Bill were on crossed a divided highway. There was no access to it: The road must simply bridge over the highway.

At the cut through which the highway passed, the fence right-angled. An extension from it ran out to meet the railing of the overpass. The overpass itself was fenced to keep people from throwing things down onto the traffic below. Between the fences, above the highway shoulder, was a gap of about eight feet. Bill ran to it and began to climb over the railing.

"Bill! Stop! Wait!" Marley stood on his brake, shouted through the side window. He threw the door open, shouting again as he stepped out. "Wait! I want to help you!"

Bill was already over the railing. The way for him to climb down to highway level was to go forward to where the angled strut girder met the overpass carrier beam, then go down the girder. Not a hard climb. The roadbed was only about fourteen feet above the highway. There were handholds, plenty of foot room. But to reach the place where he could step down onto the strut, Bill would have to go out over the inside traffic lane. Even at the distance Marley could see that melt-off from snow had refrozen over the ironwork.

Marley hesitated, paralyzed between running toward Bill and fear of driving him to desperate folly. "Bill, wait!"

Bill edged out beyond the start of the overpass fence, moving slowly, carefully. He crouched, grabbing railing stanchions. He lowered his foot, found the lip of the strut,

put his weight on it, didn't slip. He set his other foot. He
shifted one hand to the lip of the carrier beam, then the
other. He edged to his left, moving carefully down the
strut, shifting his hands one at a time.

Marley's hands gripped the top of his car door tightly
enough to keep both men from falling.

Bill took another step, slid on the ice coating the strut,
dropped to full length. He hung for an instant, then his
hands slipped, too. He fell.

Marley'd begun running before Bill hit the ground. He
might have set a record for the twenty-yard dash. His blood
rose to the strain at once, but without thinking he knew
that wasn't the source of the roar in his ears. A roar rising,
and then a shriek.

Marley reached the railing, striking it, almost hurling
himself over from the momentum of his sprint, even before
the monstrous mass of the trailer had emerged completely
from underneath him. Although it now seemed to writhe
and want to slip sideward—the driver must have been
standing on his brake, steering to keep from jackknifing—
there could not have been any way to make it swerve in
time.

Marley stared down to see Bill Wright's mangled body
on the road behind the truck, wanting desperately not to
look, but compelled to: to see the irregular splotch of that
bright red jacket, and the stain spreading from it over the
salt-white cement.

The road behind the truck was bare. There was no body.
Marley stared in disbelief, then raised his eyes to the rear
of the trailer—now halted sixty feet away on the shoulder—knowing with sick certainty what must have happened.

Dropping down from the cab, the truck driver sprinted to
the end of his rig. Then he halted, staring as Marley had
done at the bare road. He must have reached Marley's con-

clusion, too. He ran back to look at the front of the truck. He dropped to his knees to peer underneath. After a moment, he rose.

Marley watched, waiting to see the man's shoulders sag, waiting to see him slump against the front fender, drained by horror. But the driver came up only to a half crouch. Bent over, he came three steps along the side of the trailer, went down on his knees to look under. He rose and repeated the movements. Finally, he stood at the rear of the trailer, staring back toward the overpass, shaking his head. For the first time, he saw Marley. They held one another's eyes for a moment. The driver spread his arms, and shook his head again.

Marley became aware that the steel of the overpass railing was freezing his hands. He drew them away, put them into his coat pockets. Only then did his thinking seem to uncongeal. He crossed to the other side of the overpass. Leaning over the rail, he could see tracks along the bridge's abutment, going up the bank there and at an angle toward the chain link fence on that side. Not far from the overpass, erosion had cut a channel under the fence.

Bill had been doubly lucky, Marley realized. Not only had he been able to roll clear just in front of the truck, but Marley's assumption that the boy had been hit had distracted him from seeing the escape.

Marley walked back to his car, considering. The road from the condo development had curved to meet the highway: Bill probably was slogging across the water preserve to reach his place from the rear. He could get his car, perhaps pick up whatever he'd come home for in the first place, and flee. If Marley hurried, he might catch Bill inside again. He didn't want to hurry. He felt he'd had as narrow an escape as Bill had; didn't want to corner the boy another time.

After all, Bill's flight would be enough to prove to Russ

how the program had been stolen; and Bill had introduced Lily—so she *must* be involved, too. How could Russ doubt that?

Marley remembered Lily laughing, remembered the look of love she gave Russ when she set his dinner before him, remembered Russ's looks at her.

His fingers still were quivering. He gripped the steering wheel tightly as he spun it and turned his car around.

Marley was just pulling around the drive toward Bill's condo when the Corvette shot in a backward arc out of its parking place and—without seeming to stop moving—exploded forward and away in a cloud of burning rubber.

Reflexively, Marley kicked his own accelerator. His Subaru Turbo leaped forward, but it might have been standing still in comparison to the Corvette. By the time he reached Bill's house, Bill was screeching around onto the road beyond the last condo building. By the time Marley reached that corner, Bill was on his way to Mars.

Marley slowed. He wasn't ever going to catch the bomb Bill was driving, and there were patches of ice and loose sand on all the roads. He pulled to the side and sat for ten minutes, thinking what to do next. When he reached the junction with the numbered route, he paused and waited patiently for traffic before turning to go back past Russ's office on his way to Joanna's house again. He would have to be patient, he realized. Joanna could contact the police; they could put out a bulletin on Bill as a suspect; eventually—

As if his planning alone set events in motion, Marley heard a siren approaching from behind. In a moment, he saw the sparking blue lights racing up. He steered to the side of the road, went on even more slowly as the blue and gray state police car sped up and past him. Howling, it disappeared around a bend.

Eventually—probably fairly quickly, given the recognizability of Bill's car—the police would find him, and then he could be persuaded to confess. Too bad it would have to be done that way—with the police, but—

Marley started into the next curve. Near its apex the blue lights were spinning, flashing. Two sets—another car must have arrived from the other direction. One policeman stood out in the road directing traffic. He was holding oncoming cars, motioning for Marley to pass quickly, without gawking. Marley didn't gawk. One glance showed him the golden Corvette wrapped and broken around a bent utility pole, and the other policeman—grim-faced—standing with his back to it.

CHAPTER 5

"It wasn't your fault, James."

"Right." Marley spoke without turning to Joanna, not looking away from the flames in the woodstove, sitting in his usual place on the couch, staring at the fire as he had since he'd finished telling her about Bill Wright.

Joanna slid to the front of her rocker, leaning toward Marley. "I mean, it's awful, and I feel terrible, too. I'm terribly sorry about him, for him . . . but he did it to himself."

"Right."

"You weren't even chasing him when he . . . when the accident happened."

"Right."

"You weren't chasing him, he wasn't running from *you*; he was running from his own guilty conscience."

"Right."

"Don't keep saying 'Right' as if you agreed with me and weren't all on edge about it!"

Marley looked at her, then at the way she was sitting. "Wrong. *You're* on edge. I'm just relaxing, enjoying the fire." He leaned back against the couch for the first time, crossing his arms with elaborate casualness.

"If you think holding on to yourself that way looks relaxed, you're mistaken."

Marley put his hands down. He turned his head away from her, toward the bleakness outside the high windows.

Joanna moved to sit on the edge of the couch beside him. She put a hand over his.

"James . . ."

"Yeah. Well, there are the two parts: what *he* did, what *I* did." He looked at her. "The irony. Boggling. He fell from that bridge, must have missed being hit by that truck by inches—a split second. A miraculous escape. And then, not ten—fifteen—minutes later . . . So, yes, we can say, 'It was his time,' and I didn't really have anything to do with it. And it did happen because he was a thief. On the other hand, if I'd handled it differently . . ."

Joanna tightened her fingers on Marley's.

"Right," he said. "It happened; it's over." Putting on a quick smile and returning her grip, he said, "Thanks." Then he freed his hand. "So, the next move . . ." His gaze went back toward the fire.

"Yes?" she prompted.

"When I talked with Russ this morning—as I told you— he accepted my word about someone trying to beat him out on the program. He said he'd go back to work. But if Lily's there . . .

"Bill's guilt is established. That *ought* to be enough to convince Russ about Lily, but it might not. I think I'd better spend a little more time—just what's left of this afternoon, this evening: we can't afford more—trying to do better."

"How?"

"Go into Boston and see if I can find something about

her. I don't know what; anything that might tie her in with the theft of the program, or cast doubt on what she's told Russ—and me."

"And then?"

"If I discover something convincing I'll call Russ again and tell him what I know. If I don't, I'll try to persuade him at least to move her out for now. Or even to come back here."

For several moments Marley continued looking at Joanna, while she stared toward the corner of the room where a large tropical plant wasn't doing very well. Suddenly, she shuddered, and—rubbing her upper arms—said, "We should have bought a larger stove."

Silhouettes of scraggly palm trees framed a huge tropical moon. *Exotic! Torrid!* A mat woven of palm-leaf strips covered the door into the bar, its checkerboard squares highlighted by lines of powdery snow. Marley stood next to it, pretending to look at the photos of nude women on either side of the palm-tree placard. *Topless! Bottomless! Hot! Hot! Hot!* The placard was lettered with pink and orange Day-Glo paint. Despite the dead, blue-black cold of late afternoon, Marley was glad he wouldn't have to go into the place for very long.

He would have to be there for a few minutes so that the man following him wouldn't suspect he'd been seen. At each of the other four places, Marley had been inside long enough to order a beer, to be approached by one of the girls and buy her a watered drink, to put a twenty on the bar for her and one for the bartender, to be told no, they didn't know any Lily Lee.

Marley had spotted the man watching him from a stool near the end of the bar at the fourth place, the Black Pussy Lounge. Marley was using the mirror behind the bar, checking his back out of habit instead of looking at the reflection of a girl under a spotlight bouncing a short plastic fringe draped across her crotch. The guy wasn't good at his work. He stared at Marley obviously. He should have figured the mirror, that Marley might see him despite being turned away toward the "hostess" on the next stool. With dark hair tousled over his forehead, dull eyes, full lips, he was a Sylvester Stallone look-alike despite being oriental. He must have known it—he even wore a matchstick in a corner of his mouth. A bodybuilder, too, probably: He leaned over his forearms as though the bulk of his shoulders needed supporting.

Marley checked the man while putting the girl beside him at ease so he could ask her about Lily. He did that by letting her try to put him at ease. *She* was good at *her* work. She must instantly have recognized him as a square who didn't do the Combat Zone regularly, so she worked at turning him on without scaring him away. Although she'd run her tongue slowly, as though absentmindedly, along her upper lip each time she sipped her drink, and although she kept her voice soft so he had to bend close to hear her, she made the mannerisms seem like shyness. Her skin was still good, her copper-orange hair possibly natural. Young; it might have been imagined she didn't realize how leaning on her arm pushed the roundness of her breast above the line of her low-cut dress. Marley knew she wasn't a nice girl, though; and he knew what she was doing in a place like that. Still, the question did occur to him.

After he'd been given his "No" about Lily, Marley left the bar. He was apparently appraising the delights displayed in the window of a dirty bookstore half a block away on Washington Street when "Rocky" came out of the Black Pussy. Marley crossed to the Hot Palms. Using the reflection in the glass covering the placard, he watched the young man take the place in front of the bookstore and watch him.

Marley breathed deeply, enjoying the thrill of excitement and satisfaction. He hadn't really *expected* anything from his inquiry. He'd hoped, mildly, he might be told something interesting about Lily, or that his curiosity might elicit some small but useful reaction from the people he talked to. But now—a man sent to follow him was a link back to the sender. That the man was a klutz seemed a dream come true.

With the resolve of a man who has to reach a prize by wading through manure, Marley went into the bar.

Cigarette smoke thickened the air. Lamps here and there in the ceiling made it glow a pale, feverish rosy purple. At the far end of the room, a woman on a platform displayed her top- and bottomlessness, writhing to an acid-rock beat. Most of the dozen men in the bar stared at her without any evident excitement, sitting lumpily over their drinks. There were more men in that place than at any of the others Marley had checked.

He glanced at his watch. Nearly five. He guessed trade would be picking up in all of the bars now that the workday had ended. And the streets would be increasingly jammed with cars, the sidewalks packed with people hurrying to the "T" from the New England Medical Center, the Department of Agriculture building, and all the other neighboring offices and businesses.

Stepping up to the bar, he ordered yet another beer he wouldn't drink. A girl sitting at a booth with three others started to rise, pulling on a welcome like a heavy raincoat, but he waved her off. She didn't seem offended—all but two of the other men were drinking alone.

Turning so he wouldn't have to see the dancer, Marley considered the situation.

The by-the-book approach would be to slip the tail, then

tail him. If Marley's star was shining above the layer of winter cloud, the guy would go directly back to whoever had sent him. If—more likely—he reported by phone, he still could be followed, his identity learned. He might have an arrest record. Over the course of a few days'—a week's—surveillance, a network of which he was a part might be traced.

But with the clock ticking away the time for Russ to complete his program, Marley didn't have leisure to do that. Instead, he'd have to trap the man and squeeze him.

"Squeeze." Marley grimaced at the image of himself trying to grab a gorilla. But there might be a way . . .

He signaled the bartender. "Would you have a roll of nickels I could buy?"

The bartender didn't look surprised at the request. He surely already knew how a roll of coins that size fits into a fist. But he didn't look eager to accommodate Marley, either.

"Will that cover it?" Marley asked, putting a ten on the bar. The man said nothing. He took Marley's bill, put it into the cash register, deftly palmed the eight dollars' change into his own pocket, and returned with the roll. "Thanks," Marley said, putting it into the pocket of his coat.

He stepped out of the bar into the stream of people, and turned left, toward Stuart. Still across Washington Street, the tail had moved away from the bookstore a dozen feet in that direction, and was standing with his back against the graffiti-scrawled facade of a boarded-over movie theater.

Coming from the bar was like turning from one to another of Gustave Doré's engravings of the circles of Hell. Ice-white streetlamps cut the storefronts' lurid neon, revealing drawn faces of the people passing with a pitiless highlight and shadow. The commuters rushed, seemingly driven, hunched and leaning forward, forcing themselves through the invisible density of the bitter cold.

Marley stayed close to the building line, moving counter to the direction of the crowd. Pausing for a moment in an entryway—*Peepshow! Live Nudes! Private Booths!*—he looked around as though taking bearings, deciding on his next move. The follower had kept with him.

Marley continued to the corner of Stuart and Washington, turned left. That quickly, he was out of the Combat Zone. If he turned left again at Harrison Street, the next major intersection, he could pass through one of the oriental arches into Boston's Chinatown. During the years he'd lived in Boston, he'd come to Chinatown restaurants often; so although he hadn't been in any of the establishments in the Combat Zone before that day, he knew the streets around and through it well.

Glancing into an angled store window as he passed, he checked that the tail still was following. As Marley had expected, the man had crossed Washington at the corner to be behind him on the same side of Stuart.

Halfway down toward Harrison, a narrow side street cut through the block to the left. Marley turned into it. The street provided service access to the kitchens of two restaurants. Cooking-oil smell hung congealed in the air. Spilled garbage—coarse-veined Chinese cabbage leaves—had frozen to the curb. It might have been there since December.

Midway along that street, an alleyway opened—to the left again. Only a dozen feet wide, its far end blocked by a building facing Washington Street, it provided an emergency exit from the backs of the buildings flanking it. A spindly cross-hatching of fire escape ironwork clung to the brick walls, looking as brittle as the icicles that hung from window ledges. One length of ladder had fallen and lay half buried in the soot-splotched snow like a dinosaur's bones.

A dumpster hulked beside the left-hand wall near the mouth of the alley.

Marley had been walking at a moderate pace. The tail had closed the distance behind him to about thirty feet— enough so that other people screened him, not enough to lose Marley in the crowd on Stuart. But when the man turned into the side street, Marley had vanished. Only four other people were walking along it at that moment; the man couldn't miss Marley if he were among them. And Marley couldn't have reached the end of the street and disappeared around a corner even if he'd sprinted.

It must have taken the man some time to react to the surprise, and then to figure the possibilities. Perhaps he walked down the middle of the street and looked into doorways and then the alley. Marley heard footsteps of people passing, but none he could identify as Rocky's.

Marley crouched behind the end of the dumpster, listening for the crunch of a foot on the alley's lumpy, crusted snow. Light fell from upper-story windows, making the snow glow palely through its grime. The alley's doorways and corners might look dark from the street, but if the man came in as far as the end of the dumpster he'd be able to see whether Marley was hiding in one of them.

A minute. Two minutes. Maybe the trick wouldn't work, and the guy would go away. The mortuary cold was seeping through Marley's coat. Nearly three minutes, then Marley heard the step.

Setting his own feet carefully, slipping along slowly so his coat brushing the bricks and metal wouldn't make an audible scrape, thankful once again for his skinniness, Marley crept through the narrow space between the dumpster and the wall, back toward the mouth of the alley. He came out, then—moving fast—rounded that end of the dumpster and started into the alley again.

It worked better than he'd hoped. He'd expected the

man to hear him coming, and turn, and be eight feet away. He'd expected to base the fake-gun trick on the shape in his pocket. But the man had halted and stepped up to peer into the dumpster, so Marley caught him from behind and pulled out the roll of nickels and jammed its end hard against his back.

"It's a silenced forty-four, and it'll blast your backbone through your belly button! Come down slowly."

The man had stiffened, and he kept his hands on the lip of the dumpster, but he didn't comply.

"Nobody on the street's going to know what's going on here. If I shoot you, nobody'll know what happened. If they do, I'll still get away. So do like I say: Come down slowly."

Marley must have been persuasive. The man did step down slowly, keeping his hands in place on the dumpster.

"If you just keep thinking about how I can cut you in half before you could touch me, you can put your hands down—slowly! Good. Now we look like we're back here doing a dope deal, so nobody'll pay any attention to us.

"Okay," Marley went on, ever so smoothly but with his black-iron tone, "I'm going to ask you some questions, and you're going to answer me or I'll blow you away." So the man wouldn't make a mistake, he repeated his warning. "I can do that back here, and get away with it, right? You're a smart boy, right? You got the picture, right?"

"You gotta picture, right?"

Marley froze as the low voice spoke in his ear, and he felt through his coat the jab that—he knew instantly—was not a roll of nickels.

After only a split second's hesitation, Marley affirmed, "Right," very clearly.

The man behind spoke two words Marley couldn't understand, and the other turned and put his hand over Marley's "pistol." With a grunt of surprise he took the roll of nickels. He stared down at his palm for a moment. "Fucking wise-ass son of a bitch!" Suddenly, his fist closed around the coins and he hit Marley's ribs.

Marley twisted to take the blow, and his coat absorbed some of its force. He wasn't hurt, but he was glad the guy had been merely venting annoyance instead of trying seriously to punch him out.

Again the man with the gun spoke words Marley didn't comprehend to his partner, sharply. Then he said, "Okay. You turn 'roun' now. Slow, slow."

Marley did as he was told.

The man between him and the street had stepped back just out of Marley's reach. Clearly professional, he was holding a pistol concealed by his body from anyone passing on the street, pointing it casually at Marley's stomach. Much older than his partner, he wore a hat—a snappy narrow-brimmed fedora with a band that turned down to keep his ears and neck warm, a neat double-breasted car coat, suede gloves. He was Asian, too: high cheekbones, tight, papery skin. He looked Marley up and down in silence.

While he did, Marley worked at being alert to the moment, trying not to think about how he could have missed spotting the young man's partner. Actually, the explanation was simple: He'd focused on the obvious follower and missed seeing the one who wasn't obvious, because he'd never suspected there'd be two of them. Marley tried not to think about not suspecting there'd be two.

Rocky manacled Marley's upper arm with one hand, started to steer him toward the street.

"I come behind," the older man said. "Like you say, Ace, man can shoot 'nother man here, nobody catch him. Right?"

"Right. But wait just a minute. You're going to take me somewhere?"

"That's *right*," the man with the gun exclaimed, drawing

out "right" as though congratulating a dimwit for trying especially hard.

"That means you want information from me," Marley continued. "If you only wanted to lean on me, or take me out, you could do it here. If you're going to take me somewhere, you're going to question me."

"Hey, Ace, you terrific. Whatta mind. You oughta go on TV."

"So, if you want to ask me something, ask me. Maybe I'll tell you right here, and we can all go home and get our feet thawed out again."

"Terrific, terrific." The man shook his head as though in admiration, but kept his gun hand steady.

"So, why not?"

"It's nice try, Ace, but problem is, *I* don't wanna ask you *anything*."

Bad news, Marley recognized; bad, bad news. If he was questioned by someone on a higher level than these two hoods, that someone might not want Marley to be able to identify him after the questioning was over. On the other hand, if he *could* escape then, he'd have exactly the information he wanted—more than he'd hoped for. Nice to have a bright side to look on, he told himself.

As though they all were out together for *dim sum* and a night on the town, the two men led Marley down the dark side street, away from Stuart and then right at the corner. Rocky had released his grip and fallen back half a step. But his oxlike shoulder brushed the back of Marley's arm, and "Dapper Dan" was following closely with his hand on the pistol in his pocket, so Marley never allowed himself to think about trying to run or fight.

They walked two blocks into Chinatown. Only a few commuters, hunched and looking down, hurried along the ice-scabbed sidewalk there. Despite the bitter cold that seemed to have frozen their faces, some men stood outside the doors of noodle shops, smoking cigarettes they held between fingers and thumb. Bundled-up women stepped in and out of stores where the corpses of chickens, plucked and cured leather-brown, hung in the windows by their necks. Most of the people seemed not to notice Marley and the other men, and he didn't want to count on any of them as witnesses.

"Here." The younger man grabbed Marley's shoulder to direct him toward a door between a curio shop and a restaurant where the day's offerings were chalked on blackboards in Chinese characters. A tarnished plaque on the door had characters, too, and a translation in English under them—*Bright Morning Enterprises, Inc.*

"Upstairs."

Marley climbed through the smells of cooking oil and cabbage, ginger and sesame, and other reeks and pungencies he couldn't name. The men followed closely—but not so closely that he could consider throwing himself backward to topple them. Where the wall along the stairs wasn't scarred and greased and grimed from people rubbing against it, other injuries had been inflicted, staining and mottling it, flaking its paint.

At the second floor, Marley was pointed toward a door with frosted glass. It opened into an office: two old wooden desks, straight-backed visitors' chairs, olive-drab file cabinets that might have been army surplus: the headquarters, it would seem, of some shoestring—if not downright sleazy—business. Marley suspected otherwise at once, though, when his quick scan caught the closed-circuit TV camera mounted in one upper corner.

The man with the pistol said, "Wait," and then spoke a word to his partner in Chinese. The young man crossed the room and knocked at a door partially concealed by file cabinets. He spoke, and a voice inside answered curtly. The young man opened the door and nodded for Marley to come. As he passed into the inner office, Marley saw a small plaque on it. This one was polished, and—under Chinese characters—it said, "Stanley Ho."

Treasures kept within nondescript chests: Marley'd met the practice before, not only in the Orient. Despite the drabness of the stairway and outer office, he wasn't surprised when he saw the hand-tied carpet and the intricately carved dragons on the cabinet, the jewel-brilliance of the peacocks posing on a gold-leaf screen. Even the modern, Western, furniture was expensive: chrome and leather chairs, billiard-table-size desk of polished rosewood. The cashmere turtleneck sweater worn by the man sitting behind the desk; his silk-and-wool-blend jacket—soft and lightweight: They'd keep him cuddly warm but unencumbered even through a Boston February.

"Sit down," Stanley Ho said in a sandalwood voice—not quite an order, but certainly not a polite invitation, either. Marley sat in one of the chairs facing the desk. Stanley Ho looked at Marley, and Marley looked at him.

Marley didn't like what he saw. Oh, the man's face seemed pleasant enough. In his late thirties; beginning to be a little fleshy, but not overweight; his hair "styled," moderately full; his fingers manicured. His expression said he liked to cut shrewd but mutually beneficial deals. Marley could imagine him at a Rotary luncheon, mixing good fellowship and commerce without conflict; or at home with his feet up, watching Bill Cosby over his toes; or taking the family for a Sunday sail on the Charles.

But Marley didn't like the man's eyes. They looked at him like those of a scrap dealer surveying a load of crushed cars. The truth always shows in the eyes, Marley'd found. Stanley Ho prompted, "Your name is. . . ?" and by the tone of his voice seemed cordial; but the truth showed in those enameled eyes.

"James Marley."

"You're interested in Lily Lee?" He might have been asking, "You're interested in ginseng tea?" and implying he could fill a warehouse with it if the price were right.

"Yes."

"Why?"

"She's run off with a friend of mine. I'm a friend of the family, his wife, kids . . . I just want to know something about her."

After an instant, Ho's eyes swiveled from Marley's as though on gimbals; his pleasantly neutral expression didn't change. Marley understood the movement just enough not to be surprised when Rocky smashed a fist down onto his left shoulder from behind. Marley wasn't surprised, but expecting the blow didn't keep him from feeling he'd been hit with a piece of three-inch iron pipe. Despite the cushioning of his sheepskin coat, his whole arm went numb to any feeling but pain.

He pulled himself upright in the chair. Stanley Ho was looking at him again, still with affable interest on his face, still with no emotion at all in his eyes.

Ho said, "You work for David Cheyney."

"I do. I *am* a friend of the Detweillers, also."

"Why are you interested in Lily Lee?"

"For both reasons. Russ Detweiller and his family *are* my friends, and Russ is financially involved with David Cheyney." The latter information wasn't meant to be secret from anyone, and—at the cost of a nearly paralyzed left arm—Marley'd learned it certainly was no secret to Stanley Ho. "For both reasons I wanted to find out about the woman he's run off with."

"What have you found out?"

"That Lily's involved with some pretty mean people." As he sensed Ho was about to signal again, Marley added, "That's all. Nobody in the bars told me anything. I have no other information about her."

"What other information *do* you have?"

"About what?"

Too quick: Ho's eyes shifted, Rocky's sledgehammer fist hit before Marley could speak or move. He couldn't keep from gasping, and he had to use the hand he *could* feel on the arm of the chair to pull himself upright again.

"What do you want me to tell you about?"

"What do you think I would like to know?"

No way he could turn and fight from that deep chair; no chance of springing out of it and across the desk. No one outside, Marley was sure, would hear him shouting. As he appreciated Ho's style of interrogation, Marley's sweating wasn't only because of his coat and the steam heat.

On principle, of course, he didn't want to tell Ho anything. But as the microseconds before the man would signal for the next blow streamed away, Marley also decided there was nothing he needed to hide.

"I know that the codes for the program Russ Detweiller is designing were stolen by his assistant, Bill Wright. I know they were passed to somebody on the West Coast, who's using them to try to beat Russ to copyrighting the program. That's all I know."

Stanley Ho didn't take time to consider whether "That's all I know" might be true. He raised his eyes, Rocky struck, and Marley was driven down sideways in the chair.

Marley took a moment to let the wave of pain ebb. He might have hoped that two of those blows would have numbed his nerves beyond further feeling; but it hadn't happened yet. When he could, he raised himself again.

"That's all I think I know. If you have anything specific in mind"—he had to catch a breath—"I will certainly try to give you a specific answer."

"How did David Cheyney find out the codes had been stolen? How did he learn someone was working with them?"

"I don't know." Marley twisted and pitched forward just enough so that the blow only grazed his back. "I don't know!" he shouted. Then, trying to sound merely reasonable, he said, "I think this'll work better for both of us if you just ask questions and listen to my answers. Unless the point is really for you to get your jollies." Hoping he looked neither cowed nor defiant, Marley sat up again. "Now, I work for David Cheyney, but he doesn't tell me everything. He told me some competitor was working on Russ's program; he did not tell me how he knows."

"Do you know how long it will take Russell Detweiller to complete his work?"

"Two to three weeks," Marley lied. He couldn't steel himself without showing he expected to be hit, so he had to take it again, and for one instant thought he'd pass out, and for another that he'd be sick. "Two to three weeks through first-level testing," he gasped out as soon as he could. "Something less than that—a week or so—to complete the codes. That's what he told me."

Stanley Ho stared at Marley in silence, then looked up—this time over Marley's other shoulder. He spoke in Chinese. Dapper Dan gave a monosyllabic assent, then stepped into Marley's view and said in English, "Okay, Ace. We take you 'way, let you go, now."

Stanley Ho didn't say goodbye. He didn't tell Marley to "stay off the case, or else." Although he held that steady stare, he seemed to be looking at a man he knew was already dead.

When the traffic light flashed green, Rocky turned the car right. He pulled fifteen feet along Harrison Street before having to stop in the line waiting for the next light. Marley was being abducted at a speed approaching one-tenth mile per hour.

He sat stiffly in the front passenger seat, watching other cars and the commuters still on the sidewalks, trying to see a way to escape. Despite the throbbing ache, he wouldn't give the other men the satisfaction of seeing him rub his shoulder.

Escaping ought to be easy. The car was standing still or—the traffic light ahead changed to green—barely creeping forward. They were in the middle of a traffic jam and all those people were rushing along on the sidewalk. It ought to be easy for him to lift the lock button, open the door, step out. Once he was on the street again, his captors couldn't shoot him and fade into the crowd—the car imprisoned them as much as him.

"Don't think 'bout it, Ace," said Dapper, who was sitting directly behind Marley. "I shoot you right through back of seat, nobody see. Somebody look into car while we're drivin', they think you're takin' little sleep."

By going through the yellow, Rocky got around the corner without halting again. They made two long blocks—clear through Chinatown—before another light stopped them. People hurried along the sidewalks there, too—chins down, looking neither right nor left—but fewer of them; and there were no storefront lights to shine directly into the car. The time had passed when Marley might have called the gunman's bluff and made a move. He recognized that; but he hadn't thought the man was bluffing.

Again they crawled, entering the ramp down to the Expressway, which passed through cuts and tunnels below city-street level there. Then Rocky accelerated—in the style of the longtime Boston driver, without glancing to check whether there was a space for him—and entered the stream of cars speeding through the underpass.

"Can you get any more heat outta that thing?" the man behind Marley asked. "It's like freezer back here."

The driver reached to turn up the fan.

Marley considered grabbing the man's arm, struggling with him, making the car crash, and rejected the idea instantly. The man behind might shoot him before he could cause a crash. He decided to bide his time. That's how it worked, Marley knew: why victims went along quietly to a place for execution, how they were made to dig their own graves: They were biding their time, waiting for the right moment to escape. Marley's moment had always come, on other occasions. He kept himself poised between the confidence those experiences gave him and the sense he shouldn't crowd his luck.

Rush-hour traffic was heavy but fast, the feeling of speed increased by the roaring rush confined within the tunnel walls. The noise level dropped with a shocking abruptness as they flashed out of one underpass, crashed around them again as they hurtled into the next.

They swept out of the last tunnel, and around and up, rising onto the long, northern, elevated stretch of the Expressway. The regular red-dot lines of taillights ahead were gleaming brilliantly, with sporadic flashes along them. Rocky hit his brake, and brought the car to a stop inches behind the bumper of the car in front.

"Just keep it cool, now, Ace."

As a former Bostonian, Marley knew that rush-hour traffic tie-ups on the Expressway are as normal as the coming of winter, and are accepted and gotten through with the same stoical perseverance. Drivers listened to their radios or tapes, watched their chances to move ahead. Some men eyed women, some women flirted back; but most everyone observed the unwritten rule about not staring into another's car. Unless someone broke that rule, Marley might as well have been chained inside an armored truck.

Creep ahead, pause; creep ahead, pause. Sometimes cars would move faster in one or another of the three lanes. At one moment a space opened in the leftmost lane, and

Rocky seemed about to pull into it. Dapper said something to him, and he stayed in the middle one.

Marley refused to be overcome by the sense of nightmare, of being inside a clear-glass tank filled with water, drowning while a throng of people passed outside, waving his arms in slow motion, striking his fists on the glass without sound. If only he could attract the attention of someone in another car, and hold it long enough to make a move . . .

"Look 'head, Ace. Just keep your eyes front."

Marley did as he was told. He stared at the rear of the station wagon in front of them. Grime, dried salt, freezing slush coated it. Several sets of skis were racked on the roof. Suddenly the rear wiper arced back and forth twice, and then was still again. The faces of two children appeared. They looked this way and that. The wagon pulled forward one car length, Rocky closed the space up to its bumper again. The children focused on him and Marley.

In a flash, Marley goggled his eyes, stuck out his tongue, then instantly blanked his expression. The children started back in surprise. Rocky looked sideways at Marley, but Marley had resumed posing as the Great Stone Face.

The little boy pressed his face to the rear window, squashing his nose, twisting his lips. Marley retorted with three quick rabbit-wriggles of his own upper lip and nose. The little girl must have squealed with pleasure. She rocked back and clapped her hands together.

"What the fuck you doin'?" Rocky demanded.

"What?" Marley asked, all innocence.

"What he do?" from the back seat.

"What am I doing?" Marley chorused.

"I don't know what he's doin'. Must be doin' something—look at those kids."

"What am I doing?" Marley asked again, eyes wide, eyebrows straining toward his hairline.

"Cut it out, Ace."

Marley shrugged as though in bewildered incomprehension—his shoulders hunched up to his ears, his lips puckered as though about to kiss a cow.

"Cut it out!"

Marley relaxed his expression. Dapper slid to the center of the seat so he could see more of the side of Marley's face. "You watch it, Ace. Don't get cute."

"Right." Marley pulled himself up straighter in the seat, made his face a mask of determined unexpressiveness. But he stared directly at the little boy.

The boy stuck out his tongue. Marley showed no reaction. With his forefingers, the boy pulled his mouth wide, stuck out his tongue again, crossed his eyes. Marley stared straight at him, didn't react. The boy waggled his head from side to side, wiggled his tongue up and down. He couldn't make Marley break.

Marley certainly had the attention of people in another car now; but what good did it do him? Two kids five? six? seven? years old. If he started a fight, if the man behind him shot him and he made a spectacle of dying, would the kids have any understanding of what was happening?

And then even the dim hope that the children might provide a way to save himself seemed to vanish. Cars in the right-hand lane had been moving up. The station wagon driver saw an opening, darted into it.

Rocky closed the gap, coming up to the blank back of a trailer, had to halt again. In another moment, traffic on the right stopped, too. Marley tried to swivel his head slightly to see who might be in the car beside them.

"Straight 'head, Ace."

Straight ahead. The trailer back, a gray, featureless wall: Marley's future.

The wall moved forward. Rocky eased down the accelerator and followed it. Slowly, the vehicles in the center lane passed those in the now-blocked right one; so slowly that it felt as though the middle lane was standing still while the other cars were drawn past, backward. The rear of the station wagon came into sight. The children still peered from the rear window. Marley caught the eye of the little girl. Without moving any other muscles, he dropped his right eyelid in a wink. The girl poked her brother, and pointed.

"You be good, now, Ace. Straight 'head."

Marley kept his face squarely forward, but as the wagon began to slip by, he swiveled his eyes to keep them on the boy. The wagon's rear seat had been folded down. The children scrambled to the side windows as Marley passed them. Once again the boy pressed his face to the glass. Marley shifted his glance a degree to the boy's father in the driver's seat; saw him turn his head to see what the kids were looking at. In an instant, Marley twisted his head, stuck out his tongue at the man, and was looking forward again.

"Ace. . . ! Watch it!"

"You watch it, Ace," Marley snapped back without turning. "Look at them—in the wagon." Sure the man would look, Marley waited only a moment, then turned to the wagon himself. He grinned and nodded to the driver. The man grinned back, and his wife—next to him—leaned to see Marley, too.

"They see us, Ace," Marley said over his shoulder. "You punch me, shoot me: They'll see it. He stands on his horn, the whole Expressway sees you." To keep the wagon driver's attention, Marley took the chance and smiled again and waved. The gunman didn't shoot him, so—moving swiftly but not so fast as to provoke an impulsive response—Marley lifted the lock button, opened the door, and stepped out of the car. "So long, Ace. See you around."

CHAPTER 6

It couldn't be that easy, of course. Marley heard the car door slam, and knew the three seconds of shock he'd hoped for had flown. Passing the car ahead of the station wagon, he ran bent over along the narrow space between the right-hand lane of cars and the snow-banked guardrail. By the time he ran another car length, Dapper Dan would have dashed behind the wagon and been able to see him.

About a tenth of a mile ahead an access lane fed cars onto the Expressway from the right. That ramp would be Marley's only escape—the Expressway was elevated too high for him to think of jumping over the side. The line of cars on his left and the guardrail on the right walled a gauntlet for him to run—narrow, straight, harshly lighted from overhead and from the headlamps of the cars.

Man Shot on Expressway! Assailant Escapes—Motorists Too Stunned to React. Marley saw the headlines even as he sprinted alongside a van. He might hope that the man—

now undoubtedly in the lane behind him, probably halted, feet apart, both hands holding his pistol, aiming—would be thinking, too: *Despite Shock Witnesses Give Clear Description,* or *Quick-thinking Trucker Foils Gunman;* but he couldn't count on it.

Both right and center lanes of traffic were blocked somewhere up ahead. With one hand on the hood of the van and the other on a car's trunk, Marley vaulted into the space between those lanes, and sped on, sideways, scissor-stepping to avoid catching himself on projecting mirrors.

Images of escape flashed into his mind. He saw himself ducking into a sedan he passed, plopping among the four car-pooling commuters who were goggling at him. Or climbing up into the cab of a huge Mack that seemed like a rolling vault. But he wasn't giving way to panic, and he didn't think trying to hide was smarter than trying to get away.

He could get away: dash along the lines of halted cars, cut back and forth, never give the man chasing him a clear shot. Plumes of vapor rose from the exhausts of every idling vehicle. Headlamps in the three southbound lanes across the median rail cast multiple shifting shadows. He'd be hard to see, hard to hit.

Suddenly, red light flared ahead and swept back toward him. Traffic had been flowing in the leftmost northbound lane. It halted. The middle line began to move. Marley had worked his way past the Mack truck and three cars, and had reached the tail of a fourth. It rolled away from him. The driver of the car he'd just passed gawked at him in amazement, didn't move. Marley ran on into the widening gap, now cruelly spotlighted by that car's headlights.

Driving himself at a dead run, he resisted looking over his shoulder to see if the gunman had spotted him. Four feet ahead something chipped the road's surface, and Marley knew he had.

Marley leaped to the left, squeezing through a one-foot space between bumpers, ran on, bent double, between the median rail and the vehicles in the left lane. Headlights from the other side of the rail flashed on him like a strobe. A horn sounded. Another joined it. Outrage spread blaring back along the line of cars in the middle lane behind the man who hadn't moved.

Now the far right-hand line of cars was moving. A gap opened there, too, because the driver behind the gunman stayed frozen the way the first behind Marley had done. In a moment, two-thirds of the width of the highway was clear between Marley and Dapper Dan. Daring for an instant to pause, crouching next to the median rail, looking over the hood of a car halted in the left lane, Marley saw the other man silhouetted, twisting, leaning from side to side trying to find his target.

The driver in the center lane who'd stayed put behind Marley suddenly floored his pedal and sped ahead. The next three reacted fast, keeping close behind him. Then with a heavy rumble rising to a low-gear roar, the Mack trailer-truck began to lumber after them. Its mass blocked the line of sight between Marley and the gunman.

Putting a foot on a bumper, Marley sprang up and into the narrow space between the left-hand lane and the oncoming truck. The trucker took his foot from the accelerator instantly, but momentum kept the great hulk rolling. Marley pressed himself against the fender of the car, leaning backward. Although the space between the side of the car and the truck was safe enough, the truck's aura of terrible force filled it.

Then Marley flung himself through that almost crushing pressure. Even before the driver could touch his brake, Marley'd grabbed the door handle and swung up to crouch on the sill below the door. He saw the driver's face, shocked, angry; saw him mouthing curses; couldn't hear a thing above the roar except the explosive hiss of air brakes. Marley waved to try to signal the man to go on—*Go on!*— but already the truck was slowing.

But by the time it could be halted, it had reached the ramp bringing traffic onto the Expressway from the right. Marley dropped from the step, ran around the front of the truck, snapped a look back down the highway from the cover it gave him.

Dapper Dan was about seventy feet away in the empty right-hand lane, near the guardrail, trotting a few steps, pausing, bobbing from side to side, trying to find Marley again. The left-hand lane was moving once more, the center had filled with cars jamming up behind the truck. The gunman was looking across them. He hadn't seen Marley use the truck; he wasn't looking far enough ahead along the highway to see him now.

The right lane was empty between the car that still hadn't moved—back beyond the gunman—and the ramp. At the ramp two lines of vehicles were cramming themselves into that one lane as fast as they could.

Suddenly, a blast almost knocked Marley over. The driver had punched his air horn. Steadying himself, Marley peered around again. The horn had caught Dapper's attention; but he didn't see Marley and returned to the direction he had been scanning.

As though pretending he could make himself invisible by sheer confidence, Marley stepped from the cover of the truck and walked—did not run—across the lane toward the ramp. The trick of not attracting attention by sudden movement might have worked. But the truck driver hit his horn again.

Dapper Dan looked, saw, began to run. Evidently, he didn't trust his aim on a moving target in that light at that distance. How close would he think he had to be? As Marley threw himself forward and dashed toward the mouth of the ramp, he flashed glances, ready to see the gunman's arm swinging his pistol up to eye level.

Marley wasn't going to be able to run down the ramp between the line of cars and the nearer railing. He'd be a perfect target there for the man above on the Expressway. Raising a hand as if he could command the flow of steel to cease by will alone, Marley danced sideways in front of a car coming up to the head of the ramp.

The car hit him. But the driver had stamped on his brake, so his bumper barely dented Marley's shin. Marley fell toward the car's hood, caught himself with one hand, rolled across the hood, regaining balance, and coming around the side of the car.

Two of the drivers in the farther ramp-lane weren't going to let any mere pedestrian spoil their chance of getting onto the Expressway. Marley saw them see him leaning back hard against the side of the car that had hit him. True Bostonians, they never slowed, passing not twelve inches from the buttons of his coat. The next driver did pause, staring at Marley in amazement. Ducking, Marley ran in front of him, and then down the far side of the ramp.

"I don't know whether he couldn't get a clear shot at me, or didn't want to shoot into that mass of cars. At the bottom, I went under the ramp, then crossed below the Expressway. Either I lost him, or he just gave it up."

"Oh, James! My God," Joanna gasped, as she had throughout Marley's story.

Marley'd wanted powerfully not to tell it to her. But he'd had to report what he'd discovered about Lily, about Stanley Ho. No way to do that and avoid the squirmy truth of how he'd come to meet Ho. He'd tried to be brief, but she'd kept tugging and finally dragged out the whole tale.

He'd spoken most of it to his glass, and used the bite of the whiskey to cover the bitterness the words left in his mouth.

"I think you ought to have another drink!" Joanna sprang from her perch on the edge of the couch, reaching.

"Thanks."

She took the glass, but stood for another moment staring down at him.

Marley was deep in the Eames chair. He'd come into the house, plowing through her questions, asking for whiskey, straight, homing directly toward that chair, and easing himself stiffly into it—the first time ever that he'd sat there except at Russell Detweiller's express invitation.

Joanna shook her head, and turned to go to the kitchen bar. She called back, "You must have come directly here, then. You haven't told the police?"

"No. I called David's office right away, of course. Ho wanted to kill me to prevent me from telling about him; after I've told, he has no reason to. So I certainly wasn't going to keep the information to myself for very long. Ho must be smart enough to know what I'd do. I'm not in any danger from him anymore."

"You're sure?"

"Yes."

She shuddered. "Well, I'm glad the kids are away, just the same." She shook her head. "But he did try to kill you. How can you let him go—not do anything? The police . . ."

"The police would take down my story, and then they'd take down Ho's story. Which would be that he was having a Peking duck banquet with sixteen friends, who will swear to it—as will the duck. And he's never heard of me. And he'll ask, 'Who is this nut who's making such wild and libelous accusations?' And the police might believe either or neither of us, but they'd have no evidence either way.

"David will put some of his researchers onto Ho, Bright

Morning Enterprises, whatever else they turn up. If they can link him in some provable way to the theft of Russ's program—my guess is that he's the person Bill Wright called this morning, that's how he knew who I was—then, eventually, he'll get his knuckles rapped."

Joanna returned with Marley's drink. "But you sound so detached. He tried to kill *you!*"

"I am annoyed about that, Joanna. But I've learned that vengeance is not what I want to focus on. Thanks." Marley winced as he reached for the glass.

"What's wrong?"

"My shoulder's a little sore."

"What happened?"

"Nothing serious."

"James. . . !"

"Ho had one of his men lean on it a little while he was asking me things."

"*Lean* on it. You mean they *beat* you. *Tortured* you!"

"Not seriously."

"Not *seriously!* James! Oh, you make me so angry! You . . . *men!* You . . . big macho, he-man, tough-guy . . . you think you have to—"

"Could I have something to eat? Just a sandwich, maybe? If it wouldn't be too much trouble."

For another moment Joanna glared down at Marley. Then her face softened and she tipped her head to one side. "I have some baked ham. Would that be all right?"

"Great. Thanks."

Joanna crossed to the kitchen again. "And, no, it wouldn't be too much trouble."

While carrying things from the refrigerator to the counter, she asked, "What are you going to do now? Call Russ?"

"No. I'm going to go down there, to the island, in the morning. I have to call back later to confirm the times, but

I've asked David's people to arrange for one of his jets to take me to Antigua, and to have an island-hopper there fly me across to Montserrat.

"Thinking it over, I've decided that I don't want to talk to Russ on the phone. I'll send word through the security team that's watching him to identify themselves and let him know I'm coming, but I don't want to talk to him yet.

"I think I have to persuade him of two things: first, to leave that island and come back to the States. When I saw him, he mentioned that one of the reasons he and Lily went to Montserrat was because Lily knew about the place—had a friend who'd been there. I'll bet you the friend is connected with Bright Morning Enterprises—maybe Ho, himself. I'll bet you they have people there, some kind of base. I've asked David's people to watch for a connection to the island as they check out Bright Morning. Our opposition *is* starting to play rough, and I want to pull Russ out of there—hide him away until he finishes the program.

"Second—in order for there to be any point in bringing him away—I've got to detach him from Lily.

"What I have to tell him, now, *ought* to convince him about Lily. But when I tell him, he'll confront her. And she's a smart cookie. Knows how to admit enough of the truth to seem open, candid, trustworthy, then bombs you with the innocent charm. Until I knew about the program being stolen, she had me convinced about her. She made me like her even though I went there prejudiced against her. What she might do with Russ . . . I want to be there and tell him in person, and confront her myself, and not give her any chance to work on him alone."

Without looking up from her busy fingers deftly piling and poking the wafer slices of ham, Joanna asked, "He's really that far gone?"

"I think so."

"Mayonnaise?"

"Please."

"Well. If she seduced *you*—so to speak—she must be very persuasive. Mustard?"

"A little."

Joanna finished making the sandwich, in silence. Marley sipped his drink.

She brought the plate to him.

"Thanks," he said, putting his glass on the floor, sitting up straighter, reaching for the plate with his right hand, not being able to do any of it without holding his breath and tightening his jaw.

Joanna sat on the couch again, near him, watching him. After a moment she said, "Do you have any idea how much that program is worth, James? I mean, to Russ and to me? Well, I really mean to me, because—I assure you—Russ and I will divide the profits evenly. Do you have any idea?"

"Yes, but I prefer not to think about it. David can deal in those figures; you can; they make me dizzy."

"Ten million, conservatively. Very possibly, twenty or thirty. So I want you to know I'm grateful for what you're doing. If you save that program, I'll be *very* grateful. I'm already very grateful just for your trying, and I'll want to make sure you know it."

"Thanks for the thought, but I'm already being paid by David for this."

"Daily rate, nothing extra?"

"Oh, probably something, yes. David is always generous about bonuses when I've saved him some money."

"*I'll* want to do something for you, too."

"Thanks. I appreciate that. But it's not necessary."

Joanna took a breath and sighed in exasperation. "When somebody offers you something, and wants to give it to you, you should take it."

Marley looked back at her steadily for a moment.

"Okay, anytime you want to make me a ham sandwich like this one, I'll accept." He took another large bite.

For an instant she glared at him, then, smiling and shaking her head ruefully, said, "Well, as soon as you finish that one, James, you are going to soak in the hot tub, and I *am* going to give you a massage."

Joanna knocked on the tub-room door. "It's been fifteen minutes. You shouldn't stay in the hot water longer than that."

"Right. Okay. It does feel great—you were right." Reluctantly, Marley climbed out of the tub, began to dry himself with the huge, thick towel Joanna had given him.

"Are you decent?" she asked. "May I come in and give you your massage?"

"Yes," Marley answered—he'd gone into the tub wearing his bathing trunks, they were still with his clothes from his trip to the island—"but I really don't need a massage. I think I'll just—"

But she was already coming into the room. "Now you stop that. I know it's only a flesh wound, and it only hurts when you laugh. And I'm not going to put up with that. If you're going to insist on suffering in silence, then suffer from my making you feel better."

"Yes, ma'am." Marley lay facedown on one of the terry-covered mats beside the tub. Soaking in the steaming water had loosened his shoulder and taken away some of the ache. Still, he let himself down carefully.

Briskly, Joanna took a bottle of lotion from a cabinet, came to kneel beside Marley. "It's all right to feel good, despite what all your pinched-nosed ancestors told you."

"Now, come on, Joanna. You keep trying to make out that I'm a puritan. I enjoy life—I eat well, drink . . . ah . . . take pleasure from the company of women. The truth is, I'm really a hedonist."

"All puritans are really hedonists. That's what they're afraid of. I've seen you 'enjoying life'—by the measuring cup full." She had poured lotion into her palm. She began to spread it gently over Marley's shoulder. "You're afraid of what you might do if you ever really let yourself go. But don't worry, James. I'm not going to try to make you let yourself go completely. This treatment is purely medicinal; I'm not trying to seduce you."

Marley might have disbelieved her. Joanna was wearing a peacock-blue wrapper of some thin, satiny fabric. She'd tied her sash tightly; it held the crossed lapels of the wrapper in place just below her throat; she knelt on its skirts: She wasn't flaunting any flesh. But she didn't seem to have anything on under it, and as she moved and stretched, the shapes of full, firm breasts and hips showed clearly. She must have bathed, herself, while Marley soaked in the tub room; she smelled warm and of spices. Her palm glided back and forth across his back, her fingers circled, in a way that felt more like caressing than kneading out knots in sore muscles. Although Marley drifted as though on the wispy steam rising from the tub, he also was experiencing some discomfort lying facedown.

"After all, you're really not my type, James. You are an attractive man, but you don't like parties, or tennis, or going out to trendy nightclubs. I know that for thrills and satisfaction in life, you'd rate building a business—on a scale of one to ten—at about minus seventy-six. So, although you are handsome, and charming, and interesting, and strong, and mature, and you live a life full of adventure, there'd be nothing in it for me—beyond restoring some of my confidence. And—I imagine—a wildly exciting night of fantastic sex. Just something enjoyed for the pleasure of the moment. And I know you'd consider that irresponsible." She ran one fingernail down Marley's backbone. "Wouldn't you?"

It raised goose bumps on his skin. "Probably so."

"Yes. I thought so." She returned to rubbing the muscle behind his shoulder blade. "If it was really important to me, if I wanted to persuade you, I guess I could argue that it's good for you—good for everybody—to be able, sometimes, to let go and do something just because it feels good. Good for your emotional and mental health. Really, good for your *character*. *That'd* be the way to get you, James. But if I convinced you, and you did something because it was *good for you,* not because it *felt* good, then I'd actually have defeated my own argument. Wouldn't I?"

Cheek on the mat, Marley looked sideways up at her. As always, every hair on her head lay in place. The lines of the wrapper at her throat were neat and smooth. But a fine sheen of sweat glowed on her face, and—looking down at him—her eyelids were lowered. She looked like control and passion combined. Marley turned his head to face away from her.

"Russ ran off with Lily because it felt good, and because he thinks it's good for him. Good for *him*."

"Yes." Joanna's finger stiffened and jabbed. Marley winced. "Sorry, that wasn't intentional. Yes, James; and I'm very angry about it. I'm hurt, and I'm angry about being hurt; but I'm not angry—like, on principle—because he was taking care of himself. Do you understand that?"

"I'll work on it."

Marley felt a sense of unreality, as though still dreaming. He had dreamed, napping through the morning, stretched out on a feather-cushion sofa in the lounge of one of David Cheyney's corporate jets. Now, in the early afternoon, he was refreshed, alert, fully awake. Montserrat's little airport, the immigration and customs officers, were familiar to him; yet he didn't trust anything he saw.

"Too much contrast," he told himself as he looked from

the window of the taxi that was carrying him to Russ and Lily's cottage. When he'd awakened at five A.M. to drive to the airport, black night still palled Boston. His shoulder—his whole back—had stiffened: He'd felt as though his vertebrae had fused and would have to be broken joint by joint before he could bend. All the world was stiff. Ice snapped under his feet as he walked from Joanna's house to his car. The car door slammed with a flat bang instead of its usual competent thump. The gearshift stuck, the engine had solidified, the tires frozen square. The air he breathed freeze-dried the lining of his nose and lungs. To be in that sterile, blind, and brittle world one moment, and in the next—it seemed—to be gliding through this lush and supple, fecund heat, was beyond credibility.

And then there was the ease and openness and sense of goodwill of the island. It seemed to offer an invitation to bask, because nothing is worth worrying over in a land where the sun always shines but the breeze soothes in the shade under palms and mangoes; where fruit can be plucked from bushes growing wild. But the first thing Marley would do there would be to confer with the chief of the security team that was guarding Russ from physical attack—even murder. And the second thing would be to free Russ from—the clichés leaped into Marley's mind—the serpent Russ had taken to his bosom, the gorgeous, exotic flower with a fragrance that killed.

And among the contradictions that gave Marley such a sense of unreality was one more that he'd have preferred not to acknowledge: He'd be trying to persuade Russ to throw out a lover and return to a lawful wife. But Joanna clearly had invited Marley to be *her* lover, and—on the flight down—he'd had an extraordinarily detailed and vivid dream in which he'd accepted.

A man came out to meet Marley as soon as the taxi

pulled up in front of Russ's house. He waited while Marley paid the driver, then spoke. "Mr. Marley?"

"James." Marley offered his hand.

"Bob Bracciotti." The man looked to be in his mid-thirties. Dark hair cropped short, thick neck, nose bent slightly at some point in his history, probably had a box full of wrestling trophies in an attic somewhere. His muscles bulged perceptibly under his knit, short-sleeved shirt as he reached to shake Marley's hand, but not so much that he seemed to be concealing Idaho potatoes there. Dark eyes that looked straight at Marley, sizing him up exactly in the way Marley was sizing *him.*

"Have a good trip?" Bob smiled pleasantly, but not ingratiatingly as if he cared whether Marley liked him.

Marley liked him. "Very smooth. I slept most of the way down."

"Good." Bob seemed to consider niceties of greeting to be necessary, but that they'd been sufficiently observed. "Okay, James. The situation here is that everything looks okay. Obviously, we're able to provide better security now that we're inside the house than we were the way you wanted it done at first—without Russ knowing we were here."

"He's accepted it? He's not giving you any trouble?"

"Not at all. My impression is that he's one of those guys seems kind of bumble-puppy because his mind's doing something that may not show, and he doesn't attend to much otherwise. When he does click onto something, he gets right through it. By the time I came to the house last night, he'd already worked it out from what you'd told him on the phone yesterday morning that if somebody'd stolen his program, they might come after him next. He was glad to see us. I passed your word that you'd found out something more, and would be down to tell him, and that you'd sent us to look after him. He just thanked me and asked how we'd like to set up."

"How *are* you set up?"

"We're doing baby-sitter bodyguard, not full, heavy-duty security. There're four of us. Normally, one inside the house, one outside, the other two relieving or as needed. Right now, one—Ben Newman—is in town with Lily. She wanted to buy groceries. She's feeding all of us. Great little cook." Bob spoke in a voice like flannel; it couldn't have carried a foot past Marley's ear. He faced Marley obliquely, and Marley had the sense that if the man were interrupted at intervals and quizzed, he could report how many bees had visited the flowers on his left and how much the grass on his right had grown.

"It's a pretty easy layout," Bob continued. "With the bushes along the fence here nobody can drive past and see to take a shot. The house is set back far enough from the road so you couldn't toss anything you could hold in one hand and count on getting Detweiller. Big backyard—nobody can sneak in close; and we keep the drapes closed, keep him out of sight so they couldn't snipe him.

"Of course, we're not set up to fight off the A-Team. I mean, we had to come here clean—no firearms of any kind. This used to be a British island, you know: Even the cops don't pack.

"And I haven't made contact with the police. My instructions were to keep low profile. If you think this is likely to turn into some serious mud-wrestling . . ."

"I think it could, if we stayed here, Bob. I got a couple of calls in-flight from David Cheyney's East and West Coast researchers. We're starting to see a picture. First, there's a small software company on the West Coast—an operation no larger than Russ's—that's working on a program just like his. Well, David's people have traced that company's backers through several layers to some interests in Singapore. Nothing illegal about that, of course, but . . . You know about Singapore, in this context?"

"No."

"It's a major world center of the software piracy business. Now, we'd thought someone was trying to beat Russ to copyright on this program for the sake of the royalties from its use. They would be considerable. But what we're beginning to suspect is that the pirates want to copyright the program to *prevent* its being used. The profits on pirating software—which Russ's program would protect against—are about considerable-times-ten.

"Second piece of information: A guy from Boston named Stanley Ho—no connection to Singapore proven yet, but we strongly suspect—is the president of a company that owns property on—surprise—this very island.

"People with these kinds of resources *could* mount an operation—beach a hit team, swim them off again—who knows what? So I'm here to take Russ back with me—tonight or first thing tomorrow. I'm glad to hear he may be receptive to the idea; I was afraid I'd have to roll him in a carpet. We'll put him somewhere—no one will know where he is—and simply move this whole business out of the high-adventure mode."

"Suits me."

"He's working?" Marley started them along the flagstone path to the house.

"Yeah. Set up in one of the bedrooms. Really interesting to see him: He just sits there and stares at his screen for maybe fifteen minutes, half an hour. Then he scribbles on paper—lots of things with circles and squares around them, arrows back and forth between them. Then he plays his keyboard like he's on synthesizer for Bon Jovi. The computer buzzes and clicks for a couple minutes, and he waits for it to finish. And then he sits and stares at the screen again. I mean, most of the time it looks like he isn't doing anything."

Bob opened the front door for Marley. A man sitting on the living room couch who could have been a vacationing

Bears lineman looked up from a paperback. Bob introduced him, "Jeff Bowles. Jeff, this is Mr. Marley."

"James," Marley said. "Hello."

"Hi." Jeff didn't say that he was pleased to meet Marley, nor did he look as though he weren't. As Marley went toward Russ's room his eyes merely tracked without revealing any emotion at all.

"Hello, Russ," Marley said from the doorway. The bedroom window louvers had been tipped; the room was dim. Russ sat at a dressing table staring at a computer screen whose orange glow reflected faintly on his face. His trance-like concentration suggested he was generating the light, conjuring images on the screen, by his own will.

"James!" He spun in his chair. "I didn't hear you come." He started to spring up, turned back. "Wait till I save." He touched his keyboard, then came to Marley, thrusting out his hand. "How are you? Boy, am I glad to see you!"

Marley took Russ's hand firmly, "I'm glad to see you, Russ," then released it reluctantly. "But I don't know if you *will* be glad to see me when you hear what I have to tell you. Since I talked with you yesterday morning to tell you somebody's working on your program, I've found out a lot about—"

Russ raised a hand. "I know. I know all about it, James."

"What?"

"About Bill—Bill Wright—that he must have stolen the codes. And about . . . Lily."

"You know about Lily? What do you know? How?"

"She told me."

"What did she tell you?"

"The whole thing. That she was hired to distract me, keep me from working on the program. That Bill wasn't her boyfriend, he was just paid to introduce us. Well, from that I could figure that he also must have stolen the codes and passed them to someone. I really couldn't believe that, James. I mean, I didn't want to; I still don't want to. We were friends! I keep trying to think, 'Maybe it wasn't him.' But it was, wasn't it? It had to have been."

"Yes. I don't think there can be any doubt." Marley took a breath. "Russ, Bill . . ."

Russ wasn't ready for further news. He turned, walking away with his arms spread. "I just can't get over it, James. Why would he. . . ?" He stared toward his computer as though an answer might print itself on the screen. But only the prompt symbol showed there, and the pulsing cursor. "I want to talk to him, ask him. Maybe he's in some kind of trouble. I mean, he spends an awful lot of money, buys things. Maybe he overextended. If he'd only talked to me about it!" Since nothing was being entered, the computer's automatic power-saver switched, and the screen went dark. Russ turned from it. "But maybe we could still work something out. He's really a good kid. I mean, I'm pretty upset about him doing this; but if he was under pressure . . ."

"Russ, Bill's dead."

"Dead! Jesus! How. . . ?"

"I confronted him with it—that he'd stolen your program—and, briefly, he tried to get away in his car, skidded on some ice, and wrapped himself around a pole."

"Oh, no! Oh, Jesus. The poor kid. Oh, God." Russ turned from Marley, shaking his head, as if denying the message and avoiding its bearer could make it untrue. Then he turned back. "You talked to him? What happened?"

"I'll tell you about it later. For now, the immediate point is: I met a guy who's behind—involved with—this plot to steal your program. He made it clear that he's prepared even to commit murder to win. I want you to come back to the States and let us hide you away and watch over you until you finish your work."

"Holy shit! Murder! Sure, James; right! As soon as Lily

gets back we'll pack—neither of us has much—and we can
be out of here—"

Marley swept one hand, as though to cut the flow of
Russ's words through the air. "Russ—"

"What's the matter?"

"What are you talking about—Lily? You said you know
she's part of the plot."

"Yes. She was. She told me."

"She *is*. Stanley Ho—the man who's running this end of
the thing—picked me up because I was asking about her."

"No, James. I mean, I see what you're worried about.
But it's okay. Lily told me about it, about being involved.
She *told* me. Because now she's in love with me—she really
is—and she wanted me to know. She said she'd go away
now. If I wanted her to go away—if I hated her—she'd
understand, and she'd go away. Oh, James, she cried . . .
She was trying not to, so I wouldn't know how bad she felt,
and feel sorry for her, and let her stay just because I felt
sorry for her. She stood there with her head up, trying to
make her voice steady and strong, and looked me straight
in the eye; but the tears kept running down her face."

Tears filled Russ's own eyes.

"When?"

"What?"

"When did she tell you?"

"Yesterday."

"When yesterday?"

"Yesterday morning. Why?"

"Yesterday morning—after I called—right?"

"Yes. What's the matter?"

"After I called, and you told her what I'd told you: that
someone was working on your program, and you should go
back to work yourself. *Then* she confessed to you."

"James . . . I don't get what you're driving at."

"I think you do, Russ. Obviously, Lily realized it'd only

be a matter of time until I'd connect her with the plot, and
expose her to you. So she did it herself, first."

"No!"

"Yes. It's just as plain—"

"She didn't . . . she wouldn't . . ."

"Russ . . ." Marley shook his head sadly. "Russ, one of
the great things about you is that you're such a really good
person. It's been a pleasure—I'll say an *honor*—to know
you. Every time we're together— In the work I do I meet
many people who are *not* nice people, so being with you
from time to time seems a way of recharging my moral bat-
teries. But, Russ, the trouble is you're so honest yourself
you think everybody else is, too.

"Lily is *not* a good person. She was honest enough to tell
me so herself—those are her very words—because she
thought I'd discover it anyway. She was straightforward
about that. She's doing the same thing now. It's one of her
tricks: You were about to find out about her, so she tells
you and scores for being honest with you.

"So—her idea is—you keep her with you; and then she
can report back to Ho where you are, how you're doing.
Maybe find some way to stop you. Russ, I'm sorry, but
that's it."

Back in the living room the telephone rang.

The two men stood five feet apart. Short Russell, angry,
hurt, wearing one of those shirts, looking like he'd been
pelted with overripe fruit and didn't know how to fight
back but wouldn't run. Marley straight and stiff and set as a
peeled fence post that a bull could brain itself butting
against and never budge.

"No."

The phone rang again.

"Russ, I'm sorry. I understand how you feel about her.
But her telling you about herself—working on you that
way—is exactly what I expected she'd do."

Bob Bracciotti had answered the telephone. The few words he spoke—mostly he listened—reached the bedroom as a murmur the men might not have understood even if they'd heard it.

"I've met that type of woman before, Russ. I don't think you have."

"Lily isn't 'that type of woman'! She's *Lily,* and she loves me, and I love her, and I know she's telling the truth."

"Russ . . . Okay, I'm not going to argue with you. But we have to put you in a secure place, and she is not going to be there. As soon as you finish the program, you can—"

"James, excuse me," Bob spoke from the doorway in the tone of a captain preventing panic while announcing the ship is on fire. "Ben just called from town. He says Lily's gone."

CHAPTER 7

A sweet-voiced bird trilled from a palm tree beside the house, its song clear in the silence.

"Gone?" Russ seemed finally to recall the word's meaning. "Where?"

Bob turned his palms up. "Ben said she just disappeared. He said she was out of his sight for less than two minutes, and then when he looked for her she was gone. He's coming back now to tell us—"

"Where? Where could she have gone?"

"Away." Marley nodded, acknowledging to himself his own perspicacity. "Away, Russ. She's *gone*. Beat it. Skipped. She knew the game was up, so she's—"

"She's been kidnapped!"

"Russ . . . She's left you."

"No!"

Marley wouldn't be interrupted. "She's left you. I'm sorry, Russ, but it's obvious. She knew I'd found out about her, and—"

"They've kidnapped her! We've got to call the police! We've got to—"

"Russ, I'm sorry, but—"

"Hey, guys"—hands raised, Bob refereed them apart—"let's wait to hear from Ben. He'll be back in about twenty minutes. Let's wait and hear him tell what happened before we reach any conclusions. Okay?"

"No! Call the police now! We can't waste any time. I'm going to—"

Marley stopped Russ with a hand on his arm. "Russ, he's right. Even if we call the police, we have to know what to tell them. We can wait twenty minutes."

They had to wait only eighteen and a half minutes, actually. Russ sat slumping in the chair facing his computer, his fingers twisted together and clamped between his thighs, biting his lower lip, staring at the blank screen. The other men waited in the living room. Bob woke the fourth member of the team, who had been sleeping in one of the bedrooms at the opposite end of the house. In a few moments he shambled to the kitchen and stood there drinking coffee. Bob introduced him to Marley as "Kip," and the two men nodded at each other across the room. Probably Kip was still half asleep; his vagueness, and his tan and sunbleached hair, made him seem like one of those young men whose minds are in gear only when they're riding the surf. Jeff Bowles continued reading his paperback. Marley and Bob took chairs at either end of the table looking out toward the sea where the afternoon sun's heavy heat had thickened the air. Once, Bob realized he was drumming his fingers on the table, and stopped. Marley sat still.

All of them were on their feet instantly when they heard the car racing up the road toward the house, and were outside when it skidded to a stop in the driveway and Ben Newman sprang out.

Like his colleagues, Ben looked like a man accustomed
to moving heavy weights through space rapidly and skill-
fully. Seeing the others, he halted the momentum of his
own bulk and waited while they gathered around him.
"Okay," he said. Pain showed in his close-set eyes, and his
mouth seemed dry, but he made his report crisply.

"We went to the supermarket. I parked in the lot behind
it. We went in, shopped, bought a bunch of stuff—Lily said
she'd lay in a lot so we wouldn't have to come into town
again for the rest of the week. Canned goods, jars. Three
big bags full.

"You can't take shopping carts outside—the store's up
three steps above the street level. I took two bags, Lily
took the third. We went out, around the side, toward the
parking lot. There's a drugstore there, in the same building; separate entrance from the supermarket—on the side
there. Lily stopped, said she needed something. I said,
'Okay,' figured to go in with her. She said, 'Go on to the
car.' Said she had to get something for herself—kind of a
little embarrassed. I guessed she needed to get some Tam-
pax or something. I didn't want to leave her, but . . . She
shoved the bag she was carrying to me. I was afraid I'd
drop one of them. I didn't want to embarrass her . . ."

Ben ran his tongue around his mouth. "I . . . I figured
it'd only be a minute. She went into the drugstore, I went
to the car. Around the back of the building. I couldn't see
the door—only a minute, minute and a half at the outside.
Got the trunk open, bags in, slammed it, was back where I
could see the door within—couldn't have been more than
ninety seconds.

"I waited. A minute, two minutes. I went back to the
door—glass door, big window—I could see the whole inside. She wasn't there.

"I went inside, asked. They said she'd gone right out
again. Didn't see where she went. I looked back and forth

along the street. Went back to the supermarket. She wasn't there. Went back to the car. She wasn't there. Went back to the drugstore, asked if she'd left with anybody—if anybody had met her. They didn't know; said she'd walked out of the store alone, didn't see whether she met anyone outside. I checked the car again, then found a phone, called you."

Ben finished. His lips twitched as though they wanted to say something more, but he clamped them tight together.

"Anyone else on the street. . . ?" Marley paused to introduce himself. "I'm James Marley. Was there anyone else on the street who might have seen her come out of the drugstore?"

"I don't know, sir. There's a store—hardware store or something—across the street; but I didn't want to take time to ask."

"Right," Marley agreed, careful to keep the young man's focus on the event rather than on the sense of guilt that had screwed his voice tight. "But you didn't hear anything: no scream, no sound of any struggle? Any cars racing away?"

"No, sir."

"Did Lily actually buy anything in the drugstore? Did you ask that?"

"No, sir."

"Wouldn't have expected you to, Ben; you had to move too fast for that then. We can check; but if she was out of your line of sight for only ninety seconds . . . Were there other people—customers—in the store when she went in?"

"Yes, sir. Several—three or four, anyway."

Marley turned to Russ, who stood white-faced and trembling. "Russ, I'm sorry. I *am*. But look at it: To be in and out of that drugstore that quickly, she must not have bought anything. She must have left as soon as Ben was out of sight. She must have gone in only to get rid of him."

"No."

"He was supposed to— Normally, he wouldn't have let her out of his sight. She loaded him with the extra bag—"

"No."

"—And made up a reason why he shouldn't be with her. And as soon as he was out of sight—"

"No, James!" Russ's protests grew stronger, but with anguish, not anger.

"She left the store alone." Marley continued, pausing between each sentence, as inexorable as a bell tolling a loved one's death. "Either she went somewhere on her own power, or she met someone who took her away—without any struggle or outcry from her."

"She was kidnapped!"

"She left, Russ. I'm sorry."

"No! She wouldn't! She didn't. They took her!" Russ looked up at Marley, his face working, then at each of the other men. Ben and Kip dropped their eyes, Jeff Bowles stared back without expression. Bob and Marley regarded Russ with compassionate finality.

Of the six men, big Jeff reacted quickest to the sound of the telephone. Before the second ring he—without seeming to hurry—had turned and transported himself across the space to the front door. He had reached the phone and lifted the receiver by the time the others rushed in. Bob was first, Marley second; but Russ darted between them.

"It's for you," Jeff said, holding out the receiver. "It's Lily."

Russ bounded to grab the receiver. "Lily! Are you all right?"

Marley moved almost as swiftly, coming to Russ's side, leaning to put his ear next to Russ's. He heard Lily's voice, high-pitched and tense. "Russ?"

"Lily, it's me," Russ answered. "Are you all right? Where are you?"

"I can't tell you, I—"

"What happened? Where are you?"

"Listen to me, Russ! Please, just listen!" Her tone was sharp and strong, but it quivered at the edges. "Some men took me away. They're here now—right here. I can only say what they tell me to say. Please listen carefully; I'm only going to be allowed to talk to you once. They said I should tell you that there won't be another call, so don't think about trying to trace them that way." Her manner of speaking altered: As though pronouncing words of a foreign language, she seemed concerned to say each one slowly and clearly, without really understanding what they meant.

"They say you mustn't finish your protection program. They say that if you submit it for copyright within the next three days, they'll . . ." A word she did know, and her voice seemed to cower as she said it, ". . . *kill* me!"

"Lily!" Russ's agonized shout reverberated in the room, but Lily couldn't have heard it. The connection had been broken. "Lily? Lily. . . ?"

Marley slowly twisted the receiver free of Russ's grip, replaced it.

"James . . . James, you see!"

"Russ . . ." Marley put a hand on his friend's arm, and said gently, "What I see is this: People are trying to beat you to copyright on your own program. First they stole it. Then they hired Lily to distract you from working on it. Now they're using her to keep you from finishing it and filing it. She said three days—they must be almost as close to completing it as you are. It's all one plot. And Lily's part of it." He tightened his grip for an instant, then went on. "Lily's calling doesn't change the fact of what happened in town. Going into that drugstore was a pretext. She disappeared within seconds, from a public street—from right outside a glass-fronted store full of people—without any struggle or resistance at all. This call now—she's simply continuing to do her job, play her part."

"No! I don't believe it. She was kidnapped. We've got to find her!"

"Oh, I think we could find her easily enough, Russ. At least, I think I know where she is."

"Where!"

"Bright Morning Enterprises—Stanley Ho, the guy who seems to be running this end of the game . . . I got a report while I was flying down here today: The people who seem to be behind this own some kind of estate on this island. That's where Lily is—I'll bet you. I think that right this minute . . . I'm sorry, Russ; I don't want to hurt you, but I think you must realize the truth: You were taken in—so was I. We both were seduced by a very clever, experienced con artist. And betrayed. I think that right this minute we could find Lily lounging by the swimming pool there with a tall, cold drink."

Russ wrenched his arm free. "No!"

"You're a man with a sharp mind, Russ. Put it in gear."

Russ glared at Marley, then whirled to face Bob and the others. "We'll go there! We'll see."

"Put your mind in gear, Russ. I think that's where she is, but if anybody comes driving up to see . . ."

Bob nodded in agreement, and Marley continued. "This is a hoax. It's just one more part of the whole plot. The way to deal with it is to ignore it. Beat it; beat them. Finish your program, file it for copyright."

"They'll kill her."

"James . . ." Bob offered, "I think there is an alternative. I mean, I think you're probably right about Lily, but why take a chance? Did you say something about three days? They're going to beat him out and file their own program within three days? Okay, let 'em. They file, and then he files—and claims unfair, *criminal* practice on their part.

I don't know, I'm not a lawyer; but if they *kidnapped* somebody to prevent Russ from filing first . . . God, that sure ought to disqualify them from getting a copyright, at least. The kidnap—fake or real—actually, they're shooting themselves in their own foot. So Russ can wait until—hoax or not—until Lily's free."

Russ turned to Marley hopefully, but Marley shook his head. "I think they're sharper than that, Bob. Nobody saw Lily being kidnapped. There's no ransom note, just one telephone call that was heard only by Russ and myself—interested parties. So if Lily appears and says, 'Kidnapped? I was just visiting a friend,' where's the case?"

"She *was* kidnapped! She *was!*"

"It *is* one of the two possibilities, James," Bob agreed quietly. "And even if it's not true, we're all here seeing what's going on. Ben *was* in town with Lily, she *did* disappear. We know she called here—Jeff answered the phone. We know Russ *thinks* she's been kidnapped. Kidnap or hoax, either way the other side's pulling something that'll count against them."

"That's right, James!"

Marley stood for a moment weighing the argument. "No," he said. "It's not that simple. These guys are really clever. The way this works—if we ever make a claim against them to dispute the copyright—is the exact reverse of your argument. Again, there's no proof that Lily was abducted. The telephone call—she made it herself. We have no evidence of anyone else being involved. It could look like this: Russ and Lily are lovers: ran off, came here together. And then, when Russ found that someone else was developing a program similar to his—and we have no proof that it's *his* program, stolen from him—he and Lily cooked up a fake kidnapping to try to discredit his rivals.

"We cry 'Hoax!' they cry 'Hoax!' and it looks as strong from their side—stronger—than from ours.

"However"—Marley raised a hand to forestall Russ's response—"there is a way it works for us. They *have* outsmarted themselves. The one way your argument works, Bob, is if Lily *doesn't* turn up. That means, even if the abduction were real, they will *not* harm her because that *would be* evidence against them. I still say this is a hoax; but even if it isn't, it's a bluff.

"So, Russ." Marley smiled in a way intended to reassure. "Whether you're right or I'm right about Lily, no harm is going to come to her. So go back to work and finish that program, and screw the bastards."

Russ stared up at Marley uncertainly, trying to believe him, finally unable to. "No. I can't. No, we've got to try . . . We've got to call the police."

"He's right," Bob put in. "Whether it does any good . . . It'll establish that we *believe* there's been a kidnapping."

Marley accepted that. "Right. And you're right, Russ. We have to go to the police; we have to take every reasonable step we can. I'll go now, take Ben with me. Anything that can be done, we'll do. In the meantime, Russ, will you try? Try to work? You've always said you like your work because when you fire up that machine you're in another world. Okay, beam yourself into it, do your thing, and let us do ours." With a hand on Russ's shoulder, Marley turned him and started them walking toward Russ's workroom.

"You'll get her back?"

"I'll do everything I can."

See one police station, see them all. Palm trees distinguished this one's locale as tropical. It occupied one end of a long, low building that also housed the island's National Tourist Bureau and its public library, a combination unique in Marley's experience. And while Marley and Ben Newman waited, a nine-inch-long lizard waited with them.

But the lizard, with its mottled, wrinkly, sagging skin, its throat pulsing, was like the old derelict in every station, brought in and not yet booked. And the room had the customary sense of heavy use and vacancy, of being a place where everything happens and nothing changes. And of threat, because everyone since Adam and Eve has feared the police.

See three or four cops, you've seen them all. The sergeant to whom Marley spoke first was the heavyset, apparently easygoing type. The officer to whom they were taken was the ramrod: as thin as Marley, almost as tall. He stood while Marley and Ben were shown into his cubicle. The crease of his khaki trousers could have sliced beef. His tunic had been starched and pressed so smooth he might have been wearing the ironing board. His skin had the gleam of obsessively polished leather.

"Mr. Marley?" he asked.

"I'm James Marley. This is Ben Newman."

"I'm Superintendent Riley. Please sit down."

Marley and Ben sat, Riley sat. "You are reporting an abduction?" he said, more as a statement than a question. The tone suggested neither lack of interest nor alarm, incredulity nor belief. He just wanted the facts, sir; just the facts. While Marley quickly gave the man background, and told about Lily's disappearance and the phone call, Riley sat erect with hands folded on his desk, and never took his eyes from Marley's face.

As soon as Marley finished, Riley looked up to the sergeant, who had remained, leaning against the doorjamb. "The pharmacy, the shop across the street, anyone they remember being in the shops at that time, anyone you can find who was on the street."

"Sir." The sergeant shifted his bulk and was gone.

Superintendent Riley pulled a pad of lined paper to him, took a needle-pointed pencil from a shiny brass holder full of them. "Now," he said, "if we may go over this in detail . . ."

Marley began to have that sick tingle, that feeling of being pumped full of emptiness. Tell the truth about Lily— that he believed the abduction was fake—he'd look like a fool for having come to report it. He could try presenting both possibilities—maybe it's fake, maybe real; but if he did and—unavoidably—showed his certainty about his own judgment, would Riley take the matter seriously? On the other hand, if he didn't tell everything, and Riley discovered he hadn't, Riley might feel *he'd* been made a fool. Marley sensed that the superintendent wasn't a fool, and would take *that* very seriously. While Riley questioned Ben Newman, Marley thought about how much more *he* should tell. He forced himself not to think about his anger at Russ for putting him into the situation.

As soon as he got out of the car and started toward the house Marley called out, "They're going to do what they can," to answer the question Russ hadn't spoken, but which his tension seemed to scream.

Marley gestured toward the house. "Let's go in and sit down." The sun had sunk behind a bank of blue-gray clouds far out over the sea. A line of silver rimmed them; the sky above was pearly; but night would fall very soon, and Marley was tired.

Only Russ had rushed out at the sound of the car approaching, but the other men watched expectantly as Marley, Russ, and Ben came in. Bob rose from a chair. Kip looked up from the couch, where he had taken Jeff's usual place and his paperback. Jeff was in the kitchen stirring something on the stove.

Marley sat heavily into the chair at the end of the table. "It was about what I expected," he said, looking at Bob.

Then, to Russ again, "We talked with a Superintendent Riley. He seemed to me to be a very sharp, competent policeman. Wouldn't you say so, Ben?"

"Yes, sir. Very sharp." Ben stood nearby, fists clenched, leaning forward in his eagerness to help.

"Riley's put out an alarm—an alert—for Lily. I guess the police force here isn't very large, but they tap into the local grapevine, and that's terrific. He tells me the island's only about twelve miles long, and by noon tomorrow three-quarters of the population will know the police want to find Lily. He's alerted the embarkation points—which means the dock and the airfield. He's working on this very seriously, Russ."

Russ had taken a chair at the other side of the table's corner. He'd strained forward, leaning on clasped hands while Marley spoke. For one moment he continued staring at Marley eagerly, then for another, perplexed. "But James . . . if we know where she is, why doesn't he just go and get her?"

"Well, we don't *know*. Even assuming Ho has her, we don't know that he'd keep her at his estate. She could be anywhere on the island."

"But if the police arrest him . . ."

"Well, they can't do that."

"Why not!"

"There's no evidence."

Russ shook his head, not comprehending.

"Russ . . . I told Riley about Ho, that Lily might be at his estate. And, naturally, he wanted to know why I believed that.

"I had already explained the situation, basically—told him who I am, what my involvement is; about you, the program, somebody trying to steal it, copyright it first; that being the reason for Lily's abduction. I told him I'd met Ho in Boston, that we'd connected him with the pirates. Well, of course, Riley asked what evidence we had. I told him, and he listened, and he didn't try to refute it; but it is only circumstantial.

"I told him—I *had* to tell him—that we believed Lily had been working for Ho; that her abduction might be a fake."

"No! James, why. . . ! Now he won't. . . !"

"I had to. I didn't tell him right away, but he was questioning Ben about the 'abduction,' and the lack of any evidence that it *was* an abduction. And he asked more about the phone call. He had picked up, himself, that Ho and Lily might be connected since they're both from Boston, both Chinese. He just suggested it at first, didn't ask a direct question. But I could see he was thinking . . . I figured it was better to be honest than to try to deceive him and maybe turn him against us."

"No, James! It's not true! And now he won't really try. *I* should have gone. *I* would have— You did it deliberately! You're just out to get—"

Marley raised a finger. "Get hold of yourself," he said with mountainous calm. "I went there to involve the police, and they are involved. Riley's concerned that *something* is going on that may be illegal, and he is doing what he can to find Lily and solve it. I think he's doing more than if somebody had rushed in making wild accusations that might not hold up.

"Now, as far as Ho is concerned, Riley said he'd go and question him, try to smell out something. But—at this point—there is absolutely no hard evidence that would support any sort of charge. There's no evidence that Riley could take to a magistrate for a search warrant. He is putting a man to watch the road into the estate, so if she's there and they try to move her . . ."

"It's not enough!"

"It's all he can do, Russ. He can't call out the army,

search the whole island. He can't even search Ho's place without a warrant, and there's no evidence—"

"He *has to*! He— *You* could. *You* don't have to have any fucking evidence. You *know* about Ho. If Lily's not at his place, you could make him tell you where she is! *You* could do it, I know about you. David Cheyney's told me things . . . You got those people free from those kidnappers in Italy. You could rescue Lily!"

"Russ, no. I couldn't. I can't. You have an idea about me that's not true. I'm not James *Bond*. Most of the work I do for David—"

"You *could*! Please, for me, James. For Lily—they'll kill her."

"They are not going to kill Lily. You don't have to worry about *her*."

"What do you mean, I don't have to worry about *her*?"

Marley slid his thumb under the table so he could grip the edge. He was tired, he'd slipped, he needed to hold on. But anger was burning in his chest. He smiled and spoke softly. "I explained, Russ: It's a bluff. It would work against them to hurt her even if the abduction were real."

"*Even if!* What do you mean, *even if*?"

"I'm sorry. I've already told you what I think about it. But it doesn't matter. Okay, they really kidnapped her. But they won't hurt her, and the best way to get her back quickly is to call their bluff and end the charade: Finish your program, file for your copyright, and they'll let her go."

"All you care about is that fucking program!"

Marley put his other hand over the table edge and gripped tightly with both of them. "That isn't true."

"You don't give a shit about Lily! You don't give a shit about me! All you care about is that fucking program and the fucking millions it'll make for David Cheyney!"

Through his smile now thin and tight as a dead man's,

Marley replied softly, "Try not to be a complete asshole, Russ. Before you accuse me of not caring about you or Lily, try thinking and caring about somebody *other* than yourself and Lily. Try remembering David Cheyney's put money behind you, more than he's gotten in return, because he cares about *you*. Think about Joanna, *your wife,* and all the work and support and talent she's given you— you'd still be in that basement in La Jolla, without her. Think about your kids, who you're going to do so much for.

"Try thinking and caring about your responsibilities to them, instead of whining over a hired crotch who—even if she *were* kidnapped and threatened—would only be getting what she'd asked for, what she deserves!"

For a moment Russ gaped at Marley, and Marley stared back, as if neither quite believed those words had been spoken.

"Deserves?" Russ asked finally in a soft, high voice. "Oh, yeah; oh, man, yeah. I see: deserves: She's getting what she deserves. I'm getting what I deserve. Oh, you're not going to try to break *that* up, are you, James? Yeah, we were *bad*. And now we're being *punished*. And you sure wouldn't do anything to save a bad person from being punished, would you?"

Marley shouted, "Goddamn it, Russ. . .!" But then he couldn't think of anything else to say. Again, he and Russ stared eye into eye, and seconds passed.

"Aw, James. Aw, James, please don't punish us." Tears rose in Russ's eyes, and his voice began to tremble. "Please. We just wanted to love. That's not bad . . . if we *were* bad, don't punish . . ." he sobbed, ". . . Lily."

The tears ran down Russ's face; he was crying; sitting there staring straight at Marley, not trying to choke back, or to cover his face, be a good little soldier. Marley looked at him, but was aware that all of the other men had their eyes averted.

"Please . . . oh, please . . . save her, James . . ." Russ's words came brokenly through his sobbing. "Please."

Marley sprang up so abruptly his chair crashed over backward. Slamming aside the screened panel, he stalked out onto the terrace. He strode across the flagstones, past the swimming pool, and down onto the thick lawn, halting finally halfway across the yard toward the lower wall.

He took a full breath, held it tight—an anvil for his pulse to hammer and exhaust itself—then exhaled slowly. He sought something to focus on. The hedge of flowering shrubs obscured the wall. In the thickening dusk he couldn't distinguish patches of painted brick from blossoms. Out beyond the hedge, the sea had darkened to an inky blue-purple, and blended with no horizon into the bank of cloud. The cloud did still stand separate from clear sky above, but had lost its bright, hard outline. Looking straight up, he could see three stars—no, four—and then, possibly, others. They shimmered, as though he were seeing them from the bottom of a deep, clear pool.

He took another breath. The air did feel like liquid, eddying gently, soft, neither warm nor cool, sweetly fragrant and rank with fertility. If he'd let himself go, it seemed, he'd rise and float, drifting where the zephyr currents carried him.

But his fists were clenched, his arms stiff, his back tight, like clamps and rods and cables straining to bend an iron bar. He was a bar; he was an iron man, a statue standing on the bottom of that pool.

Marley opened his fingers, shook out his hands, flexed his shoulders, loosened his neck by looking from side to side.

Off to the left, the cluster of lights that was Plymouth town gleamed softly below the dark but not yet black shape of the mountains. As with so many mountains, those two peaks could be imagined to look like a woman's breasts. Although the just-past-full moon wouldn't rise for several hours, the picture was essentially the same as when he'd been there two nights earlier, when he'd seen Russ and Lily making love: Lily floating in the pool; Russ and Lily floating, together, in the night. Floating, as he never had, never—iron man, granite man—never would.

For several minutes he stood looking over the landscape, thinking and then not thinking. Then he sighed and turned and went back into the house.

"Where's Russ?"

From where he'd been standing, looking at Marley through the window wall, Bob nodded toward the bedroom. Ben and Kip were perched on stools at the kitchen counter, Jeff stood behind it. They all stared at Marley.

"Maybe I'm wrong," Marley said. "It's been known to happen."

No one commented.

"I guess Lily ought to have the benefit of the doubt. I guess she—they—ought to have a chance."

All four of the other men continued to stare at Marley in silence.

"I don't know . . . It really runs against all my better judgment, but . . . Somehow it does feel like—if they can—they *ought* to be together."

Jeff had frozen in the act of ladling soup into Kip's bowl. He seemed to remember. He completed the action.

"So," Marley went on, "I'm going to go in and see if I can get her back."

Jeff put the empty ladle down onto the counter with a soft click. That was the only sound.

Finally, Bob asked, "Ah . . . how do you figure to do that?"

"Well, obviously I haven't got much of a plan. I'm sure I can go into town, ask a cabdriver for directions, find Ho's estate. I'll just have to go there and see what I can see. I don't have in mind breaking down the door, slinging her over my shoulder, and running out with her through a hail of bullets."

"Glad to hear that, James."

"If she's there, if I can establish that, then I can come back and get the police to act. If I don't locate her, maybe I can arrange a few minutes' private conversation with Mr. Ho. We've talked before, so he knows that I know the method of questioning that *he* thinks appropriate for this business."

Bob regarded Marley, and then said, "While you were outside, I explained to Russ what he was asking you to do. The odds, the risk. Like, it would really be a job for Superman; and that—whatever you may have pulled off in Italy or anyplace else—you aren't Superman. You *aren't* Superman, are you, James?"

"I've done some poking around after dark, Bob. That's all I have in mind."

Bob's eyes shifted from Marley to the three men at the counter. "Our contract doesn't call for us to play offense, but . . ." Ben started to blurt, "*Anything* I can . . ." then he caught himself and simply nodded. Kip nodded. As usual Jeff merely stared back, looking like an Olmec head.

"No, it doesn't," Marley agreed, "and—although I appreciate the thought—I think we'd better keep it that way."

"Look, James, if you're serious, be serious. You'll need support, somebody to watch your back—"

"No. The bigger the intrusion, the more likelihood—"

"James?" Russ's voice interrupted them. He was standing in the arch leading from the bedrooms. All the men looked at him, and for a pin-drop moment he and Marley held each other's eyes. "I heard your voice . . . I . . ."

"I want to apologize, Russ. I'm sorry for what I said, and—"

"No. I'm sorry. I—"

"I'm going to find Lily," Marley said.

"No. It's too dangerous, James. I understand that. I was crazy to think you could."

"Well, I think I can without too much risk. I'm only going to do some scouting."

"Thanks, James. Thank you. But you can't, it's just too—"

"Don't worry about him, Russ," Bob broke in. "We're going to look after him."

"No," Marley said firmly. "What I want you to do is—if you have to—to be accessories-before-the-fact to the crime of trespassing. You make a formal note of my intention to go into Ho's estate. One of you drives me to the place, and leaves me there and comes back here, making note of the time I started into the grounds, and that I wasn't carrying any kind of weapon. If you don't hear from me by . . . I'll give you a time . . . you call Superintendent Riley."

"James, come on—"

"That's it, Bob! I'm in charge of this operation."

Russ stumbled forward a step. "James, you can't. I don't want you to!"

"Well, *I* want to. As I told you, I *don't* do this kind of thing often. But when you have a skill, it's nice to practice it." He smiled. "It'll be fun," he said.

No one in the room believed it.

CHAPTER 8

"What's it look like?" Kip asked, peering past Marley from behind the steering wheel.

"Like the old days—before the revolution." Marley sat twisted, his elbows braced on the frame of the passenger-side window, holding the big night-glasses Bob had given him. "Big white house; two—maybe three—floors. Porch and balcony running all around." With the light-gathering power of the binoculars he could see that much. In the last of twilight, the house in the middle distance appeared to the unaided eye only as a small, pale patch on the dark velvet landscape.

Marley and Kip were parked on the shoulder of the road, looking at a slight angle downward and across a deep gully.

"The approach looks good," Marley said. "All the slope is clear over there for . . . must be a half mile on one side of the house, at least a quarter in front down to the gully, much farther—looks like fields under cultivation—on the other side. Forest is closer in back. Wall around the house, but doesn't look very impressive."

"You can walk right up to it," Kip observed encouragingly. Then he added dryly, "As long as they don't have a patrol, or night scopes, or just a dog."

"I doubt they're set up with night vision. A patrol—I'll have to be careful. If they have a trained dog . . . you're right: I'm in trouble."

Marley scanned to the side of the house. "Lights showing, off to the right at the back of the fields. I'm seeing them through some kind of foliage, can't make what they are; but I'd guess some outbuildings. I think I'll check them first—come along the edge of the forest behind the main house. If Lily is being held, it would make sense to keep her in a place like that: They could take her back into the woods if anybody showed up looking for her."

He returned to the mansion. "Lights in the main house, but only a few. And night's coming fast now—I can hardly make out the balcony." Putting the glasses down, he looked up at the sky. "And I should have at least four hours before the moon rises. Looks good. Let's go."

Kip put his hand on the gearshift, but paused. "You really think this is a good idea, James?" Pale green light from the dashboard showed his face expressionless. He and his three colleagues were of that tribe of men trained to reveal no feeling.

And Marley was their elder brother. That light deepened the lines in his face, made it graver than the younger man's, but his voice was as neutral as he answered. "Well, frankly, no."

The men regarded one another for a further moment, and then Kip pulled the car back onto the road and took them down the hill into the gully's darkness.

Marley wore his dark blue windbreaker zipped up to his chin. Ben Newman had loaned him a pair of black jeans that were a little loose in the waist and a little short, but comfortable. The outfit wasn't a commando's blacks, but with some dirt rubbed on his face, he thought he'd be hard to see in the night.

In fact, he was virtually invisible as he made his way along the edge of the forest. He had entered the estate a quarter mile beyond where its driveway met the public road—out of sight of Superintendent Riley's man, who sat in a car watching the entrance. He crossed several hundred yards of open land to reach the wood, then turned right. He'd made good time, despite moving cautiously.

He'd paused often to listen for any guards who might be abroad. He'd heard none. He didn't really expect patrols. Nothing about the place was fortresslike. Superintendent Riley had indicated that Stanley Ho was an absentee landowner who contributed substantially to the island's economy and was well liked. The estate had no outer wall—only a wire fence along its border with the road, obviously meant to keep livestock in rather than intruders out. And Ho had no reason to suspect that Marley would come to break into it.

Marley moved cautiously less in fear of possible guards than because of the terrain. Not a lawn, as it had appeared from a distance, the ground was rough—lumpy and stony—probably used for livestock grazing. He had to be careful not to trip or turn an ankle. And the old Vietnam fear of stepping on a snake tightened his guts. He'd read that the island's poisonous snakes lived only back in the jungle, away from any human habitation. Still, the scurryings and slitherings he heard as he walked shot cold jolts up his spine.

As he approached the big house, and when he passed perhaps fifty yards behind it, he stopped often to use the binoculars. The wall he'd seen from the road seemed not to be topped with spikes or wires or the like. It was no more than five or six feet tall, so from the high ground at the edge of the woods he could see all of the house over it.

The house was two full stories high, with a line of low dormers along the slanted roof indicating a floor of cramped-ceiling attic rooms. The wide porch and pillar-supported balcony did run around the entire building, connected by a wrought-iron spiral stairway at one rear corner.

French doors gave access from porch or balcony into every room. Lights shone in several rooms on the ground floor; all but one on the second were dark. None of the doors seemed to be screened—maybe the constant breeze kept bugs away. They did seem to have curtains that could be pulled across them. Those for the room on the upper floor were drawn. Slipping inside the house ought to be easy, if he had to do it.

Looking into one of the lighted rooms on the lower level, Marley saw a man sitting in a big chair, evidently watching television. It was the young hammerhand he'd called Rocky. In the kitchen two black women were working.

Down from the porch, at the rear of the house, patio furniture had been placed around a swimming pool. From the darkness of the trees, Marley could see directly across it, through the center pair of French doors. He could see enough of the interior, of a stairway rising on the right, to sense the simple plan of the building: It was a rectangle with a two-story atrium in the middle. The stairway probably led up to an inner balcony from which all the second-floor rooms would open. Virtually every room in the house, then, would have two ways to enter or leave. Possibly there would be doors between rooms, too. Couldn't be better for what he'd want to do—if he had to go inside.

Marley hoped, though, that he wouldn't have to go in. Staying close under the trees so no illumination from the house could reach him, he continued carefully toward where he'd seen the dim lights of possible outbuildings.

Suddenly, something whished by close to his head. He ducked, whirling, ready to fight. Against the not-quite-black horizon, a shape swooped and wheeled. A bat. Marley straightened, regulated his breathing, and went on.

A little beyond the far side of the house he came upon a distinct path through the turf. It led from the house into the woods. He followed it, now moving even more slowly, silently. Trees rose high and thickly above him, brush filled the forest's lower story. For three or four minutes he had to grope, one hand guarding his face, the other outstretched, walking into leaves, catching himself against a tree trunk, able to keep the path at all only by feeling the softness of the earth when he strayed. He pushed a branch aside and saw lights.

They came from three small tin-roofed shacks. The buildings were set squarely, all with their backs to the hillside, facing the same direction, but stepped along a diagonal axis at the edge of the trees. Kerosene-lamp light shone through the unglazed window openings in each, and through the open doors of the first and third. People lounged outside those two—two women sitting on the wooden stoop of that closest to Marley, four men at the farthest one. Someone moved past the lamp in the middle shack.

The people looked like field workers taking their hard-earned ease in the rich and languid evening. They chatted and chuckled, women's talk, men's talk. Only fifty feet away from the nearer cabin, Marley could hear the voices distinctly without understanding a single word—he'd been told the islanders spoke no other language but English, but their inflection and dialect made it sound to him like some speech of Africa.

The people probably were workers for the estate. Probably there was nothing strange about whoever occupied the middle cabin wanting privacy for a time, keeping the door closed. So there *probably* was nothing sinister in the men's keeping the tools of their trade near them: Even at the distance to the farthest shack, Marley could see light gleaming on the machetes' blades.

From concealment behind a tree trunk, he focused the binoculars on the middle cabin. The window opening was about three feet by two. A shutter, hinged to its top, was hooked up under the roof's overhang. He could look through to the bare-board back wall, and see an edge of what must be a similar window there.

For several minutes he watched, tantalized by that momentary interruption of the light that had told him someone was inside. He crouched, shifting his weight so his legs wouldn't go to sleep, being patient, trying not to think that the person might have lain down on a bunk to sleep for the night. Suddenly, he was rewarded. A woman's shadow appeared on the back wall. She turned and sat—evidently at the table where the lamp was. He couldn't see her, but she must have been close to the lamp because her shadow loomed.

Could she be Lily? The outline of her head, from crown to shoulders, was that of a woman with long, straight hair—a silhouette completely unlike that of the two black women outside the nearer cabin. Yet when her profile had been projected, her bust had seemed larger than Lily's. But he had seen it for only an instant, and her shadow might have been distorted.

Marley put down the glasses and considered. No, he could not go back to Superintendent Riley with the information that *some* long-haired woman was sitting in a cabin on Ho's estate. He'd have to see the woman, not her shadow.

How? The two women at the nearer shack could look directly at the front of the middle one. Indeed, one of them sat turned toward her companion so that its window and door were continually within her view. The men outside the farthest building could see along the back of the center one.

Well, if he couldn't creep close and look in, logic suggested that the woman be made to come out. Fleetingly and regretfully, Marley imagined having tear gas or a smoke grenade. However, he thought, there was a simpler way: If he moved around behind the cabin and tossed stones onto the tin roof, the woman would certainly react.

However . . . if the woman did come out, she'd come through the front door; he'd be in the woods behind the shack. Furthermore, the men just next door would hear, too. They'd probably quickly comprehend what was happening, move swiftly to find the stone-thrower. Marley puzzled for a moment, then saw what to do.

He backed into the wood, began moving to his left on a curve behind the shacks. What faint and broken light reached him gave no help beyond fixing their location. He had to find his way in nearly total darkness. The forest wasn't any solid jungle; he could go around trees and between bushes—when he found them. He found them by walking into them. He did that very slowly, very carefully, moving one cautious step at a time, with his right palm shielding his face and his left outstretched. He'd touch a trunk or branch, feel out its extent, go around. He concentrated on not tripping or stumbling, not crashing into anything: quite reasonably afraid of making noise. He concentrated also on suppressing that unreasonable (he told himself) fear of snakes, of putting his hand on a trunk and touching something many-legged, hairy, stinging, of walking straight into a broad, sticky web—

Stop it! he commanded himself. There's nothing like that here. Stop thinking like that, and just go on. He did go on, every nerve in his skin tingling.

The forest, the night, helped him in one way: They were

filled with sounds: croaks and trills, whirs and drones and constant chitterings. They gave him confidence that the small blundering noises he couldn't completely avoid making wouldn't be heard. But as evidence of the jungle's teeming life they also screeched against the slate of his self-control.

After ten or fifteen minutes—or as many hours, it seemed—he pushed aside a branch to check the lights and saw that he had put himself directly in line with the back of the middle cabin. He approached it with even greater care, halting behind the last screen of underbrush about twenty feet away from its back wall.

Then he had to find something to throw. Some light penetrated the foliage, but still he had to feel across the ground, brushing aside layers of leaf mold, digging for stones, a piece of broken branch. Thick and damp, the humus was warm beneath its surface, and stank of decay and generation. Marley's fingers touched cool and slimy things, too; worms or slugs; and he tried not to think what else might live under rocks.

When he'd found half a dozen missiles, he stood and positioned himself, imagined the trajectory and force needed, and threw a stone. A moment later, he heard it clunk onto the far end of the roof of the shack to his right, and rattle-roll down the tin roof to drop off the front eave. He heard the women's talk cease for an instant, then one exclaimed to the other, who responded. He waited five seconds, tossed another stone.

Clunk—the voices stopped again—rattle-rattle-rattle, thud. First one woman, then the other came out far enough from the front of the cabin to be in Marley's sight. They were looking up at the roof. He tossed the piece of wood.

One of the women shouted to the men. The other did, too. While alarm and questions went back and forth, Marley threw a fourth projectile.

The first woman seemed frightened, the other laughed and called out, apparently sure someone was playing a friendly trick. The four men also seemed amused. They laughed and jibed. But they did get up and stroll over—past the middle shack—to the one at the other end. Their calmness and good humor suggested they weren't on guard; however, they all carried their machetes as they came.

Marley tossed one more stone, dropped the others, and—bent low—pushed through the brush and sprinted toward the back of the middle cabin. He was in line of sight of the people gathered at the end one for barely more than a second. During that exposure he counted on no one looking his way, or on not being seen against the blackness of the forest.

In four bounds he reached the shack. He tried to run quietly, but speed seemed more important. His last step was heard. As his white but mud-streaked, wide-eyed, strain-distorted face appeared in the window, the black woman at the table turned. Her hands flew up to her kerchief-draped head, and she screamed.

Marley whirled, dashing for the forest. Every sense straining, he heard the bang of the cabin door thrown back, heard the terrified woman fleeing down the three wooden steps shrieking for help, heard the men responding. Light from the cabin behind him let him see well enough to leap headlong through the screen of brush without fear of braining himself against a tree. Crashing into the wood for another two yards enveloped him once more in darkness. He couldn't run farther.

He didn't want to run, because of the noise it made. At first, all the people had been shouting—even as the men began running, smashing through the brush. Now the men were blind, too, and slowed. One of them called back to the women, whose voices dropped to a murmur. The men moved deeper into the forest. They weren't silent. They spoke to one another constantly: a word or two, grunts; but softly, low-pitched. They shoved branches out of their way. They hacked them off cleanly with single slashes of their machetes. They weren't silent, but they were quiet. *Marley* had to be the silent one.

The men were listening, Marley knew. They'd hear any sound that wasn't their own. He crept, crouched to the ground, one hand on the ground taking part of his weight, the other arm extended to feel from side to side. Touch a tree, slip around it. Touch a bush, push it aside, go under. Brush the ground ahead, find a fallen, dried, and brittle palm frond, step carefully—carefully!—over it. Creep deeply bent-kneed, one hand down and then the other, feeling with one hand out and then the other, the twisting locomotion of an alien creature with all its sensory organs at the tips of its forward limbs.

The hunters moved quicker, side by side. If they came upon him that way, close together, they'd catch him. Marley could only hope that their line of search would angle away from his direction, or that they'd drift apart enough to comb past and miss him.

Neither was happening. Having to go where the forest let him kept Marley from cutting to one side sharply, quickly enough to escape them. And with their low-voiced signals back and forth, they were keeping their places next to one another.

Marley's hand touched a tree trunk. Which way to go around it? He groped from side to side. The trunk was broad, many times the width of its neighbors. Rough bark—some different kind of tree altogether. He ran his hand up it, then cautiously stood upright. Perhaps it had limbs. Perhaps he could climb up into it.

No branches, not as far as he could reach on that side. The hunters couldn't have been more than thirty feet away, hacking toward him inexorably. Carefully, he moved around the trunk. Broad as a wall: For a moment he was tempted to flatten his back against it in the hope they'd divide and pass without suspecting someone might hide behind it.

If only there were a branch! He circled the trunk, feeling desperately for that branch—that one branch that could save him. That branch on the tree he'd found in the middle of a pitch-black forest at the absolute last minute. Finding it might be implausible, but why not? Why shouldn't he have a miraculous escape? He'd been told that one can make miracles simply by believing in them strongly. Marley believed. With each machete slash he believed more strongly. He circumnavigated the tree, stretching for that branch.

There was no branch. In desperation, he dropped to his knees and scurried on, another six feet, until he encountered a bush. Many-stalked, thick: possibly—*possibly*—the hunter who came to it would go around instead of hacking through. Marley crawled under and around behind it, and crouched as low and tightly as he could.

Slash! "Yah." Branch-crack. "*Oh*-kay." Thud and metallic ring. "Uhh, *hey!*" Marley heard one voice exclaim what he thought might be, "Be here the Granddaddy Tree!"

The men halted, talking softly. Evidently that tree marked their location for them. From the tones of their voices, Marley guessed they were discussing whether to go deeper into the forest. One spoke commandingly, and they fell silent.

Marley froze absolutely still. He kept his breathing slow and even so they couldn't hear it as he heard theirs. A tiny, high-pitched whine passed his ear, returned, and drew closer. A mosquito. Maddeningly, it hovered, drifting back and forth, brushed his cheek without landing. A second drone joined it, homing on him. The first insect landed, and he felt its sharp needle-sting. The second seemed to be waiting its turn. He heard a third.

All around, he imagined, mosquitoes were sensing him, smelling him. He wondered if the four men—the nearest must be standing not eight feet away on the other side of the bush—could smell him.

The men spoke again, softly to one another. One raised his voice in what sounded like a warning: "Something . . . this tree . . . my cutlass!" Then, *thunk*! In his mind Marley saw a machete swung backhand, biting into the bark at the waist level of a man hiding behind the trunk.

The men laughed. Maybe they still thought it was all a trick, a joke by some friend. Maybe the machete-wielder had used the flat of his blade. Marley was very glad he hadn't tried to hide there and found out.

Still laughing, the men turned and started hacking back the way they'd come. At least, it *sounded* as though they *all* went back. But Marley knew how farmers shoot crows: Four men cross a cornfield and enter the woods, three leave; crows can't count above three, they land again. Marley waited. Now there were too many whines around his head to keep track of. With his body hot, his blood pumping close to the surface, he must seem to all the mosquitoes within a square mile to be a neon-lit banquet. They'd risen like a mist thickening into a fog. They tickled and itched and bit his forehead and cheeks, the hairline at the back of his neck above his turned-up collar. When one found his eye he chanced waving his palm to fan it away. He screwed his lids tight-closed—couldn't see anything anyway. He fanned his face with one hand, cupped the other over his nose and mouth. There seemed to be nothing he could do to keep them from behind his ears. He gritted his teeth, waited another three minutes. By then he felt sure none of the men had stayed to trap him, but wasn't sure he cared.

Crawling out from under the bush, he rose and con-

sidered which way to go. To head on what he believed
would be a direct line toward the big house was a daunting
thought. While the hill's slope oriented him generally, the
difficulty of moving through the forest might keep him wan-
dering for who could say how long. Less rationally, but
more powerfully, he felt an unaccustomed claustrophobia.
Just as the mosquito swarm seemed not a gathering of indi-
vidual insects but a single, many-barbed, bloodsucking
creature, so the whole forest itself had become one thickening, enveloping, constricting, increasingly hostile entity.

The house ought to lie on a diagonal line ahead and toward his right. The hunters had retreated at an angle toward the left. If he cut sharply left, he should come out of
the wood and into the cleared land, and be able to swing
around the cabins downhill of them and in darkness. He
began to make his groping way in that direction. The mosquito swarm moved with him, constant, intensifying, as did
the feeling of the jungle as a hostile being that sensed him.
He had to stop frequently and reassure himself that he did
know which way he was going, that the jungle wasn't drawing him into its center—like a pitcher plant drawing a fly.
When he finally stepped out into the cleared land, he felt a
sense of escape as palpable as the open, starry sky and the
fresh breeze.

As he'd hoped, he'd emerged from the woods fifty yards
or so beyond the cabins. All of the people were gathered in
front of the one farthest from him, excitedly telling and
retelling, gesturing, reenacting, caricaturing—always several speaking at once. But laughing, too. Evidently, they
didn't consider the incident truly alarming—so they probably hadn't reported it to anyone at the big house.

Marley didn't think that any light from the shacks could
reach him, but he kept low at first as he circled well out
over the open ground and down the hill. The mosquitoes—
like the stink, like the sense of animate threat—seemed

confined within the forest's heavy shadow. The gentle breeze blew them away, and—although balmy—cooled Marley. After a little while he rose, confident of invisibility.

He came toward the house from the downhill corner, so that he wouldn't have to enter the woods again. Starlight alone made the wall and the upper part of the white building glow palely. Lights in first-floor rooms, which he couldn't see directly, were reflected up on the stucco as soft, amber patches. Especially in contrast to the dense, black menace of the jungle, the house seemed serene, peaceful, inviting. But Marley wasn't deceived: The dangers of the forest were potential, perhaps imagined; those inside the house would be real and active.

Bending low again so his silhouette wouldn't show against the lighter background of the wall, he moved uphill. As he expected, he found a gate near the back corner, where the path from the cabins entered the house grounds. The gate stood open. Marley crouched and waited for several minutes, then scurried through it and into the garden. He ducked behind a bush and waited again. After five minutes he crept out and toward the spiral staircase at the corner of the porch.

Obviously, the people in the house weren't expecting trouble. Either Lily wasn't there, which the lack of precautions seemed to indicate, or—even more likely—Stanley Ho never imagined anyone would attempt intruding. Marley tried to convince himself that he was cleverly taking advantage of a miscalculation, not confirming his own foolhardiness.

Flowering shrubs grew here and there between the wall and the house. Marley slipped from the cover of one to another, subconsciously aware of their fragrances. He paused for another minute at the one nearest the house, then dashed for the porch. Once on it, he prowled slowly, careful of his footfalls. He climbed the stairway to the balcony. Wrought-iron railing, wide-board floor. The lighted second-floor room was three-quarters of the length of the house away from him.

The boards flooring the balcony seemed solid, but were uneven. Marley, suspecting some might creak, trod carefully, lightly, close to the wall of the house where they'd have the most support. Clearly, his situation was dangerous. Every movement, every step toward that lighted room, made it more so. The level of risk would rise exponentially if he went inside the house. Yet he felt a tranquillity that seemed to be the place's character: the gracefulness of the building's proportions, the scent of its garden, the caress of air it must always enjoy. He could hear a soft clatter of dishes, a murmur of voices, chuckling, from the kitchen. He could hear television—not loudly enough for him to distinguish words, but from the rhythms of speech—setup, punch line, topper—and the surflike rushes of laughter, he guessed it was a sitcom. Comfortable domesticity.

He ghosted along the balcony. At the side of each of the French doors leading into a darkened room, he paused, sinking to his knees so that he could peer in from a level where he'd least likely be noticed if anyone were inside. No one seemed to be.

As he'd seen with the binoculars, curtains covered the door to the lighted room. A diffused glow shone through them; he'd hoped they might be sheer enough so he could see through when close to them. They weren't. Nor was there any gap at sides or center. Nor did the gentle breeze, which made them billow slightly and sway, open any slit between their panels.

A television set was playing in the room. Marley heard a stadium full of people chuckle, chortle, and guffaw and applaud. He heard why he should launder his clothes with Tide and brush with Crest. With an exhilarating shock, he heard someone inside the room run water in a sink. But he heard nothing by which he could identify the person.

Perhaps if he waited longer he would hear some such sound. Perhaps if he waited, the person would open the curtains. Or, if he waited long enough, the person—or some other—would come out on the balcony to enjoy the luxurious evening air and find him squatting there like a frog. He decided he'd have to go inside.

He rose, returned to the adjacent room that he'd already passed. Its door was closed but not locked. Carefully, he pressed down the latch, opened the door, stepped inside, leaving the glass open behind him. For several moments he stood, blind until his pupils opened fully. Just enough light entered the room through the balcony doors, and from under the door to the hallway inside the house, for him to make out the furniture. A canopied four-poster stood centered against the wall to his left, bedstand tables at either side of it. There seemed to be a chest of drawers beyond the bed, on the hallway wall. To his right was a vanity; above that a huge mirror, located suitably either for primping at the vanity or reflecting on how one looked in bed.

A thick rug covered the floor. Marley padded silently across it, and put his ear to the wall opposite the bed. The old house had thick partitions; he could hear the TV only as the barest murmur. He moved to the hallway door, cracked it open.

As he'd imagined, an inner balcony ran around the second story, providing a hallway access to all the rooms there. The staircase to the ground floor descended on his right. A huge, electrified crystal chandelier lighted the core of the house.

Marley closed the door again while he considered what to do. There seemed to be few options. He tried to think of at least one. Suddenly, he heard a voice downstairs. He opened the door just a slit again.

Stanley Ho had come out of an archway to the right of the bottom of the staircase. He was holding several business-size envelopes. He might have been working in an office in the house—a businessman never completely free from his affairs—but he looked like a man on vacation, too: white shorts, sandals, white knit shirt with some designer's logo, a gold chain around his neck. He called out again, and in a moment another man appeared from the rear of the house. Marley recognized him at once, even from above and behind. Dapper Dan.

Ho spoke to him, mostly in Chinese but with an occasional English word. He handed over the envelopes, and Marley caught "post office." They chatted for another moment. Ho said something, and nodded, indicating the second floor. Dapper replied with a suggestive chuckle. Ho shrugged, and started up the stairs.

Marley closed the door and retreated across the room to the balcony door. He paused. He ought to get out of there, he knew. Ho might be coming to that very room. But Marley's instinct told him where Ho was going. He waited. He heard the door to the next room being opened and closed, heard Ho speak. With the TV on, Marley couldn't distinguish the words. He couldn't understand the reply, either, but he knew the answering voice was Lily's.

Step silently out onto the balcony, creep to the spiral stairway; down, across the garden, back over the fields. Once outside the wall, there wouldn't be any need for caution to slow him. He could be at the road, with Superintendent Riley's watcher, within fifteen minutes.

". . . Get some air," Ho said, sweeping aside the curtains at the adjoining room door. "Yeah!" he said, exhaling. "Smell the flowers from the garden." He stepped out onto the balcony.

Counting on the softness of the rug, Marley backed a step, and then another, to one side, out of view.

". . . Stars. No stars like that in Boston. I don't know why I don't come down here more often. Ought to retire is what I ought to do, you know? I ought to just— Somebody left the goddamned door here open. I tell them, you can't leave the goddamned doors open at night without a light on, the bats come in."

Pressed tight into the corner, Marley saw Ho's white-clad bulk appear in the arch of the balcony doorway six feet away. Ho stepped forward, across the threshold, his arm stretching into the room. His hand took hold of the door handle. He turned to pull the door closed. For an instant he looked straight toward Marley.

In the next half second, as Ho started back in shock, beginning to exclaim, to shout for help, to come on guard, Marley would have hurled himself forward and struck. But Ho didn't start. His glance passed the corner of the room in the natural sweep of a man pivoting. "Goddamned blacks just don't pay attention," he said as he pulled the door closed behind him.

The TV was turned off. After a few moments, Marley remembered to breathe again. Then he considered what to do. Plan A: He could wait five minutes, then sneak mouselike out onto the balcony. Plan B: He could slip into the hallway and then brazenly stride down the stairs and out the front door. Or . . . Staring across the room, he suddenly became aware of doors in the wall at either side of the bed. They might be closets, but one of them might connect with the next room. His best route of escape would be out onto the balcony through a room farther away from Ho.

Quickly, he crossed the room. He was standing beside the bed, his arm reaching for the door handle, when the door to the hallway opened.

CHAPTER 9

A blade of yellow light slashed across the bed and up the wall beyond. It widened as the door swung inward, framing the shadow of a man who stood silhouetted in the arch. Then the light narrowed again and was gone, and the man's figure was one with the darkness.

At the soft click of the first quiet latch lift, Marley had spun and dropped to the floor. Looking below the bed, he'd watched the man's feet step across the threshold. But even if he hadn't seen those steps, Marley would have known that another person was in the room. That instinct, more than the visual knowledge, raised hairs on the back of his neck. In another moment, he realized he could hear the man breathing.

Marley didn't think the man had seen him. Kneeling low to the floor, he stayed where he was.

The softest of shuffles crossed the carpet, then halted. A dim light came into the room. And then Marley heard Stanley Ho's voice.

". . . Paperwork. Can't get away from it, no matter where I go." The voice was tinny.

Marley cautiously raised his head to peer over the bed.

Dapper Dan stood at the vanity wall opposite the bed, staring at the big mirror that wasn't a mirror now. It was a window. Through it, he—and Marley—could see into the adjacent room.

". . . Pain in the ass, pain in the neck." Ho sat on the side of the bed there, clutching the back of his neck with one hand, twisting his head against his grip. "Missed my swim, talking to that cop this afternoon. I really *need* a swim every afternoon."

"Break my heart, Stanley. I missed mine, too." Lily spoke from somewhere out of sight.

"*You* can't go out where somebody could see you, so you didn't *miss* it. I *could've* had a swim, so I did."

"Break my heart. I'm gonna come out now."

"Just a second. I'll close the curtains."

The light through the mirror-window had a strange, colorless quality, an emotionlessness out of keeping with the obvious purpose of the device. For an instant, Marley wondered whether the view was a one-sided joke on people who used the other room, or whether the see-through could be reversed, and guests at the estate took turns watching one another.

Dapper Dan was watching with a blankness of expression to match the neutrality of the light. His skin had the color of old, unpolished ivory. Nothing was happening in the next room to arouse excitement, but Marley assumed that Dan expected something would happen. From his stealth, he clearly wanted to watch without Ho's knowing.

Ho came into sight again, returning to the side of the bed, flexing his shoulders. "Feels like somebody stuck a key in my back and wound everything up tight."

"The cop worry you?"

"No. I just acted mystified. I mean, 'No, I don't know anything about this woman. Never heard of her. James Marley? Who's he?' Riley didn't have anything; I could see he was only fishing, wanted to see my reaction. No problem.

"No, it's the paperwork—three hours at that goddamned desk. I need some relaxation. How about a treatment?"

"How about 'no'? How about you get out of here and let me get some sleep?" Lily appeared. She was wearing a long, dark red, silk dressing gown splotched with pinky white carnivorous-looking flowers.

Her true colors, Marley thought; no longer the deception of daisies and dancing beagles. Vindication! He'd been right about her all along. Once again, he'd proven that although he made mistakes, his basic instincts and judgments were rock. Marley felt very pleased with himself about that. Surprisingly, he also felt disappointment weighting him like water seeping through sand.

"Lily, I'm stiff. I want a rub."

Lily had come to the mirror on her side. She glared into it, evidently at Ho's reflection. Her eyes might have burned holes through the glass. She drew herself up. Crossing her arms, she turned to face him. "That's not what I do for you anymore, Stanley."

Ho put his palms very precisely onto the tops of his thighs, fingertips just across the hems of the white tennis shorts. He regarded Lily for several moments with his scrap dealer's stare. Finally, he spoke the way a snake uncoils. "Lily, you are one of my people. You're on my payroll, you're under my protection. Just like Shen and Johnny, and the rest in Boston. Just like Big Joseph and Geraldine and all the other help here. Just like I'm one of Richard Chee's people. When Mr. Chee calls me from the Coast and tells me he wants me to handle something, I don't say, 'Hey, Mr. Chee, I don't do windows.' I don't always like doing it, Lily—what he asks me to do. But I'm one of his people, so Mr. Chee says, 'Shit,' I squat.

"Now, a couple more days, you get your bonus. You set yourself up—get up off your back and start making your living off other girls'—okay. Then you're not on my payroll, I won't ask you to rub my neck: I'll respect your position.

"But when you start running your own service you'll still be one of my people. I'll be protecting you. I'll be sending you clients. And you'll still owe me obedience. I have somebody special, you'll do him for me, personally. That's how we operate. That's our way of life. Mutual respect. Taking care of the people who work for you, being obedient to the people you work for.

"I can't believe you've forgotten that, Lily. I guess you had your mind on the way things are going to be, instead of the way they still are now. I'd hate to think you had forgotten about obedience, because I don't see how we could go on with our arrangement if that was the case. Which would be a shame, considering all you've done up to this point. Now, I need a neck rub, okay?"

After a long moment Lily replied, "Okay, Stanley." She didn't sag physically, but her voice sounded old and tired. "You want me to take my robe off now?"

"You got anything on under?"

"Just my underpants."

"Okay, take off the robe. You know I don't like it all at once."

Lily walked two steps toward the bed. Pausing, she hooked her thumbs under the dressing gown's sash, slowly pulled outward to loosen it.

Dapper Dan's jaw muscle tightened. He moved to his right, across the vanity, trying to see Lily more at an angle. Marley abandoned his binoculars, shoving them under the bed. He rocked up onto his heels, then rose slowly into a crouch.

Holding the right side of the gown in place across her, Lily let the left shoulder slip down. Dapper leaned closer to the window. Marley began creeping toward him.

With both hands closing the gown just above her breasts, Lily let the right side slip off that shoulder. Dapper licked his lip. Marley rose half upright with one forward step, fully with a second.

For a moment, Lily stood motionless. All at once she dropped her arms to her sides, letting the gown slide to the floor. Dapper gasped at the sight of Lily, and then the breath exploded as Marley struck him across the base of his skull.

As the small man collapsed, Marley caught him, let him down softly. Spinning around, he grabbed the bedspread, dragging it over the end of the bed and to the floor. He rolled the unconscious body onto the spread, then rolled both together once and again. Not the same as tying him, but didn't take as long, either. When the man awoke in a few minutes, the spread would bind him for another one or two. That would be all Marley would need.

Rising, Marley glanced once more through the window into the next room. Lily was standing, one leg between Stanley Ho's as he sat on the edge of the bed, her other knee on the bed, her thigh pressed against him. She was holding his head to her breasts as her fingers worked into the back of his neck. She wasn't looking down at Ho; her head was lifted and her hair fell away from her face. She was staring across the room, evidently at nothing, because nothing showed in her face. Least of all, life.

A great heaviness dragged at Marley, but despite it he moved quickly to the balcony door and outside. No need now to make an escape through adjoining rooms. He had taken three careful steps, close to the house, toward the spiral staircase, when something scraped on the porch below. He froze, then crept on. Reaching the staircase, he let himself down and lay so he could look upside down through its opening and back along the lower level.

The young muscleman was sitting in a wicker rocker outside the rear entrance to the ground floor.

Marley pushed himself up to his knees, and quietly took a deep lungful of the cooling night air. He saw a million brilliant stars in the swath of sky beyond the overhang of roof above; but lower down, off over the fields to the right, the mountains' silhouette loomed clearly against a brightening grayness where the moon was about to rise.

Then he stood again, and feather-footed back to the room he'd just left. He stepped past the bedspread roll silently, wondering how many moments more he had before the man cocooned in it began to groan, to fish-flop. In the other room, Stanley Ho sprawled facedown on the bed while Lily, kneeling astride him, massaged his back.

Ho and Lily were occupied, Dapper Dan slept at least for a time, Rocky was relaxing in the great out-of-doors. If the kitchen women still toiled in the building, it seemed unlikely that they'd come into the lobby. Marley cracked the hallway door, checked, then stepped boldly out and started to stride like the master of the house along the inner balcony toward the stairway.

Halfway to its head, he heard a car approaching, coming fast. He hesitated only for an instant. He might race back and hide, but Dan would be coming to very soon, or might be missed and looked for. Better to go on, cannonballing through whoever was arriving. He half loped along the hallway, still trying to be silent. As he grabbed the top of the banister railing and spun himself onto the stairway, he heard the car skid around the circular drive outside. As he bounded down the first two steps, he heard the car door slam and the sound of heavy footsteps running up those to the porch outside. Marley leaped out, taking the stairs two at a time. As he hit the floor at the bottom and began driving toward the doorway, a figure lit from above appeared at the open door and raised his fist to knock on its casing. Building momentum, Marley hunched his shoulders and lowered his head, preparing to smash the man aside.

"James!" Russ Detweiller shouted. "Where's Lily!" He jerked the door open.

Shock checked Marley for one instant. And then he was throwing himself forward again, "Come on, Russ! Run!" reaching for Russ to shove him, drag him away. Russ stood dumbfounded, not responding. A hand grabbing Marley's arm jerked him. Marley spun. It was Rocky, shouting, "Stanley! Shen!" his voice ringing from the stair-hall walls. Then the men were twisting, gripping, jabbing, parrying. Stanley Ho, in shorts, no shirt, was standing at the railing above shouting, "Shen! Shen!" and more. Marley landed a punch. He took one in the ribs. It hurt him. He gasped, twisted away to get breath. Stanley Ho had vanished. Russ, jumping in, was clawing at Rocky's shoulder. "Stop! Stop it!" Rocky back-armed him, knocking him aside. The movement opened him. Marley shot a punch to his stomach. The blow hurt Marley's hand, broke Rocky's grip. He staggered a step. Then they were slashing again, ducking, feinting. Marley, skillful, scoring more hits, not seeming to hurt with them, blocking but jolted with pain every time the other man connected. Russ was shouting, "Don't! Stop it! James!" Rocky was shouting, "Stanley! Shen!" shouting at Marley, "Fucking bastard!" raging constantly as he fought. They struck a table, knocking it crashing to the floor, smashing a vase. Marley and Rocky were throwing punches, grappling, Russ was trying to separate them, to hit at Rocky, shouting, "Stop it! Stop it! You don't have to!" Rocky was still bellowing curses. All at once, someone else was yelling, his voice sounding over the pandemonium. Rocky sprang back. Russ froze. Marley darted a look, then held it.

Stanley Ho stood halfway down the stairway, pointing a large revolver straight at Marley's head.

During the next long moment, all four men were statues in a silence louder than the noise had been. Stanley Ho stood on two steps, balanced, firm. He held the pistol in both hands, his arms out stiffly in front, sighting along the barrel. Light from the chandelier glinted on it, and in the obsidian pupil of Ho's eye. Then, never letting his aim waver, Ho lowered his hands to rest them on the banister. "Johnny?"

The young man answered, "I was out on the back porch. I heard a car tearin' up around the front, came in. This guy"—he indicated Russ—"was comin' up to the front door. *This* guy was comin' down the stairs. He musta been inside the house."

Ho regarded Marley, his dark clothing, his mud-smeared face. He didn't ask Marley to confirm or deny.

"Where's Shen?" Ho didn't look away from Marley, but the question seemed to be directed to Rocky-Johnny.

"I don't know. I was watchin' TV, and then I went out back."

Ho tipped the pistol, sighting it at Marley's leg. He held the angle carefully when he raised his eyes again. "Where's Shen?"

Experienced as he was with Ho's questioning, Marley answered directly. "If you mean Dapper Dan, he's on the floor in the bedroom next to the one you were using."

By the tiniest of nods, Ho suggested he understood completely. "You hit him?"

"Yes."

"You hurt him?"

"Not seriously."

"Too bad." Another nod indicated Russ. "Who's this?"

In the instant while Marley was thinking what lie might succeed, Russ answered, "I'm Russell Detweiller. You're Stanley Ho?"

"That's right, Mr. Detweiller. You came here to see me?"

"I came here to get Lily. I know you kidnapped her. If you aren't holding her here, then you're hiding her somewhere else. I came to get her, and to stop James—" Russ turned to Marley. "I couldn't let you, James. It was too much of a risk. I shouldn't have asked you. I had no right. It's my responsibility, and I'm going to—" To Ho again, he said, "Here." He extended the diskette he'd been holding in one hand. "This is it: what you want. It's my program."

"Russ—" Marley kept himself from moving, sure that Ho would shoot him.

"It's the best thing, James. It's only a fucking piece of software! It's only money. If he wants it, he can have it— the whole thing, no backup, no competition, it's all his. So there's no point in holding Lily, or you . . . or me."

"Russ, Lily—"

"Marley!" Ho snapped. "One word, I'll kill you. You know what I mean? One word. One move, one word."

Once again Russ turned to Ho. "I don't know, Mr. Ho: Maybe you think as soon as we're safe we'll tell the police. Okay, so what? With what this is worth—what James says it must be worth to you and whoever you're working for— there must be enough in it for you so you can go anywhere in the world, change your identity. What do you care if you can't go back to Boston? Take the fucking program, get rich, and let us go."

Ho allowed himself a razor's edge smile. "Johnny . . ."

Johnny stepped toward Russ. Russ handed the diskette to him. And Marley stood still and silent so Stanley Ho wouldn't kill him right then, containing his rage, calculating the probability that Ho would surely kill both him and Russ in the very near future.

The thick wooden door shut with a solid clunk. The wrought-iron bolt was slammed home to hold it. Two sets of footsteps tapped, overlapping, away along the corridor outside. At the bottom of the door the thin line of yellow went black, and Marley and Russ stood imprisoned in a large closet.

At once, Russ asked, "Did you find Lily?"

Marley had his palm to the door, feeling all around it. "She's in the house."

"You saw her?"

The door had no casing. It had been set into a wall boarded tightly on both sides. "Yes."

"Is she okay? Are they hurting her?"

"She's okay—safe." Although the rooms on the third floor must have been used for servants' quarters or storage—bare boards, no trim—the construction was solid. There'd be no breaking through.

"But will they . . . now that. . . ?"

"She's okay, Russ." Marley offered his friend what death-row comfort he could. "Don't worry. We'll get ourselves out of this, then we'll worry about her." He began running his hand over the wall to his left, took a step to feel the back one. The closet must have been about four feet deep. "Solid boards here. Same on your side?"

"Yeah. How are we going to get ourselves out of this?"

"I don't know. We'll have to think about it." Marley reached up, stretching on tiptoe.

"I'm sorry, James. I'm really sorry. I thought it was the best thing—that it would get everybody *out* of danger, and doing that was worth more . . ."

Marley's fingertips found no ceiling. "We'll talk about it later."

"Jesus Christ, James, Ho's probably going to *kill* us, isn't he? He really is probably going to kill us. And I don't understand why. I mean, I thought it through. Like I told him, he doesn't have to kill us. But if I was wrong, then why hasn't he done it already?"

Marley wished he could tape Russ's mouth shut. But he made himself relax.

"He's keeping his options open, Russ. He's covering himself both ways. First, I imagine he'll try to blank-face it through. Superintendent Riley's stakeout man sees a car come flying down the road and into Ho's estate; twenty minutes later it comes flying out again. I imagine it heads back toward your house, but—going so fast—it doesn't make one of those corners above the coast, goes over a cliff into the sea. No body is found. Who can prove anything against Ho?

"And Bob and his team say I went into the estate grounds. But there's no trace of me. Maybe I got lost in the jungle. Maybe the mosquitoes and the ants ate me down to the marrow. Who can prove anything against Ho?

"They may try. Just possibly both of us disappearing, plus the tie-in between Ho and your competitor on the program, will convince a court. Frankly, I doubt it. Everybody may realize Ho is rotten . . . But everybody knew Al Capone was rotten, and they only got him—finally—on tax evasion."

Russ objected, "But you were counting on it that Ho would let you go if he caught you, because people knew you'd snuck in on him. You told Bob . . . That was your safety line when you went in, wasn't it?"

"Well, Russ, maybe I didn't think it through carefully enough."

"But . . . No, James. That *was* your safety line, and I broke it, didn't I? I mean, now that I've given Ho everything he wants . . . *now* he can split if he has to. He's just willing to try bluffing it out and not have to run. That's it, isn't it?"

Marley was leaning on the back wall of the closet, staring into the darkness as though he could see Russ. "Yes. Giving Ho the program probably shifted the balance."

In the next silent moment, Russ must have sagged and leaned against a wall, too. "Then why hasn't he killed us already?" he asked as though he merely wanted to know, not to argue.

"I don't know. Maybe he figures that if Riley does try to lock him up, he can trade us for free passage out."

Marley could almost hear the circuits in Russ's head connecting. "More likely—with that gorilla of his out getting rid of my car, and the guy you hit still groggy—he just couldn't handle disposing of our bodies at the moment. I mean, he doesn't seem to have any other people around, does he?"

"No. There are field workers, out at some shacks a few hundred yards away; but it appears he doesn't involve them with this part of his business."

"So he could just be waiting for his strongman to come back to get rid of us."

"It is another possibility, Russ."

"So, we'd better figure a way out of here," Russ concluded. "Where are we? I lost my sense of direction, coming upstairs."

"We're on the top floor, on the inside of the house. There seems to be a ring of rooms around the outside— there are dormers all along the roof. Then the corridor we came through, then these storage closets. All of that would be over the rooms below. In back of us here would be the space over the big central hall. There aren't any supports under that, of course; so it's probably just empty space around the structure that holds up the roof."

"Any chance of getting out that way? I mean, the walls seem solid, but maybe . . ."

"Right. I can't reach the ceiling, but—"

"On my back."

"Can you. . . ?"

"Sure." Russ went down to hands and knees, his head braced against the front wall. "Okay."

Steadying himself with a hand to the wall, trying to think himself lighter, Marley stepped up onto Russ's back.

"Okay?"

"Okay."

Marley's hand found the ceiling less than a foot above his head. "Yeah. Boards. Wide ones. Solid." He felt from side to side. "Wait—here's one with some give!"

"Can you lift it?" Russ grunted.

"Maybe." Marley strained, pushing upward against the board. He heard Russ grunt, taking a breath and holding it. Relaxing for an instant, Marley struck upward with the heels of both hands. Again. Each blow knocked a gasp out of Russ.

One end of the board lifted. With steady pressure, Marley raised it, prying, loosening the nails at the other end. "I'm getting it. How're you doing?"

"Okay."

Marley twisted the board one way and then the other. Suddenly, with a pop, it was free. He laid the board to one side above the ceiling, stepped down.

Russ sucked in a breath, straightened his back. "What did you get?"

"About ten inches. If I can lift one next to it, I can climb through. Can you hold up?"

"I can hold up."

Russ moved to a new position, Marley stepped up on his back again. He pressed against the board to one side of the opening. He struck it. Twice. A third time, and the old, dry lumber split at the nail holes. Marley wrenched away the pieces until the main part of the board fell onto Russ's back, then to the floor.

Russ grunted. "Can you get up through?"

"I think so. And then if I can go across the ceiling and drop down into the corridor or a room—anyplace—I can come back and let you out."

"Go, man!" This time Russ laced his fingers and Marley

stepped into his hands. Russ boosted him with a gasp and in a moment Marley was rolling up onto the floor above the closet.

He paused. He could see, if only very dimly. Semicircular vents were set in a row all around the roof of the house. Moonlight slatted between the louvers of those to the east; pale sky light filtered through the ones on the other sides. Although the great space still seemed one of limitless darkness, Marley could—after a few moments—comprehend the structure that filled it. What at first looked like a huge maze of dark bars he understood as trusses—a complex geometry of beams and braces—running across the entire house, holding up the roof, spanning the central atrium.

He rose and carefully made his way a few steps, until sure he was above the corridor outside the closet. Kneeling, he felt the boards that made its ceiling. They were nailed down. To lift them he'd have to draw their nails from above—and he had no hammer or crowbar—or get between two boards and pull or lever upward—and all the boards he touched were set close together.

Possibly if he felt around he'd find one pair of boards with a wide enough gap between them. Possibly he'd find that gap soon. Or . . . there had to be a way up into the attic from the floor below: Probably there was a trapdoor through the ceiling of a room or some other closet. But possibly he'd scrabble around the entire perimeter of the house and find nothing. Meanwhile, Johnny of the triphammer triceps would be drawing ever nearer. Marley didn't know what provisions Ho had made, but doubted he'd let his henchman spend the remainder of the night walking back from disposing of Russ's car. And Russ was right: Ho might only be waiting for Johnny's return to dispose of *them*.

He pivoted on his heels, surveying the cavernous attic.

The posts and angled braces of the struts made a petrified forest within it. Ages of dust coated them like frost, glowing palely where the moonlight touched them. A short length of rope looped like a vine. Ancient cobwebs were a desiccated, silver Spanish moss. The dust he'd raised held the moonlight as a deep-night mist does, seeming to make the light a substance, yet seeming also to dissolve, rarefy to invisibility, anything that passed into it.

For a moment, Marley yearned to disappear that way; or to climb high among the branches where he'd never be found. The feeling was instinctive, not a thought. Thinking, he moved through narrow bars of moonlight to get the rope.

The hemp was dry but seemed sound. It wasn't as long as he'd hoped—only about a dozen feet. Carrying it, he crawled back to the nearest vent.

The vents were semicircular, vertical to the angle of the roof, a yard in diameter, their canopies protruding from the steep pitch, appearing from outside like a row of half-submerged alligator eyes. Marley could crouch comfortably at the one he reached and look out between its slats. As he expected, the vent was directly above the ridge of one of the dormers. The distance to the ridge was less than six feet, that to the front of the dormer about the same again. The rope might be just long enough.

He tore away the wire screening that was stretched across the opening, tested a slat. It was wood, set into slots in the sides of the vent, old, weathered. Pulling on it, he was able to break it inward, remove it. He broke another. Like the first, it came out easily, but snapped as it did. In the stillness of the attic, the cracks sounded to Marley like shots from a .45. He wondered how loud they would be to someone inside the house, or outside below. He had to wonder, and hope, six times. Then he could lean out through the opening.

He turned, put a foot through, straddling the sill, and set the bottom of his shoe against the metal sheathing. Weathered and corroded, the surface seemed just rough enough to give grip for his feet so that he'd be able to walk down backward holding the rope. He looked around the vent opening for a place to secure it. There wasn't anything he trusted close to the opening, and the rope wasn't long enough to reach the front of the dormer if he tied it to a truss.

Quickly, he pulled himself back inside the attic and scuttled over to the opening in the closet ceiling.

"Russ," he called down, "I'm going to need your help up here."

CHAPTER 10

"What's the matter?"

"I'll explain when you're up here."

After a second's pause, Russ asked mildly, "How am I going to get up there, James?"

"I found a rope." Marley tossed one end of the rope down into the darkness. "Here. Come on, Russ, we've got to hurry."

"You think I'm Tarzan? I can't climb a rope, James. I'm sorry."

"Just hold on. I'll pull you up."

"You know how much I weigh?"

"Don't tell me. Ready?"

"Do it."

Taking a breath, letting half out, Marley straightened his back, bringing all the weight onto his legs. Then he began to rise.

Russ's hand, arm, head, and then the tops of his shoulders emerged out of the blackness like a tortoise being hauled from a pond. "Okay, James, okay! I'm up enough. Don't let go!"

Marley stepped quickly across the opening so Russ could support himself by his upper arms. Dropping to his knees, he reached down and caught hold of Russ's belt and heaved.

Gasping, Russ wormed forward, bringing his chest over the floor. Again Marley pulled.

"Okay, I got it! Okay!" Russ rolled, and for a moment lay on his back, gasping.

"Would you believe two hundred pounds, James?"

"More. You are not just overweight, Russ. You are grossly fat. Unless you lose weight I am never going to take you anywhere again. Come on. Let's move!"

Marley led Russ to the vent and explained the situation. ". . . So I'm going to need help to reach that dormer: For me to have enough length, you're going to have to hold the rope—I'll tie it around your wrist—and lean out of the vent."

"You're crazy! The whole idea is crazy!"

"You want to stay here?"

Russ opened his mouth and closed it again.

"You have a better idea?" Marley demanded. "You have a better idea, you tell me. I'd surely be pleased to hear it. Otherwise, let's go."

Russ seemed to be thinking, but after one moment he said only, "Jesus, man," and extended his wrist toward Marley.

Marley looped the rope around it, twisting once so that it couldn't slip over the hand. "It'll tighten up and hurt. I'm sorry."

"Don't worry about it. What're you going to hold on to? You're just going to hold the end? That's crazy. You should have a loop around your wrist, too."

"Right. But I don't think I can afford to lose the length. I figure what we have will just barely do it."

"Do what? Get you down beside that dormer, no farther."

"If I've estimated the distance correctly, it'll get me close enough to the front that I can punch out a windowpane and reach inside and grip the casing. That's all I'll need."

"Then you let go of the rope and swing like a chimpanzee."

"Exactly."

"You're out of your fucking mind."

"Consider the alternative."

Again Russ was silent.

"Okay," Marley directed. "I go out backward, holding on to the bottom of the vent. Then you get in position. Throw the free end of the line straight down the roof, and brace yourself. One security I have is that there's no way I could pull *you* through a hole that small."

Legs straight out, Marley wriggled backward through the opening. He brought his feet up so that he could squat, his full weight on his soles flat against the roof, but also still hanging, secure, from handholds on the sill.

Russ came into the opening, tossed the line down to Marley's right, braced himself, extended his arm.

Marley lifted his right hand from the sill, took hold of Russ's arm, clutching it under his own. Now, he knew, he had to release his left-hand grip and straighten his legs. From working on roofs, from hiking in mountains, he knew he'd be less likely to slip with his full weight pressing his feet against the pitch. His mind knew that, understood the physical principles; but his body never believed it, never accepted that it wasn't safer hunkering as much of itself as possible against the slippery surface.

Focusing on a two-inch length of the seam between sections of sheathing that lay directly in front of him, he straightened his legs, lifted his left hand, and moved it to grip Russ's arm. His feet didn't slip. He felt perfectly secure. Shifting his holds, hand over hand, he came fully upright. Stretching down behind, he let the line slide through his right hand, then through the left. Now—should his feet go out from under him—he was completely out of reach of the sill, or Russ's arm, or anything else solid that he could grab.

Well, he wasn't going to slip, and even if he did, even if his line broke, he'd only fall as far as the dormer ridge. A picture flashed into his mind of himself sliding, striking the ridge, being deflected before he could grab it, going sideways, dropping to the main roof beside the dormer, avalanching down the last few feet, and hurtling over the edge. It had the vividness—not merely in sight, but in feeling—of an event not imagined but remembered.

For a long moment he stood still, alternating between the terror of that image and the night's sense of tranquillity and assurance. Then he took a breath, looked hard at the sheathing seam, felt the bond between his boots and the roof, and began to move down again, hand over hand, foot after foot.

His foot touched the dormer ridge. Putting full weight on it, he paused, shifted his hand-grips, worked his way to the side of the dormer.

His right hand reached the end of the rope. Two more steps backward and he could plant himself against the roof just about a foot from the dormer's front edge. Then all he'd have to do would be to grip the end of the line in his left hand, lean backward, and punch out the window. All he'd have to do would be to grip the last six inches of that rope in his sweaty palm, lean backward toward a fifty-foot precipice, his feet on a steep, untrustworthy, semi-slick surface, and exert vigorous lateral and twisting movements.

Marley shifted his right hand above the left. He wiped

his left palm thoroughly on his trousers. He took hold of
the end of the rope with a grip that could have compressed
steel. Then he leaned backward.

The dormer windows were made to open outward: two
sashes, each with four panes. Using his teeth, Marley
pulled the elastic cuff of his windbreaker over his fist, then
with the heel struck the mullion cross of the nearer sash.
Wood cracked, glass snapped. Well, you can't punch
through a window quietly, Marley thought, and hit again.

Glass fell to the floor inside, making that unmistakable
tinkle. Marley paused to listen. Nobody below called out
an alarm. He hit twice more, knocking out the larger pieces
of glass, which shattered, ringing, as they struck the floor
inside. Then he began to work at the pointed shards that
remained.

His left arm was beginning to ache. His hand—clamping
so tightly around the end of the rope—was losing its feeling. Soon he might not be able to sense the grip, soon his
muscles would become exhausted and relax without his
knowing. But he had to remove those points. He could
have unlatched the casement, but swung out it would be an
obstacle. Literally at the end of his rope, he couldn't go
around it; he had to go through.

He tried to be quick, careful, thorough. From wetness on
his fingers, rather than pain, he realized he hadn't been
careful enough. From the sensations in his arm and hand he
decided after another thirty seconds that he'd been as thorough as he could be.

Reaching through and around, he gripped the casing inside, trying to find a hold that didn't press his wrist hard to
the sash still studded with tiny dagger-points. Using that
contact more for balance and confidence than to hold himself, firmly forcing from his mind the images of how he
could slip, Marley put all his weight on his left foot,
brought the right up, and set it on the windowsill.

Okay, he told himself, it's monkey time.

Pressing himself tight to the dormer, he dropped the rope. For an instant he clung to the building, then got his left arm around the window casing, his left foot on the sill, and stepped inside.

Staggering into the room, he found a wall, leaned his back to it, let himself slide down and sit for almost a minute until his arms and legs stopped quivering and he felt sure he wouldn't throw up. He sucked his fingertips. They stung, but the cuts weren't deep.

A plain lumber pallet-bed had been built into one corner; otherwise the cramped room was bare. When Marley stood again he had to take care not to bump his head against the slanted ceiling. He opened the door cautiously, listened, then stepped out. By leaving the room door ajar, he let in enough light so that he could make out the closet across the narrow hallway. He threw back the bolt, opened the closet door, stepped in, called softly, "Russ?"

"Right here." Russ had come back to the opening in the ceiling. "Everything okay?" he whispered down.

"Looks good. Come on down, and let's get out of here."

"How do I get down?"

After a beat, Marley said, "Either you go down the roof the way I did, or you drop through the hole here."

"Yeah. I mean, how do I do that? I'm sorry, James. I'm not very good at this."

"You sit at one end, let your legs hang down."

Marley could see Russ's bulk against the paler darkness above. "Now lean forward," he directed, "one hand on either side of the opening. Slide your butt forward, come down on your forearms. I'll grab your legs, take some of your weight. Then let yourself down more, hang by your hands, and let go. And try to come down quietly, Russ, okay?"

"Okay, okay. You're going to grab my legs? Okay, here I come, softly as a fucking moonbeam."

Russ began to lower himself, Marley clutched him around both legs: The maneuver went just as Marley had instructed until the point where Russ had to release his hold on the ceiling.

"Wait! Wait, I can't!"

"Let go!"

Russ let go, started to fall backward. Trying to save himself, he broke his legs free of Marley's grip. He crashed to the floor.

"You okay?"

"I broke my fucking ankle!"

"Broke it?"

"Oww, Jesus! Wait a minute."

"Can you move it?"

"Yeah. Yeah, I can move it."

"Can you put weight on it?" Marley helped Russ to rise on one foot, leaning against the wall.

Tentatively, Russ put his foot to the floor. He gasped. "No, it's not broken. Probably just twisted, sprained. Shit!"

Marley asked in a level tone, "Do you think—if I help you—can you walk?"

Russ tried his weight again, gasped again. After a moment of silence in the darkness he said, "Well, I fucking well have to, don't I?"

"Put your arm across my shoulder."

"Do you think anybody heard me fall?"

"Back in town? On the other side of the mountains? Probably not."

"I'm sorry, James. I'm really fucking up."

"Only so-so. When we're out of this, I'll repair your computer and show you how it's really done."

"Okay. Give me a hand."

Marley helped Russ stand again. "Let's go."

Marley bolted the closet door behind them, "in case somebody comes up to check on us." They reached the door to the back stairway by which they'd been brought to the third floor. "Now," Marley said, "we want to try to start doing things quietly. We'll take it slow. They probably heard you fall, but that won't necessarily worry them too much—we could have been just bouncing ourselves off the door or something. If they don't hear anything else, maybe they won't come up to check. I'm more worried about the noise I made breaking the window. Let me go a step ahead, you lean on me."

The narrow service stair wound in tight squares in one corner of the house. One step down and they were in total blackness except when they could see a slit of light showing under the door to the hallway at the second floor. Marley kept his back to the wall, descending sideways one step at a time, taking most of Russ's weight each time Russ moved. Russ caught his breath with pain at every step, but kept the sound low.

They lost all sense of time. Step down, step down, step down, step down, then two side steps to a corner, two along the adjacent wall to the next flight, four steps down again. Marley counted to himself, knowing the rhythm prevented a misstep in the darkness. As important, it seemed, counting and keeping track of the landings counteracted the sense that the stairs were winding endlessly in a shaft of infinite depth.

Like all old, enclosed stairways, this one held in the pores of its wood the stink of ancient sweat. It creaked. Marley and Russ kept their footsteps light—even Russ, despite the pain; and Russ's soft grunts were barely audible. Yet anyone listening for them would hear their progress.

Other than their own movements, there was no sound. Marley listened, expecting to hear men pounding up the stairs from below, or running pell-mell along the second-floor hallway to cut them off. He heard nothing. The house might have been abandoned. He didn't believe that.

As they approached the second floor, he expected the stairway door to be thrown open, certain Ho and Shen and Johnny would appear framed in the arch. He tried to visualize what he'd do. If alone, he'd whirl and race back upstairs before a trigger could be pulled. Or hurl himself onto the first figure, knocking it back into the other two. Neither idea gave much hope, but being encumbered with Russ offered none at all.

He and Russ reached that level. Marley's ear twitched. But there weren't whispers on the other side. No black breaks in the yellow line under the door. Marley and Russ passed the door, started down the next flight. What if the door opened then? No promising plan of action formed. But the door wasn't thrown open. So Marley began to run the pictures over again as they went on down toward the bottom of the stairway and the door there which would certainly open into the kitchen.

As they reached the last landing before the bottom, Marley halted them for nearly a minute. He could hear, faintly, the sounds of the night and the forest. Nothing else. Even more slowly, cautiously, he took Russ down the final four steps, halting there again.

Except for those muffled night-creature noises, there was silence. Maybe Stanley Ho was packing, gathering papers he wouldn't want found if the house was searched, preparing his escape in case he had to make one. Perhaps he was with Lily, getting her ready for a move to some other hiding place. Despite the quiet, Marley never believed that Ho had simply fled.

Finally, putting his face close to Russ's ear, he whispered, "Okay, we're going to do it. I'll swing this door open, spot the one going to the outside. Then we'll move together—*very quietly*. Once we're outside, we'll run for the nearest bush. I'll help you run. Then we'll figure where to go from there."

Marley lifted the latch as if it might trigger a bomb, swung the door into the room degree by heart-in-mouth degree. Inch by inch the back wall of the kitchen appeared, and that blessed door to the outside. Before stepping from the stairwell, Marley opened the door as far as he could—a cabinet prevented it from swinging around to the wall.

"Okay," he whispered, and—with Russ leaning on his shoulder, moving in step—came into the room.

Stanley Ho stepped from behind the cabinet beyond the door holding his revolver level and said, "Stop there."

Russ started. "Jesus!" Off balance, he put his weight on his injured foot and winced.

"He hurt himself?"

"Sprained his ankle," Marley replied.

"Too bad," Ho observed in a tone with all the compassion of a bug squasher. "Sit down."

Marley nodded to Russ, helped him to sit on the stone floor. "Could we get some ice for the ankle?"

"Sit down."

Marley joined Russ. "Let me look at it. I think if you rub it lightly it'll help." Then he sat back, arms loosely around his knees, regarding Stanley Ho.

Ho tipped his head to one side very slightly—but his pistol pointed unwaveringly toward the center of Marley's chest. "You really thought you were going to tippy-toe out of here?"

"Seemed worth a chance."

Ho kept his focus on Marley as he sidestepped to the plank worktable that stood in the middle of the room. Moving behind it, he sat on a stool at a corner so he could rest his forearms on the table. He had changed clothes. Now he was wearing jeans and a knitted, crewneck cotton pullover and jogging shoes—casual wear, but all the best quality: He looked like an ad in *GQ*. Except for the pistol.

"No chance," he said. "I heard you all the way down the stairs."

"You must have been listening."

"I knew you'd come down this way when you got out of the closet."

"You heard me fall," Russ said dejectedly.

"Couldn't miss it, Mr. Detweiller. But I heard the glass break before that."

"I was afraid of that," Marley said.

"You really came down the roof? Scary?"

"A little."

"You must have gone up through the closet ceiling. How'd you reach it?"

"Stood on Russ's back."

"Ah. Well, nice try."

"What are you going to do with us?" Russ demanded.

Ho looked at him for a moment. The table was far enough away that he could shift his eyes without losing sight of Marley, and the aim of the gun never varied. Ho didn't say anything; the dead flatness of his stare was his reply.

"What are you going to do to Lily!"

Ho actually registered an expression: surprise. His eyes snapped back to Marley.

"I told Russ that Lily was here. I told him she'd be all right. He loves her, he wants to be sure about that."

"Don't hurt her, Mr. Ho! You don't have to hurt her. You don't have to hurt any of us; you can disappear and nobody will ever . . . But even if you think you have to kill *me*, please don't hurt Lily!"

"True love," Ho observed to Marley dryly.

"A beautiful thing," Marley replied. "Be terrible to spoil it pointlessly."

That slightest change in the line of Ho's lips might have been a sardonic smile. To Russ he said, "Don't worry, Mr. Detweiller; Lily's going to be o-kay."

"Thank you, Mr. Ho. Thank you."

Since it seemed they all were going to sit there for a

while, Marley decided he might as well try Russ's argument, futile as he knew it to be. "Russ is right, Ho: You don't have to eliminate us. Take the program and run."

"Oh? And what am I going to do with you two? Put you in a closet and think you'll stay there?"

"What does it matter?"

"Maybe I don't want to have to disappear—did you think of that? And if I did, how would I do it, Marley, with a resourceful, never-say-die guy like you behind me? You're impressive, Marley. I wouldn't count on getting five minutes' lead even if I chained you up in a milk can like those pictures of Houdini."

"There's a cop watching the entrance to this estate."

"Yeah. I know. He see you come in here?"

"No. But the security team back at Russ's house knows."

"Oh? Any of them see you come into the house?"

Ho's rebuttals were welded tight, and he knew they'd take the stress. Marley didn't debate.

After a minute of quiet, Russ asked, "Are you really working for software pirates in Singapore?" He might as well have been moving his lips in a vacuum chamber.

They all sat in silence for another minute. Russ rubbed his ankle, looking down at it with glazed eyes the way he stared at his computer screen, perhaps diagraming the situation in his mind, hoping the arrows would point a way out. Marley looked around the room. At one moment his eyes fixed on the open doorway into the rest of the house, behind Ho's back. Then he stared at the ceiling over Ho's head, his eyes growing wide. "You may not believe this, Ho, but there's a snake up there going to drop on you."

"No, Marley, I don't believe that."

"Would you believe cracks are appearing, and the ceiling's about to collapse?"

"No. I had all the structure checked over, two years ago. All solid. I don't think a bolt of lightning would make it all the way down here, either."

"Could come through the window," Marley said hopefully.

Ho shook his head.

"Maybe your guys'll have an accident on the way back. You sent that natty dresser after the other one, didn't you? That's why we're just sitting here, waiting."

"Yeah."

"How? Is there another road? It'll compromise your story about Russ driving away again if the cop out there saw your man leave soon after and come back again."

"Dirt track leads back around through the fields. There's a way to reach the road, but it's all overgrown—we hardly ever use it. I had Johnny check earlier today, after that cop was here, just in case. The cops aren't covering it. Probably didn't even remember it."

"Rough road?" Marley asked. "Maybe the car will break a spring. Your men won't make it back. You'll sit there all night waiting for them. You'll get sleepy. Your eyes will get heavy, heavy, so heavy. Your hands will get heavy, heavy."

"Marley, you're a character. A real comedian."

Marley looked long and speculatively at the light fixture in the ceiling to Ho's right. "Maybe that light bulb will suddenly burn out."

"If the lights go out, I'll shoot."

"Right. It would have to be something bigger."

"Floor *could* give way," Ho suggested. "Not likely, though."

"How's your heart?" Marley asked.

"Tip-top, tick-tock," Ho assured him. "No fainting spells, either. You're going to have to think of something else."

Russ had been drawn out of his trance by the banter, and was looking back and forth between the two men. Suddenly, shock showed on his face. Instantly, he controlled it, but couldn't keep his eyes from a point behind Ho's shoulder.

Marley glanced at Russ, then smiled at Ho. "Well, there is someone coming into the room behind you, Ho."

Russ looked at Marley, incredulous, then back to Ho and beyond him.

Ho really did smile broadly for once. "You're a team," he said. "Mutt and Jeff, Laurel and Hardy."

"We're going to get him, Russ," Marley said, fixing his own stare over Ho's shoulder. "Just keep looking back there. We both keep looking, he'll turn. He'll start to hear things—a quiet footstep. He won't be able to resist looking. He'll fight it, but sooner or later, he'll look. Then we'll jump him."

"I'm going to miss you, Marley. I really am."

Russ stared, wide-eyed with apparent hope and anxiety. Marley stared, smiling confidently. Ho's head twitched as though he might have heard something—or thought he did; as though an animal reflex was trying to impel him to turn, but his rational will overrode it.

"I'm not going to turn, Marley. Even if I did, I could shoot you before you reached me. But I'm not going to—"

Then a hand sweeping down full force struck Ho's head with a bottle.

Marley threw himself sideward, flat, just as the bottle connected. The movement alone wouldn't have saved him from the bullet fired when Ho's finger gripped reflexively, but that convulsive squeeze jerked the muzzle up, too.

"Lily!" Russ shouted, trying to struggle to his feet.

Marley was scrambling up, lurching to reach Ho in case the blow hadn't stunned him. It had. Ho lay arms out, the side of his head on the table, the pistol loose in his open hand.

"Lily! Are you all right?"

"Don't hurt yourself, Russ!" she warned. Then, at once, to Marley, "Is he out?" holding the bottle up beside her head with a tension that made it quiver, ready to strike again.

"Yes." Marley was taking the gun from Ho.

"Is he dead? Did I kill him?"

"No. I don't think so." Marley opened Ho's eyelid.

For an instant Lily looked as though she'd hit another time and finish the job. "Bastard," she hissed. She was dressed now in the blouse and shorts she'd worn shopping that afternoon. With her hair pulled back, she looked like Little Miss Wholesome again—except for the kill in her eyes.

"Lily, how did you—" Russ began.

"Where's Russ's program?" Marley broke in.

"In the safe. In his office."

Marley's talents didn't include safecracking. He thought about calling the police, waiting for them to arrive. He thought about Ho's men reappearing at any moment. He thought about using Ho's pistol to control them; trying to do that without risk to his team, without having to kill somebody on theirs while they waited. "We'll have to leave it for now. Let's get out of here."

Lily started to protest, "What about Stanley?"

"When we're safe we'll worry about him." Marley shoved the pistol into his waistband behind his back.

"Kill him!"

For an instant Lily's vehemence shocked Marley. An image of what he'd seen through the mirror-window flashed to explain it. "He's not worth it, Lily."

"Yes! You got to—"

"I'm not killing anybody!"

Lily stared at Marley with a look of agonized disbelief. "You don't understand . . ." Suddenly she swung the bottle above her head.

"No!" Marley shouted. "That's murder! He's not worth going to prison for murder!"

For a full second Lily held the bottle as though she still might smash it down on Ho's skull. Then she lowered it and stood it on the table. "You don't understand," she repeated almost despairingly.

"Shouldn't we tie him, or something?" Russ asked.

Marley looked down at Ho, again running pictures in his head. He thought about tying Ho securely enough to hold him there. He thought about looking for a rope long enough to do that. He thought about locking Ho in a closet, thought about finding a closet with a lock, thought about moving Ho to it with only Lily's help, having to drag or carry him to another room. And again, he thought mostly about Johnny and Shen.

Dish towels had been draped over a counter to dry. Marley strode to them. "We can't take time . . . this will have to do." Grabbing one of the towels, he sprang back to Ho. He seized one of Ho's wrists, then the other, tied them together and then to a rung of the chair behind him. "That won't keep him, but it'll slow him. We've got to move. Depending on how long he stays out . . .

"There's a cop out on the road." Striding to Russ's side, he put his arm across his friend's waist. "Get on the other side of him, Lily. Come on." He started them toward the back door as fast as Russ could hop. "We can radio in, call for help."

None of them spoke again. By the time they'd gone around the house and reached the gate beyond the driveway circle, they were all panting from the effort.

"Slow down," Marley ordered. "We've got nearly a half mile to the road. We'll never make it this way."

"I can walk." Russ pulled to free himself from their grips. He put weight onto his injured foot, gasped, lurched.

"Don't, Russ!" Lily caught him.

"Easy, buddy." Marley tightened his grip again.

"I can walk a little. Just let me lean on you a little. I think I can go faster that way."

"Okay, try it."

With Marley taking most of his weight when he stepped on the bad foot, Lily on the other side helping him balance, Russ was able to limp. He did move faster, with less strain on all of them. Still, they were covering ground only at the speed of a slow stroll.

Marley tried to calculate. It must have been over an hour since he and Russ had been shut into that closet while Johnny was sent speeding off in Russ's car. Shen must have left within the next ten minutes. No matter where on the small island they'd chosen to stage the accident, they should be returning soon. When he could, without breaking the rhythm of their five-and-a-half-legged stride, he watched back over his shoulder. Each time he felt relief at not seeing any headlamps moving across the moonlit gray fields.

They might just make it, he thought, committing the folly of provoking fate. Fate responded. A bell clanged back at the house, strokes ringing as fast as a hand could swing the clapper bing-banging back and forth, frantically side-to-side.

"The fire alarm!" Lily exclaimed in dismay.

CHAPTER 11

The bell's frenzy stopped them still.

"The field hands!" Marley thought aloud. "Will they—? Do they know—?"

"They're not like Shen and Johnny," Lily answered, "but if Stanley tells them to catch us and bring us back, they will, James!"

"He could tell them we stole something," Russ suggested.

"They won't ask. He's the boss."

"Let's go!" Marley started them moving again.

"That cop out on the road . . ." Russ started hopefully.

"I don't know. He'll call in, but whether he'll leave his stake-out . . . We've got to keep moving."

Despite their heartbeats pounding to the wild beat of the bell—fighting down their animal terror of that furious clangor as much as their rational fear of the hunters it would rouse—they kept a controlled, efficient pace.

But after four more steps Russ protested, "Leave me! You and Lily run ahead."

"No."

Russ halted, jerking his arm from Marley's shoulder, tottering but catching himself. "Yes! It's the only thing makes any sense. You and Lily get away, get help. Ho won't do anything to me if you're free."

"Russ, move while we talk!" Marley grabbed Russ across the waist, urging him forward. "If Ho catches you, Russ, he will kill you. I didn't want to say that before, but it was certain the minute you came in there and gave him your program. If what you told him is true—you didn't make a copy—then nobody but you knows how it works. If he kills you, there'll be no contest, no competition. The guy who's been working with what they stole can finish it, copyright it. No one can prove his program is like yours at all."

Russ processed that thought through the next half dozen steps. He didn't counter it directly, or stop them again; he simply said, "At this speed, none of us are going to get away."

"I don't know." Marley was again scanning over his shoulder. "It depends on how quickly the field hands come to the house, how long it takes Ho . . ."

"What's the matter?"

"Nothing. Just keep moving."

No, Marley hadn't seen the headlights of a car twisting along the dirt track from the other direction. Of course Shen and Johnny wouldn't drive across the fields using lights—that would beacon their movement to half the island. Marley realized he hadn't been thinking when he'd watched for lights. He realized it as he saw the dark and glinting shape beetling around a wide curve up to the house.

Under the merciless straight-down moonlight, the pasture on either side of the driveway glowed palely gray. The asphalted drive was smooth, hard, darkly sparkling. Neither offered any concealment for Russ and Lily. In his pseudo night-combat outfit, Marley might have avoided being seen if he'd lain off to one side in the pasture, curled next to a hump in the ground, posing as its shadow; but Russ and Lily both wore clothes of colors light enough they might as well be white. Running, lying down, or hunched and pretending to be rocks—no matter what they did, they'd be glowingly visible to anyone looking from the gate in the wall around the house.

"Should we cut off"—Russ gasped as he put weight on his injured foot—"to the side? Try to make the woods?"

"Ground's too rough. Uphill. Too far."

"What're we going to do, James?" Lily's voice sounded frightened, but firm.

"Keep moving," Marley commanded, as though that really answered the question. The car had entered the gate. It would reappear, speeding toward them—he guessed—in about one minute. In little more than that, the four men who even now were dashing out from the gate would catch up.

Russ, Lily, and Marley had found a stride that let them cover ground much faster than Marley would have expected; but there was no way they could cover enough to escape the pursuers. Continuing to watch behind, he could see the dark figures clearly. He could see glints of moonlight from their machetes.

"Lily has to get away!" Russ said vehemently. He didn't break the stride, but Marley could feel Russ's arm across his shoulder jerk with determination.

"Right. Lily, you—" Marley was scanning ahead, and to the right, up toward the forest, estimating which direction gave her the better chance. He'd been watching behind until then, and the forest made a black background, and the dark figures still were far enough away to be small: That's

why he hadn't seen them running down the hillside toward
the driveway. "There's more of them! They're cutting us
off!"

Marley released Russ, spinning from under his arm.
Light struck him as the car roared out of the gate, its high
beams now blazing. They silhouetted the men sprinting not
fifty feet away from him. The light hurled the men's
writhing shadows along the road and onto Russ and Lily
holding one another, onto Marley standing as if he imagined he could protect the other two.

The field workers came pounding down the final yards,
dividing into pairs. The car hurtled into the gap between
them as though to smash into the three figures frozen in the
roadway like jacklighted deer. At the last moment—sliding, scrunching—it stopped.

Marley didn't reach behind his back for the revolver.
Dazzled by the headlights, he couldn't see any of the men.
Firing blindly would be futile; shooting at the lights might
provoke return fire. Knowing he had more opponents than
bullets, he had to try for surprise. He waited, his hands in
sight.

All seemed still. The field workers stood back, silent but
for their heavy breathing. The car's motor idled, humming
quietly, one valve sticking, ticking rapidly, softly. Ho's
voice spoke very quietly to someone in the car, "He hasn't
got the gun." Then one of the car's doors opened and
slammed. But no one seemed to move. A thin fog of dust
drifted from behind the car, making the edges of the light
beams hard, catching the flare around them. Marley stood
squinting against the brightness, a cornered animal ready to
fight, not in hope of escape but because that's what it does.

Four moments: The scene played in four brief but distinct segments. In the first, the quarry was run down and
caught, surrounded, pinned against the wall of night by the
white shafts of those headlights. The next was that stasis. In

the third, Johnny loomed, a broad chunk of darkness solidified, materializing, breaking into the headlamp light. His
shadow struck Marley like a black club.

"Hey, asshole," Johnny said, "I'm gonna pound you."
Showing what he meant, he brought his hand up from beside his leg and—making sure the light glinted from it—
slapped the tire iron he held into the other palm.

Two of the field hands grunted as though this wasn't
what they expected, but they didn't move.

Johnny tried to make his moment last. Slowly, he lifted
the iron and slapped it again. From the darkness behind the
lights, Stanley Ho's voice ordered, "Just do it, Johnny!"

In the fourth moment, Johnny seemed to swell, spreading his arms and lowering his head for the charge. The field
workers muttered uneasily. Marley set himself to duck, to
draw the pistol and fire while throwing himself sideways out
of the light. And the men Marley had spotted running
downhill from the forest's shadow struck.

Bob Bracciotti and Ben Newman, sprinting hard with
shoulders down, hit two of the field workers like runaway
boulders. Kip drove into one of the men on the other side
of the drive, knocking him sprawling. The other man there
jumped back, raising his machete, but didn't leap into any
attack.

Arm wide, Johnny was about to strike at Marley when a
huge hand seized his wrist, and Jeff Bowles stepped into
the light.

Marley spun out of the headlamp light, the pistol in his
hand. Jeff and Johnny, still in the light, were grappling like
Godzilla and King Kong. No longer blinded, Marley could
see the men at either side of the drive. One of the field
workers lay flat, wind knocked out of him. Bob gripped
another from behind, twisting the man's arm to make him
drop his machete. The man Kip had knocked down tried to
rise. Kip chopped him once, turned to face the fourth.

"We're police officers!" Marley shouted. "Stop fighting, in the name of the law! Stanley Ho is under arrest!"

Perhaps the field workers believed Marley. At least, the fourth one backed away; and after Bob's man dropped his machete he didn't continue struggling. Perhaps Stanley Ho, himself, believed. Engine screaming, tires screeching, the car shot backward, pulling its light after it through blue rubber-smoke like the flame of a rocket. The light slashed in an arc across the pasture, and then blasted through the soft moonlight up the drive to the house.

Marley caught himself from firing after it. He turned. Jeff had Johnny's arm twisted. He spun half around like the tractor of an eighteen-wheeler on ice. Johnny, the trailer, swung out, flipping tail over head, crashing down on his back. All the battles seemed to be over.

"The rest are okay!" Marley shouted. "Don't hurt them!" He pointed at the field worker still on his feet. "You! Run out to—"

"You not the police!" The man was holding his machete defensively, level in front of himself.

"We're Americans working with the police. There's a policeman in a car out on the road. Run out there and tell him to call Superintendent Riley. Bring some cops here; send an ambulance. Go on! *Get* the police!"

The man took off toward the road. His companions seemed to be recovering. Perhaps Ho's actions had raised doubts enough so they accepted Marley's words. They showed no sign of wanting to resume fighting.

"I'm glad to see you," Marley said to Bob.

"Looks like we got here just in the nick of time."

"Anytime in the last two hours would have been the nick."

"Sorry. Russ just ducked out. Didn't tell us anything, took the car. It took us a while to put it together, get it together."

"I'm sorry," Russ said. "I'm really sorry about everything."

No one told him it was okay. Marley did nod to indicate he'd heard. Then he turned. "Bob and Jeff, you stay here. Bob, deal with the cops when they come. Tell them exactly what happened—everything you know about everything—and send them after us." To Russ he said, "When they question you—whenever—you tell them the whole story, too." Then he shifted to Lily.

Her head was raised to look at him, he could see her eyes clearly. In the straight-down moonlight, his own might be shadowed by his brow, but he was sure she'd feel his look even if she didn't see it. "Lily, you tell them nothing. They probably won't stop to question you now, but when they do, you tell them nothing until after I've talked with Riley."

Lily's eyes widened, then she nodded.

"Okay," he ordered, "Ben and Kip come with me."

Bob objected, "Let the cops take him."

"I don't care about Ho, but he has Russ's program."

"James. . . !" Russ started to protest.

"It's okay, Russ. We don't have to catch him, we just have to keep him from getting away." Wheeling, Marley started at a brisk trot back toward the house. The two men caught up to run beside him.

The car stood at the porch steps directly in front of the house. Its motor had been switched off, but the automatic cooling fan hummed, audible in the night's quiet even at the wall thirty yards away. Marley, Kip, and Ben peered around the corner of the open gate there. The porch light had been turned off; the chandelier in the entrance hall, too. A yellow glow came from a corner room only.

Kip asked quietly, "Okay, chief: What do we do?"

Marley deliberated. "I'd like just to bottle him till the police come, or—if we have to engage—catch him out here, leaving."

"You suppose this closes?" Kip indicated the wrought-iron gate, its single wide leaf swung open against the back of the wall at one side of the opening. "Hinges are pretty rusty."

"We can try, but . . ."

"Could he get out another way?" Ben interrupted. "Is there another gate?"

"Yes. At the back corner, on the right."

"You want me to go around and cover it?"

Marley shook his head. "There are a lot of other ways out. Too many. If he knows we're trying to keep him in there, he can come out of any room, onto the porch on any side, go bush-to-bush and over the wall just like we'd do going in."

"Then how are we going to bottle him, if that's what you want to do?"

"That's what I want to do. But I haven't figured a way."

"So, looks like we'd better go in," Kip concluded.

"I'm afraid so. But the other problem is, he's not alone. He has another man, who—I'll bet—is watching the car and this gate from back inside the hallway there. They had this pistol; we'll have to assume they might have another."

Kip laid out the options. "So, to take him, we'll have to sneak up 'round-about. But if—while we're doing that—he comes blasting out in that car, he goes past us. On the other hand, if we close the gate now, he knows we're here, he slips out the back. We should have brought Jeff. He could have hidden here and then jumped out and tackled the car as it went by."

Marley decided. "Okay, here's what we do: *You* hide here behind the wall. Ben and I go back to the corner, up along the side, and over at a place where we can't be seen if Shen is watching through the front door. We try to make it to that lit room, catch Ho while he's still packing, or shredding, or whatever he's doing. If we miss him, and they come out and get into the car, you try to close the gate. Try to do it fast, Kip, and make an effort to avoid being shot, okay? If you can't do it fast, don't do it at all: We'll let them have the inning. If they don't use the car, if something else happens, you be ready to render what assistance you can. Okay?"

"Yes, sir! You really think this is a good idea?"

"Frankly, no. Okay, Ben, let's go."

Marley turned, then froze. "Wait!"

"What?"

"What happened?"

"What. . . ?"

"It's the car," Marley whispered with recognition and relief. "The fan shut off." Now the only sounds were from crickets and the trilling toads: sounds not breaking the night's silence, but of it.

Marley nodded to Ben, and the two men scuttled along the wall and around the corner. When they'd gone far enough up the side, Marley stopped them. "Okay, we're past the front corner of the house. Let's look."

Marley and Ben came up carefully until they could look over the wall, like prey-seeking creatures raising eyes above the surface of a pond without making a ripple. Then Marley stood fully upright. "Looks good," he whispered. If he'd had more men than Ho and Shen to worry about, the bushes here and there, with their dark shadows, might have troubled him. "I don't think either of them will be looking this way—and as long as Ho has the light on in that room he won't be able to see us out here even if he does look. Just the same, we'll move from cover to cover until we're as close as we can get. Then make it fast up to the porch— but quiet. Be careful, some of the boards squeak."

"Then what?"

"If we can see in, see Ho, see we can take him, we'll go right in. If we can't try that, we'll work around the porch—close up against the house—to the front door. Take them when they come out."

"Okay."

"Let's go." Marley vaulted up to the top of the wall, rolled over, dropped to the ground, and darted behind a shrub. He checked for movement in the house, sighting over the pistol he held in both hands. Ben waited another few seconds, then followed. They worked their way toward the house quickly but cautiously, one at a time, pausing to look and listen before each advance.

Seeing Ben move increased Marley's confidence. He'd known nothing about the background of the men on the security team, but clearly they were experienced. Suddenly, Ben demonstrated his experience further.

"Shen!" Ho shouted from inside the house, calling the man's name and some order in Chinese.

Ben was running. He hit the ground, rolled, and lay still. Marley froze behind his bush.

A moment later, Marley heard footsteps from the front of the house. They crossed the porch, clumped quickly down the three steps. Shen must be going to start the car. They'd shut it off so Shen might hear anyone approaching. Now Ho must be about to dash out. But before a slam sounded to reveal Shen was inside, there came a grinding squeak from across the lawn. Kip must be swinging the gate. Then gunshots—one, two! Footsteps pounding back up, and across the porch, Shen shouting. The light in Ho's office snapped out. Ho shouted. Silence.

The widely overhanging, column-supported roof shadowed the sides of the house with a plumb-straight darkness like a dense veil. Just enough moonlight reflected up from the silvery lawn to distinguish glass doors from white-washed walls. But Marley couldn't tell whether someone might be peering out through an inch-wide gap in the curtains. Ben lay flat. A hasty glance from the house might miss him; a careful survey wouldn't. If Ho or Shen did see him, would they shoot?

"Ben," Marley called softly, "on three, break for the bush to your left. One . . . two . . . *three!*" Marley bounded from his cover toward a tree four yards to his right, not looking to see Ben spring up and hurl himself left.

No shot: Had the moves been too quick? Had he drawn attention, distracted, as he'd intended? Or wasn't anybody even watching?

There might not have been anyone watching—the house stood still and silent as a mausoleum. Instantly, when that single lamp had been extinguished, all life seemed to have left it.

"Kip?" Marley shouted. "Are you okay?"

"Okay. Gate's closed," Kip called back.

Well, now, Marley thought, I have three men pinned down on two sides of this house, only one of us armed. Ho has two inside, armed, and has four sides to come out of. My plan is . . .

When in danger, fear, or doubt, throw up your hands and scream and shout. "Ho!" he shouted. "Stanley Ho! You are surrounded. I have two men in place on every side of this house. We are armed. Come out with your hands up!"

Silence. Marley's shouting must have frightened the nearer toads into stillness. The trilling of some came from farther away. From the house, there was nothing.

It wasn't possible that those in the house couldn't have heard, but to be even more certain, Marley megaphoned his hands when he shouted again. "The police will be here in a few minutes. They'll bring tear gas. You don't have a chance, Stanley. Come out now, before this heats up and somebody kills you."

Silence. That silence should have been stiff with tension and threat. Only a minute before, a gun had been fired; men had shouted. Surely the men and the gun were inside now. Yet Marley felt foolish, shouting at the house, not because of the thinness of his bluff but because of a sense that no one heard it. In one instant the house had become vacant. Shrouded by shadow, its curtained windows blank as the eyes of the dead, it looked derelict. It seemed like an ancient villa, still standing centuries after its builders had perished and their bones had powdered and blown away, and their ghosts with them.

Of course his shout had been heard. Ho and Shen were lying low, calling his bluff, daring him to storm their fortress with his instantly acquired army. All Marley had to do was to keep them doing that.

Of course that's what they were doing: lying low, letting themselves be bottled, waiting for the police—who surely weren't a fiction—to come. Waiting for that tear gas. Waiting for the island's militia to be called in, if need be. Of course.

Or, of course, they could have dashed at once for the rear of the house and the forest gate, without waiting to listen to Marley's bellowing. They could have run down into the cellar and out through any of the network of tunnels that Marley suddenly imagined.

Crickets chirped, and in another moment the frogs sang again, and overhead a breeze brushed the palm's leaves against one another. But the house was a block of silence. And Marley wouldn't know whether Ho was in it until— sooner or later—someone went inside.

"Ben," he called in a voice meant to reach the man twenty-five feet to one side, but not the two others who might be only twenty in front of him. "I'm going up on the porch. When I'm in place, you come."

"Roger."

Marley spun out from behind the tree, sprinted, leaped

up to the porch, and caught himself against the wall between two French doors, the pistol held up beside his head.
No one shot at him. He waited a moment, listening, then
signaled Ben.

Ben made his dash, and with a bound flattened himself
on the other side of the door toward the rear of the house.
No one shot at Ben.

Ho *had* been in the office, might still be there crouched
behind a desk, his sights lined on the glass door. While
Marley and Ben couldn't really count on entering the house
through another room and creeping up on the office un-
detected, it did seem better to try something like that than
to crash directly through that door. Marley reached,
opened the door to his right, pushed to swing it inward. He
and Ben looked at one another. Marley shrugged, and—
ducking—spun through the doorway and to one side.

Although shadow obscured the room to anyone looking
from outside, enough indirect light came in to allow Marley
to see once he was inside. He found himself in an informal
sitting room, the one where Johnny had been watching
television earlier. There were comfortable-looking arm-
chairs, a couch, covered in flower-print. Marley bobbed
from side to side until sure no one was hiding behind one.
"Okay," he whispered, and Ben came through the door.

Marley prowled across the room to its open door into the
central hall. From the right side, he peered cautiously into
the hall, and then up the stairway, which began just beyond
the door. Then he stepped back, crossed the opening, and
from the left side looked over the gunsight toward the front
of the house.

Stanley Ho and Shen weren't silhouetted against the
open doorway, as he'd hoped they'd be. Marley waited,
listening, for over a minute. Nothing.

Well, the office, then.

Nodding to Ben, Marley slipped through the doorway.

Ben took the place at the arch, from which he could watch Marley's back while keeping some cover for himself.

Close to the wall on his right, ready to fire at any movement, Marley crept toward the office doorway. He tried to breathe slowly, without any sound. Inside the house, with the night noises muffled, the silence was like a crystal sphere.

Reaching the arch into the office, Marley knelt by the jamb. The door into the room stood open. It must have previously been closed, he realized, because no light had come from the room into the hall to show through the front door.

Now Marley's feeling that Ho had escaped was growing. He wanted to hurry—every moment spent searching the house was wasted. But if he was wrong, rushing into the office would be a very, very bad idea. Carefully, he looked around the arch. Then he stood, stepped inside.

The wall safe in Ho's office wall stood open. The center drawer of Ho's desk was pulled out.

Tension drained from Marley. Suddenly, he felt very tired. He tried to brace himself up, to generate a new supply of energy. Maybe Ho hadn't gotten out *yet*. Maybe he was in some other room—the kitchen—still checking whether Marley did have the rear covered, still deciding whether to run and risk being shot.

Back in the hall, Marley spoke to Ben, then led the way to the rear of the house, through the corridor to the kitchen. They moved quietly, took precautions, but Marley wasn't really fearful. He knew Ho had gone.

CHAPTER 12

Marley didn't have to wait long; not nearly long enough. Sitting on the top step of the porch, leaning against a pillar, he gazed out across the liquid-silver and black-velvet landscape. Ben and Kip, in wicker chairs behind him, speculated quietly on what might happen next. They noted when the sound of cars—coming in from the road and then stopping along the driveway—reached them. After a few moments, when the cars started again, Kip observed unnecessarily, "Well, here they come." Marley simply sat, absorbing the moonlight, for that all-too-little time of mindless rest.

Three cars wheeled around the drive and stopped behind the one Ho and Shen had abandoned. Superintendent Riley and the sergeant Marley had met that afternoon got out of the first. The car's interior light showed Russ and Lily sitting in the rear. The second car held two policemen and Johnny. The third was the one that had been parked out on the road to watch the estate's entrance. Bob and Jeff were in it, sitting behind the stakeout man. Marley suspected he might be seeing the island's entire police force.

Superintendent Riley strode toward the porch. Presumably, the man had been roused from bed and had to step quickly into his uniform. It must have been ready for him, standing in a corner like armor. Ben and Kip rose respectfully. Marley felt just too tired.

"Mr. Marley," Riley said, "Mr. Marley, exactly what's been going on here?" His tone was as mild as the moonlight, but Marley wasn't deceived.

"Some things about which you can be justifiably angry, Superintendent." In half a dozen sentences, Marley outlined the story.

Riley was silent for several moments, as though not trusting himself to speak. Then he gave low-voiced instructions to his sergeant. Turning back he said, "All right, Mr. Marley: Let's go inside and hear this in full."

At a little past nine the next morning, Marley, Russ and Lily were brought back to Russ's house. After being questioned, they had been taken to the emergency room at the hospital, where Russ had been examined and provided with a crutch and some commonsense advice about his ankle. Since two policemen had stayed with them the entire time, they'd hardly spoken.

Bob and his men were already at the house, sitting, dozing, in the living room. Kip and Ben moved to give Russ and Lily the couch. Marley, trying not to look the way he felt—like a sackful of bruised grapefruit—let himself down into the chair at the head of the table.

"Well," he said, "Superintendent Riley is angry."

Jeff gave a quiet snort, and Bob said, "James, I don't think you'd lose your position as World Champion Understater if you said Riley was as mad as a tiger with a crocodile chewing its tail.''

"Well, yes," Marley conceded, "he is *very* angry. But he can't really find anything he wants to charge us with. Ho isn't going to show up and file 'breaking and entering.' We're not quite 'obstruction of justice,' especially since—I pointed this out as tactfully as possible—we uncovered a crime and a criminal when Riley couldn't. Riley suggested they might find something like 'interfering in police business,' but I think he's decided the penalty wouldn't be severe enough, so he'd rather just be rid of us.''

"Start packing?" Bob asked.

"Not right away. They want to catch Ho, of course; and if they do we'll be needed."

"For how long?"

"If they catch him? I don't know. If they don't . . . If they don't catch him within a day or two, we'll have to figure he got away."

"How can he get away?" Ben demanded. "Swim?"

"Maybe. I suggested to Riley that he check with the telephone company—Ho was back in his house longer than it would've taken just to grab Russ's program out of the safe. Ho called a number in California, talked for three minutes. We have to assume they were arranging a way out of here for him. Whoever he talked to may not care about *him,* but they do want that program."

"What're they going to do, James?" Bob asked skeptically. "Surface the nuclear submarine they've had waiting off the coast here?"

"I don't think it'd be too difficult for them to bring in a powerboat—even if they had to fly someone down from the States to Antigua this morning to do it. Look out there"— Marley waved toward the window wall behind him—"there are a couple of them in sight almost anytime you look. I think Ho swims . . ." He turned to Lily for confirmation. She nodded.

"What's Riley doing?"

"He has people watching the dock, the airport, the beaches. He's put out an alert through the grapevine. What else can he do?"

"You think he'll catch him?"

"Fifty-fifty."

After a moment while they all pondered that, Bob asked, "What happens if he gets away? I mean, about the program?"

Marley looked at Russ.

"It's gone," Russ replied dismally. Then with a forced optimism, "But if they file for copyright, we can contest it. I mean, I do have some printouts of subroutines. I'm sure we could establish prior—"

"Right," Marley cut him off. "But I doubt that's an issue now. After all that's happened here, they're not going in straight-faced for copyright. But let me ask you, Russ . . . I've heard about writers losing their manuscripts, giving up a whole book because they simply couldn't recapture it. Can you start over?"

Russ hesitated, looking even sicker than he had. "Probably, going back, working up again from what I do still have. But . . . Oh, God, I don't know. And . . . I mean . . . I wouldn't just have to recall the program. The *real* problem . . . I'd have to *rework* it some way—almost reinvent it— so they couldn't beat it by knowing exactly how it functions. I don't know if . . ." Russ gestured vaguely, then dropped his hands as though the nothing in them was too heavy to hold.

After a silence, Bob said, "Well, how about we start getting organized. We're still on security, right?"

"Right. It's hard to believe that Ho or Shen would try walking right into civilization here, but"—Marley turned to Russ—"it continues to be to their advantage to have you out."

Russ nodded.

"Two on, two off," Bob directed. "Anybody not sleepy?"

"I'll do the first trick," Jeff said, rising.

"Me, too." Ben stood up.

"Okay. Two hours, first trick; then we'll extend to four again." Bob yawned. "Thanks." He and Kip headed toward the bedrooms.

"Inside, outside?" Jeff asked Marley.

"Both outside, I think. Front and back."

"I'll take back," Jeff said, and the two men started for the doors.

While they were leaving, and for a moment after, Marley, Russ, and Lily sat in silence. Then Marley began to edge into what had to be said. "There's something more we have to talk about."

Before going on, Marley glanced at Lily. She had followed the conversation among the men with evident interest, but now her eyes seemed even keener, like those of an accused told to rise and hear the verdict. No, Marley thought, she knows the verdict. She's up to hear the sentence—and she's already planning her appeal. He was annoyed that she wasn't downcast, abject in her guilt, and at the same time found himself admiring her.

He made a further sideways approach. "It worked out as I hoped—that I was able to talk with Riley before—"

Russ interrupted. Very calmly, he asked, "What's going to happen to Lily, James?"

Marley blinked.

"I know she wasn't kidnapped."

"You know?"

"Of course."

Marley looked rapidly back and forth between the two of them. Lily seemed to be as surprised as he was, although she must have known Russ would learn the truth eventually. They'd all been questioned separately by Superintendent Riley. Marley knew she'd told him the truth about her 'abduction,' and that Riley hadn't told Russ. Perhaps she'd been planning another nine-lives way to tell Russ herself.

"How. . . ?"

"Come on, James. Give me a little credit. I didn't want to believe; I didn't believe. But last night, when she came up behind Ho . . . I mean, if she'd been kidnapped, how could she have gotten free right at that moment? If she got free while they weren't watching, how would she have known where we were—back there in the kitchen? That Ho was holding us? If she hadn't known, if she'd really been kidnapped and gotten free, she'd have run for it. I mean, as soon as I saw her I knew she had to have been involved with Ho."

Lily now was staring at Russ steadily, appraisingly.

"But . . ." His mind on fast rewind, Marley replayed the previous night. "But after that—while we were trying to run—you kept insisting that Lily had to get away."

"That was after she'd hit Ho," Russ explained patiently. "She'd changed sides—no going back. If he was going to kill us, he'd kill her, too. *You* wanted her to get away."

"Yes . . ." Marley said slowly. "But it wasn't *me* she'd . . ."

"So, what's going to happen to her now?"

"Riley finally agreed that if they catch Ho and try him for extortion, he'll recommend clemency for Lily for having been Ho's accomplice in exchange for her turning state's evidence. If they don't catch Ho, in consideration of what she did for us he'll just let the matter drop."

Russ nodded, looking pleased. He turned to Lily and smiled. "Well, then, everything will be okay."

After a moment, Lily lowered her eyes. A flush began to come into her face. Marley sat almost gaping at them, too dumbfounded to move or speak.

"I think we all ought to get some sleep," Russ said. "You go on in, Lily; I'll be right there."

Without replying or looking at him, Lily rose and went into the hall leading to their bedroom. After hearing her close the door, Russ said, "I just wanted to thank you, James. For everything. And I wanted to apologize. For not believing you—you were right, about all of it. And for going crazy and rushing into the middle, and screwing things up, and nearly getting us killed. I'm really sorry, and I'm really grateful."

Marley collected his wits enough to say, "Don't mention it, Russ. Don't think about it."

"Oh, I will."

For a moment they sat in silence. Then Marley asked in a tone both dubious and wondering, "You really don't care about what Lily did?"

Russ tipped his head. "Oh, I care, James. Sure. When I saw her, and realized . . . all night . . . Yeah, I care. It hurts. But she did make her choice last night, James. She chose me instead of Ho. That proves—despite every-thing—she really loves me."

"So you forgive her—you forgave her even last night, even as soon as you understood the truth—because you're sure she loves you."

"No, James." Russ shook his head sadly. "You just don't understand, James. I forgive her—it doesn't matter—be-cause *I* love *her*."

"James? James?"

Marley rose to consciousness realizing someone was whispering his name. He'd been in a sleep as deep, black, and oblivious as any Hell-fearing sinner might hope to find death. At some single instant he was awake, but he didn't move; and when he did open his eyelids, he might have thought himself still submerged, merely nearer the surface, dreaming.

Before going to bed, he'd closed the window louvers against increasing brightness and heat. Although the time was nearly noon, the dim light in the room now was brownish, directionless. The air was warm; he was sweating. Sprawled facedown on the bed, he might have been floating within a pond. The figure clad in a pale green gown kneeling beside him calling his name softly, caressingly, could have been an ondine. Each time she spoke she swayed toward him as though on an eddying current. Marley had folded back the sheet. He wore only his undershorts. The woman's gown was thin; she might twist and it would slip from her shoulders. Marley could have been dreaming a sweetly drifting, undulating, erotic dream. Knowing the woman was Lily only increased the possibility.

"James?"

"Yeah." He raised himself on crossed forearms enough to show he was awake and attending. "What is it?"

"I got to talk to you."

He almost said, "Now?" but the urgency in her voice already carried her answer. "What is it?"

"James, we've got to try to talk to Stanley."

"Ho?"

"Yes. Before he gets away—or the police catch him."

"Why?" Marley realized his responses weren't very sharp. "Wait a minute." He got up and put on his trousers, then sat on the edge of the bed. "Okay." He indicated the bed, and Lily sat beside him. She smoothed the skirts of the dressing gown primly over her thighs, but as she leaned forward the robe gaped enough for him to see her breasts. He raised his eyes to hers. "Why?"

"If we don't talk to Stanley, James, I'm dead."

"Why? Because of what you did?"

"Yes. Everything in the—we call it our association—everything is loyalty and obedience. What I did—hitting Stanley, helping you get away . . . I'm a traitor, James. They'll never let me live. They'll hunt me, no matter where I go." Lily's voice had the tension of fear under control. The grip almost broke as she said, "And just *killing* me won't be the worst of it."

"I see," Marley said. "This operation was really that important? Obviously, a lot of money was at stake; but if Ho escapes with the program, they'll still—"

"That doesn't matter. It doesn't matter how much money is involved, or even whether Stanley escapes. The point is, they never let anyone get away with betraying them. I mean, that's why nobody hardly ever does. But if they let *me* get away, then somebody else . . ."

"I see. Were you thinking about that when you hit Ho last night?"

"Sure."

"Well, I thanked you before, Lily; but I guess I didn't realize how grateful I should be. Why did you do it?"

"I couldn't let him kill Russ. I mean, I wouldn't have wanted him to kill *you* either, but . . ."

"I understand. I'm glad you care that much about Russ."

"I do. Stanley told me . . . he said you were in the next room: You saw us through the mirror."

"Yes."

"So you know: Stanley is a scumbag pig. But I had to do whatever he . . . But when Russ came to save me . . . I couldn't let *him* kill *Russ*."

"I thought you wanted me to kill Ho because of the way he treated you. I really didn't understand, did I?"

"No. If you—if we'd killed him right then, I thought they—the association—wouldn't have to know how . . . that I . . . But you were right, James."

"It would have been a murder charge," he reminded her, in case she was agreeing without being convinced.

"Yeah."

"And the story would come out, anyway. Your 'association' would know."

"Yeah."

"And as a famous man once said, 'It would have been wrong.'"

Lily nodded.

"Well, what are we going to do? If they're going to come after you, what can we do other than try to protect you?"

"We can try to make a deal with Stanley."

Marley must still have been partly asleep. It took him until that moment to put things together. "You know where he is."

"I think so. I don't *know,* but I think so."

"Where?"

Lily evaded the question. "We've got to see him, try to work something out."

"What can we do?"

"Let him get away."

"How? I don't think we could get Riley to call off the search."

"No. But that's between him and Riley. But if he's where I think he is, then we can make a deal not to tell Riley—to leave Stanley clear to take his chance. If he won't deal, then we put Riley on him."

"Which leaves him no worse off than he is now."

"No. I mean, James, right *now*—if I'm right—he's in a real good place. He's got a place to hide; he can see what's going on around him; he's in position to get to a boat when it comes. If he has to really be on the run, his chances go way down."

"And not revealing where he is will buy you off?"

"If he agrees. If he accepts it."

"How do you know he'll honor his side of the bargain?"

"Because he has to. That's part of how the system works.

This has been going on for—I don't know, James—maybe a thousand years. Longer. If somebody who has the authority—and Stanley has enough for this—if somebody gives his word on a bargain, then the association has to honor it. Otherwise, the next time they try to make a deal . . . I mean, you understand, the association isn't some kind of one-shot syndicate or anything. The thing is, you have to be very careful about your deal: They'll honor just exactly what they say."

"Like an insurance policy."

"You got the idea. Only more so. You got to know exactly what to say, and hear exactly what they're saying."

"And Stanley will give his word to . . . what? forgive you? in return for not telling where he's hiding?"

"I don't know, but maybe. It's my only chance."

"What happens if he's caught?"

"He still made the deal; we would have kept our part. I mean, he'd have to tell people that, whether he gets away and sees them or whether he sends word from jail."

"What happens if he's killed trying to escape?"

"Then I'm dead, too."

Marley spoke briefly with Bob Bracciotti while Lily dressed. They left the house without waking Russ.

The late morning sun stood high above the island, stood *on* the island with a crushing weight of heat and brightness. Those people who had to work or walk under it moved slowly, bent over. Cattle sheltered in shadow beneath the ledgelike branches of isolated trees. A snowy egret startled from a pasture beside the road rose only a few feet, then glided to earth again as though pressed down.

Marley had turned on the car's air-conditioning as soon as he'd started the engine; within three minutes it had begun pumping in coolness. But by then he and Lily were already soaking. Marley wore khaki trousers, a thin cotton short-sleeved shirt, and no undershirt; yet sweat ran down his face, and his forearms shone with it. And Lily's skin gleamed as though oiled, although she had on even less: white shorts so brief they showed the bottoms of her buttocks, a Stanley Kowalski undershirt with—obviously—nothing under it.

She hadn't dressed just to beat the heat, Marley suspected. Nor—when she'd come to his room—had she worn the thin, loosely tied dressing gown that parted to reveal her thigh as she knelt by his bed and her breast whenever she leaned forward while sitting beside him, merely because that robe was handy when she got up. Did she really think a flash of bum would influence Stanley Ho to trade for her life? Did she think a flash of boob before and tight undershirt now would win Marley's help? Probably she did, on the basis of long experience. Possibly she was right. Lily might be treacherous, devious, selfish, greedy—he could imagine an entire Devil's Girl Scouts' code—but he couldn't deny she aroused him. He could only assure himself that wasn't his only reason for helping her.

Both Marley and Lily wore sunglasses, and kept the car's visors down; still they squinted against the brightness. It glowed in the heavy haze out over the sea, shimmered above the road, ricocheted and struck at them from sloping, grassy fields. Even on the higher slopes of the mountains, light glanced off the dense foliage as though all the trees' leaves were armor-plated scales shielding the forest floor.

They passed a few other cars at first, and people working or sitting in the shade. After Lily directed him to cross to the eastern side of the island they saw no one. They had the whole highway to themselves, as far as they could see down the coast. Their car raised a little dust from the surface of the asphalted road. It didn't billow, but hung in a layer and settled quickly again.

"That must be it," Lily said. Marley looked where she pointed, up the hillside ahead and to the right. They had driven down the east side of the island, past the airport, and wound hairpinning back and forth up a mountainside. Passing through what seemed to be the last settlement—a hamlet of shanties—they'd curved around a wide shoulder of the mountain on an obviously recently paved road.

A three-story building sprawled across a level gashed in the slope. Even from a mile away Marley knew it was vacant, unfinished, by the emptiness of its window sockets staring blankly at the sea.

"Yes," he agreed, "it would be a good hideout. Clear view of the road and across the fields: no way to approach it without being seen. Forest close enough behind to duck into if anybody does come. Of course, someone could sneak down through the forest."

"Sure," Lily agreed, "but why would they? I mean, if nobody knows Stanley's there, why would they?"

"Nobody else knows it's Stanley's place? You're sure?"

"Yeah. I mean, actually it isn't his place. Just his idea— he advised them about it. From what he said, I guess the whole point of building it was to be some kind of write-off: Some dummy corporation bought the land, said they were going to put in this big development. That's the hotel; and there were supposed to be condos and cottages around it. Then they fake the costs, say they're going bankrupt. Every time they want to lose some money—on paper—they start it up again. It's kind of like the estate, only in reverse. The estate is a fake money-*maker*. Since Stanley's officially connected with that, his name's probably not connected with this place. He just mentioned it to me one time."

"There's a way down to the water?"

"Yeah. I mean, if they've finished it. There was supposed

to be. They were making a beach. Of course, they picked the wrong side of the island—storms keep washing away the sand. So they have to redo it, bring in rocks. Costs a mint."

"Must be a mile away from the house."

"They were going to build a road."

"Money no object."

"That's the point."

Marley drove at a crawl, looking up toward the building. Lily advised him, "Looks like the turn's just ahead."

They turned into the drive that curved to the house through a scrubby field where half a dozen goats grazed, and halted. "I would still rather handle this all myself, Lily. It would be much safer—for both of us—if you stayed in the car the whole time."

"It's my life, James. I got to read the fine print."

"I've done some pretty tight negotiating myself, Lily."

"Yeah? So what would you ask Stanley? To guarantee nobody will come and kill me? So he says, 'Oh, yeah, sure: deal.' And then somebody throws acid in my eyes."

"I think I'd probably ask him to guarantee that no one will harm you in any way."

"Great, James. And so one night they pick up Russ and me together, and they say, 'Don't worry, Lily; nobody's going to harm *you.*' And then they beat Russ to death right in front of me. Or maybe they wait five years—when maybe Russ and I have a kid."

Marley couldn't see Lily's eyes behind the dark lenses. He wondered if they would have the same hard shine as the glass. "You seem to know all the tricks of the trade," he said. "I think I probably do know most of them myself; but—I guess you're right—it is your life."

"Yeah. But if you think it's safer if one of us stays in the car, you can stay."

"I have my own negotiating to do. I want to get that program back."

Nothing showed in Lily's face. After a moment she said, "A chance to get away *with* the program makes *my* deal better for Stanley. He's in trouble—I mean, even if he gets away from here—because he lost control of the situation. Like you say, the association is not going to get the copyright on Russ's program. Stanley is blown—here and in Boston. He's in trouble. But he's been a good man for them in the past, so maybe they'll overlook one fuckup—like he over-looked Shen losing you on the Expressway—if he proves he can still deliver. If he makes a deal with me so he can get away *with* the program, that's a smart move. If he makes a deal with me, and gives you the program, too, just to save himself . . . Well, the only reason for going back to them at all would be so they'll kill him quick."

"Well," Marley said quietly. His glasses were just as opaque as Lily's; if her face was ivory, his was stone. "I am being paid—essentially—to safeguard that program. I can see how letting Stanley keep it could be a chip for you in your bargain, but I would prefer for it not to be used."

"I'd prefer not to be dead."

"Of course. But if I could persuade Stanley that he should give the program to me, that would be in your inter-est, too. After all, that program could make Russ a multi-millionaire. I imagine you have thought about that."

"Sure. But it won't do me any good if they kill me. You're really having trouble making up your mind, aren't you, James? I mean, you believe me that saving you and Russ put my life in danger. But you think I did it only for Russ's money. But you think I'll give away the money—the program—just to save myself. But if I have to give away the money to save myself, why did I bother saving you?"

"Those things aren't mutually exclusive, Lily. Russ has a lot of money already, and maybe he can rework the program, and even if he can't there will be other programs. You'll do well with him, anyway."

"Yeah, I will."

"Undoubtedly a lot better than as—what? the madam of a whorehouse in Dorchester? That must have made your choice last night easier: When Lochinvar rode up to save you from the 'scumbag pig,' his armor was shining all right; not only with true love, but because it's solid gold."

"You're never going to trust me, are you, James?"

"Probably not."

"And it looks like I was pretty stupid to have trusted you. You had me bring you here, show you Stanley's hideout, just so you could try to get that program back. That's why you wanted me to wait in the car, and you go alone to talk to him—you wanted to make a deal for the program. You probably weren't going to try to make a deal for me at all, were you?"

"Isn't that the way *you* do it, Lily? Say anything, do anything, betray anybody if it's a good deal for you?"

"Isn't that the way everybody does it? It's the way everybody's always done it to me. Everybody except Russ. So you don't like it? So you don't like *me*? So what? You're just the same. What do you want from me?"

No outburst: Lily's voice was tempered like steel hammered into unbreakability; it had the low gleam of anger beaten deeply into the alloy.

But Marley was twice Lily's age, and even more case-hardened. After a moment he said, "I want you to take off your glasses."

She didn't move. But then she must have realized that if she wanted his help she'd have to do as he said. The tightness of her jaw didn't change, nor the clenched-lip line of her mouth; yet when she pulled away and lowered her sunglasses her entire expression seemed transformed. The tightness of her face suddenly showed as a desperate con-

tainment of the fear now unshielded in her eyes. And behind that, hurt. Marley knew the look; he'd seen it in the
eyes of Vietnamese children.

"That's better," Marley said. "Thanks. I wanted to
check something; that's why I've been giving you a bad
time. I'm sorry.

"I probably won't ever trust you, Lily; and I'm not over-
looking anything about you; but on the whole"—he took
off his own glasses—"actually, I do like you." He smiled at
her.

Lily's big eyes grew huge, and then she jerked her sunglasses back up to cover her nakedness. Still without actual
change, her face was hard and tough once more. "So, what
are you going to do?" she demanded.

Marley smiled again and slowly put on his own glasses.
"Keep an eye on Stanley while you're making your deal. If
I can get in a word about the program, I'd like to. Maybe
he doesn't see things the way you do. Maybe he can be
conned."

"Stanley? Maybe pigs shit diamonds."

"Well, if you don't mind, I'd like at least to raise the
subject. I'd like to be able to tell David Cheyney I tried.
However, the main thing for me to do, I think, is to stand
behind you and hulk. Stanley might not believe we won't
give him away after you have your deal. After all, we *could*
arrange it that Riley 'gets lucky' and 'just happens' to catch
Stanley after he leaves this place on his way to meet his
boat."

"You do know something about this business, don't you,
James?"

"I told you I did. So, Stanley may figure that his hideout
is blown, and he's better off hunkering down in the bush—
with hostages—than relying on an agreement."

After a moment Lily nodded. "How do we do this?"
While the tone of her voice gave nothing away, the ques-

tion did. Taking the control she had relinquished, Marley answered, "We leave the car here, leave the doors on the uphill side open so that Stanley can see there's no one hiding in the car. You stay by the car at first, so he can see it's you. We're about a hundred yards—straight-line distance—from the house; technically that's within pistol range, but the likelihood of anyone hitting you is small. I walk up halfway to the house, call to him. If he'll come out to meet me I'll signal you to come up to us."

Lily nodded again, put her hand on the door. "Thanks, James," she said softly.

"My pleasure," he replied.

They opened their doors and stepped out of the car.

Heat struck them like a physical force. In an instant what coolness clung to their skin was stripped away. Marley almost gasped, taking hot air into his lungs to equalize the pressure that seemed to bear on him like the weight of water in the depths of an ocean. He walked around the car to the uphill side, opened the rear door next to Lily.

"Okay," he said. "I've left the keys in the ignition. If anything goes wrong, or if I wave my hand from side to side instead of 'Come on,' you jump in and lay rubber out of here, and call in the army."

Lily nodded, and Marley turned and started toward the hotel.

It had been placed just below where the steep rise of the mountains broke into a long, gentler shelf sloping toward the sea. Although the mountainside was heavily forested, the shelf was open, scrubby field for several miles in either direction. The land undulated between gullies running down to the shore. Patches of the slope, in the distance, seemed to be planted in some crop; but the nearer fields were rough pasture. Three cows lay in the shade of a lone tree half a mile away. Four goats, apparently oblivious of the heat, grazed to Marley's left near a line of bushes growing along a gully. Several snowy egrets stalked among them with a slow-motion high-step.

Marley headed directly across the pasture rather than following the curve of the drive. Although—with the sun riding on his back—climbing the slightly steeper rise cost more effort, the blacktop seemed a path of molten lava. When he'd covered half the distance, he halted.

In time, when the cheap stucco over the building's shoddily laid concrete block had cracked and chipped more extensively, and its pale peach color was further bleached and sun-blotched, stained and mottled, and creeping vines had begun to arabesque it, the place might pass for a ruined temple. Now it was only an eyesore, a heap of terraces and thick-walled rooms with undoored arches and openings for picture windows—entire sections of wall—unglassed. Marley probably wouldn't have liked the place if it were finished. He certainly disliked it now—especially as he considered all the places it offered for someone to hide, and watch him, and take aim.

"Ho!" he called. "Stanley Ho! I know you're there. We want to talk with you."

Clink-clank. One of the goats—with a bell around its neck—pulled at a twig on a bush beside the gully. There was no other sound.

"Stanley Ho! You can see me, you can see Lily, you can see there's nobody else. We need to talk."

Marley imagined he could hear waves on the shore a mile behind him. He realized the sound was his own pulse. What if he hasn't gotten here yet? Marley wondered. Do we wait? Come back?

"We want to make a deal with you, Stanley."

No one answered, nothing at the house moved. Marley began to feel he might be trapped in a repetitive nightmare—condemned to stand shouting at empty houses while Stanley Ho slipped into forests behind them.

No, Marley tried to reassure himself, if he's there, he'll talk.

"Stanley Ho! If we don't talk to you, we're going back and tell the police to come here and watch this place—and this section of coast. You want that?"

For a last moment Marley stared up at the unfinished, already ruined structure, trying to hold the faith that Ho must be inside. Then, feeling disappointment heavier than the heat, he turned.

"Marley!" Ho called from inside the building.

CHAPTER 13

Marley spun around. He saw no one. "Ho?" he called back.

"You want to talk?" The voice came to him disembodied. The building might have been speaking. Perhaps Ho was trying for a daunting effect, but the sound wasn't the solemn reverberating bass of a ruined temple; it had the flat ring of an abandoned barn.

"Right. Come out."

"You come up here."

"No chance."

"No talk."

Marley shrugged, turned away as though to go downhill again.

"*You're* the one wanted to talk," the voice called after him.

"That's right. So do you, or you wouldn't have answered."

"I'm not going to come out there in the open."

"Yes, you are. You can see everything, all around. You can see it's safe. You know I'm not going to go up inside there."

"How do I know you haven't got a gun?"

With his arms out to each side, Marley turned a full circle, slowly.

"Stuck down in your sock, under your pants leg."

Marley pulled one trouser leg and then the other up to his calf. "Come on, Stanley."

"Okay, but no tricks. Shen is right here with a bead on you."

Marley clasped his fingers together and rested his hands on his head. Just the narrow shadow of an arm on his cheek gave relief from the high noon sun.

Ho came down a flight of steps leading from a side terrace to the ground in front of the building.

"Keep your own hands up," Marley called to him.

With his palms outward at shoulder level, Ho walked down the slope to Marley. When he was twenty feet away, Marley stopped him. "Wait. Lift up your sweater, turn around." Ho pulled up the waistband of his pullover, pivoted. "Okay. Come on. And let's put our hands down."

Ho came up to Marley, halted just out of reach. "Okay, Marley: What're we going to talk about—as if I couldn't guess?"

"Lily wants to talk."

"I figured. You don't want to talk?"

"Sure. But I'll let her speak first." Marley started to turn, then paused. "Ah, from what I've seen of Shen's marksmanship, there's no way he could hit any of us at this distance except by inaccurate aim. But if he tries, I can reach you before you make cover."

"He's not going to try. I don't think you're going to try anything with me, either, because I know why Lily wants to talk to me. Shen's just my insurance. But don't sell his aim short: He's in a good position up there—got his hands braced on a box, clear view of you."

Marley waved to Lily. She started up the slope toward them.

"Fucking cunt," Ho said without apparent emotion.

"She worked for you a long time?" Marley asked.

"Nine years. I gave her her first regular job—when her father died. Got a job for her mother, too."

"Nine years; she must have been—what? Thirteen, fourteen?"

"Something like that."

"I wonder how she could have turned out the way she did, given all you must have done for her—the things you taught her, the example you set."

"Fuck off, Marley."

For several moments the two men stood silently, watching Lily approach, watching each other out of the corners of their eyes. Suddenly, Ho made a move toward his hip pocket. Marley sprang on guard.

"Just getting my handkerchief," Ho explained. While Marley watched, he reached slowly and brought it out. "Jesus, it's hot. This is crazy, meeting out here. We'll all die of sunstroke before any of us says anything."

"We could go over and sit under the bushes," Marley suggested, gesturing toward the gully thirty feet away.

"I think we'll stay where Shen can see us."

Ho mopped his forehead and neck. He must have been roasting, Marley thought, dressed as he was in that sweater against the coolness of the previous night. Marley took out his own handkerchief, wiped his brow.

The men said nothing more to one another as they watched Lily climb through the field to them. Even wearing his sunglasses, Marley had to squint, staring down toward her. Ho didn't have dark glasses. He shielded his eyes with one hand. The sea and hazy sky behind her figure were a blue-white, steamed-over mirror. The grass was pale whitish green, absolutely still yet shimmering. Lily, in her bleached cotton shorts and shirt, with her white-gold skin, seemed incandescent.

When she reached them, perspiration was running down her face, it slathered her arms and legs. It had soaked her undershirt, which clung to her even more tightly, revealingly. But Marley saw her not as overheated and sweating, but as she'd looked coming out of the swimming pool on the first evening he'd met her. The illusion came from the coolness, the composure in her face.

"Hello, Stanley," she said.

"Hello, cunt."

"You want to talk, Stanley, or you just want to mouth-shit me?"

"I want to see them screw you with a piece of red-hot pipe, Lily; but for now we'll talk."

Lily's glasses hid her eyes, but Marley believed that no fear would have shown in them now, even though he was sure Ho meant what he'd said literally. Marley admired her for that. Matching her control, he regarded the two of them as though disinterested, setting to one side an intense regret that he hadn't killed Ho the night before.

"Me for you, Stanley," Lily said.

"I figured. How're you going to get me a safe conduct? You fucking the police chief?"

"I really do think Shen's too far away"—Marley interrupted quietly and with his deadly smile—"to shoot me if I break your mouth, Stanley."

"Oh? Sir Galahad." Ho looked back and forth between Marley and Lily, seemed about to make an obvious comment, seemed to think better of it. He dabbed his face with his handkerchief instead.

"No safe conduct," Lily went on as if there'd been no

break. "But you got a better chance staying here than if you got to hide up there in the jungle with the snakes."

Ho wiped his neck. He looked at his handkerchief ruefully, waved it back and forth as though in hope of drying it enough to make it useful again. "Selling me what I've already got, huh? How'd you know about this place?"

Ho was standing with his back to the hotel, Lily facing him, two steps away. Marley had placed himself closer to Lily but to one side so that he could look back and forth between them. Up the hill, in sight along a line past Ho's back, an egret suddenly flapped up from beside the bushes and then—wings stretched wide, neck curled back in an "S"—glided across the pasture and landed again.

"You told me about it. You were impressing me how smart you are."

"I guess I wasn't so smart, was I?"

"Most men aren't as smart as they think they are. Are you going to deal?"

"What're you offering?—you got no safe conduct. And what're you asking from me?"

"I'm offering we won't tell where you are. Whatever plan you've got, you get a clear shot at it."

"I've got a clear shot at *you* right now. Shen could pick you off from the house: bang, bang. Then nobody knows I'm here. Or do they?"

Another egret rose from near the gully, downhill of where the first had been.

Marley told him, "We left a note. Lily wrote out where this place is. If we're not back in . . . soon . . . my security man will call Superintendent Riley."

Ho mopped with his handkerchief back and forth across his forehead. "So I give you my word, make a deal, you go back, and *then* you call Riley."

"No, Stanley," Lily picked up the discussion again. "We'll keep the deal because you'll keep the deal. That's how it's done. You and me will both stick to it because we know that."

Ho tipped his head toward Marley. "What about him?"

"We can make a deal, too," Marley replied.

"Like what?"

"Russ's program. For myself, Stanley, I think I'd like to see the police take you regardless of what happens to the program. But the people I'm working for probably feel differently."

"I give you that program, Marley—just give it to you, to try to get myself out of here . . . Believe me, I'm better off cracking coconuts, or weaving baskets, or whatever they'd have me doing *if* they put me away. No, no deal. You want to call the cops, okay. By the time they find me—*if* they find me—that diskette Detweiller gave me will be hidden where they'll never find it. But our people will find it. And in return for me doing my job, they'll get me out—one way or another—long before I start getting homesick for the Boston winter.

"So, you and I don't have any deal to make, Marley. Lily and me . . . maybe. But how do I know you'll go along with hers?"

After a moment of apparent deliberation, Marley replied, "I owe Lily. I'll keep your bargain."

Turning back to Lily, Ho asked, "What kind of bargain are we going to make? What guarantee do you want?"

"No harm to me, or anybody connected with me. Not by you, or the association, or anybody put onto it by the association. Complete clean slate. No revenge of any kind. Never."

"Total amnesty."

"That's right."

Tipping his head to one side, then the other, Ho seemed to be thinking it over. "Okay, I guess so," he said finally.

"You say it, Stanley. You say, 'I guarantee, in the name

of the association . . .' All of it, in English so James is a witness, and Chinese. And I'll—"

The third egret sprang into the air, and Marley understood. "Shen!" he shouted.

In the one moment Ho leaped, crashing into Lily, knocking her to the ground, falling on top of her; Shen started breaking through the bushes, pistol pointed out ahead of him; and Marley—knowing instantly the futility of trying to stand and fight—whirled and ran. Bounding, shifting like a broken-field runner, increasing his chance to stay alive with every five-foot leap, he sprinted across the field and then curved around to head for the car. But no shot followed him.

"Marley!" Ho shouted "Marley! Listen!"

Still running, Marley flashed a glance over his shoulder. Then he halted. He'd put nearly forty yards between himself and the others. Ho was standing, looking down across the distance at him. Lily was on her knees, with Shen behind her twisting her hair in one hand and pointing his pistol at her pulled-back head.

"Marley! You hear me all right?"

"I can hear you."

"Then hear this: You go on back and stop your people from calling the cops. Or you *can* call them, if you want. I think it's better if you don't, but you want to call them, you do it. But if any of them come here, if anybody gets between me and my way out of here, she dies. You understand that?"

"I understand." Marley stood glaring up the slope at Ho. He felt his chest heaving, heat engulfing him like swirling steam. He knew his anger and chagrin, even more searing than the sun. He focused on countering Ho.

For a moment Marley tried to imagine some way to barter Lily's release for Ho's. He pictured one of those exchanges of spies: Two men pass on a bridge. But the freed agents cross into places where they can't be pursued and recaptured. No matter what assurance Marley might give—what the police might give if they were involved—Ho wouldn't trust it and leave Lily safe on shore while he sailed away. He'd believe, as Marley did, that the police wouldn't keep any promise made in this case—if they'd agree to making one at all it would be a trick, and a patrol boat would speed out from hiding to intercept him.

In the next moment, Marley imagined a siege of the hotel: "You can't escape, Ho. If you kill her, you'll hang. Let her go, and you'll get off lightly." That might work; especially if Ho was willing to delay his revenge on Lily, knowing someone else would track her down and kill her for him. But equally, Ho's code—the law of his ancient association—might require him to kill her and himself rather than fall into enemy hands; who knew?

With a sudden flare of intuition, Marley realized he couldn't counter Ho—he'd have to counter *attack*.

"When you kill her, you're finished!" he shouted. "Remember that: You have a chance only while she's alive!" Then he turned and loped down the field to the car.

Slamming the doors on the uphill side, dashing around and throwing himself into the driver's seat, slamming that door, Marley started the motor. He shot one last look up toward Ho and the others. They hadn't moved from their tableau: Ho stood, feet apart, arms folded, the victorious warrior-emperor glaring down at his routed foe. His lackey held in thrall the beauteous captive maiden. Evidently, Ho was playing out the scene, enjoying his triumph, waiting to see Marley turn the car around and begin a long, ignominious retreat to the other side of the island.

Then Marley dropped into gear, floored the pedal, and—tires shrieking, laying down smoking black tracks—rocketed *up* the driveway. In a constant, wheel-spinning skid he whipped the car around the long curve. For an instant, Ho seemed too stunned to react. By the time he did, shouting to Shen, beginning to dash uphill himself, Marley was accelerating through the final straight to the hotel.

Lily squirmed, trying to rise. She drove an elbow toward Shen's ribs. He jerked back, avoiding the full force of the jab. Twisting his hand still locked in her hair, he struck down, hitting her with the pistol barrel. The blow knocked her to her hands and knees. Before she could recover, Shen had caught one of her wrists, bending her arm up cruelly behind her back. He hooked his fingers over the yoke of her shirt so she couldn't writhe away from him. Using her pain, not his strength, he made her come up onto her feet. She might yet have struggled, but he brandished the pistol, threatening to hit her again. Then he looked up the hill to Ho for direction.

By then Ho had halted, panting, standing at the edge of the drive, staring with fury over the empty car at the building.

"Ho!" The structure seemed to shout at him with Marley's voice. "Think about it! You have no cover. If you kill her, you have no hostage. You don't have the program. You have nothing. The police will be here if I don't stop the call. Give up."

Marley didn't really expect Ho to give up. Clearly, Ho wasn't a quitter; and his situation wasn't as weak as Marley'd suggested. Calling out that way, though, might make Marley's seem stronger.

While Ho deliberated, and then waited for Shen to reach him, Marley began to go through the rooms on the ground floor. The diskette would be there, somewhere.

Ho wanted that program; wanted it more than immediate escape or immediate revenge—his two reasons for holding Lily. If Marley could find the diskette—and keep out of Ho's reach—he could trade.

Marley moved quickly through the zigzag of connecting

rooms. Some of their walls had been stuccoed, others still showed bare concrete block. They echoed back the soft scrape of his footsteps from the raw cement floors. Each room had at least one large window opening facing the sea; others looked to the sides as well. He could keep Ho in view almost continually, see Shen and Lily approaching. Ho seemed to catch his movement for an instant, then lost him again.

None of the rooms or closets had doors. There were a few piles of building materials—sand, gravel, blocks; not many, not large. A single glance showed every cubicle essentially as bare as a robbed tomb. The rooms did feel like chambers in a tomb. Perhaps in the morning, when the sun shone through the window openings, that wouldn't be true. Now, despite the brightness outside and the warmth the masonry had absorbed, a clammy chill seemed to emanate from the dead-gray concrete, a smell of decay.

Marley moved swiftly through the rooms until he came to a staircase leading to the floor above. Ho had come out from the second floor; it was the logical place for him to have sheltered—giving both a good view along the coast and a quick exit to the jungle behind. Marley dashed up the stairs.

He found himself in a huge room two stories high. As in Ho's estate house, a balcony ran all around it inside, providing access to rooms on the upper floor—an architectural plan common in the tropics. Likewise, an outside terrace ran along the front and sides of the rooms. Two free-standing staircases connected the floors, one at either side of the big room, toward its rear. Other rooms opened to the sides beyond the stairways. Nearer the front, wide hallways led away to wings. An opening across the rear wall, obviously intended for sliding glass panels, gave out to a broad patio behind the building.

Probably Ho had been hiding out here. The room commanded the best view, unblocked by the building's wings. Marley considered the possibility with dismay. Boxes of construction materials covered much of the floor—crates of flooring tiles, pipes, and plumbing hardware. The program could be hidden in any of them.

He strode across enough of the room so he could peer through the balustrade of the terrace outside. Shen and Lily were just reaching Ho. Wheeling left and right, looking through window openings, Marley could see into some of the rooms in the wings of the building. Supplies were piled there, too.

He doubted that Ho had seriously hidden the program before coming out to talk. Those boxes wouldn't all have to be emptied, the piles disassembled, the heaps probed. The building wouldn't really have to be *searched*. A quick scanning would be enough. Even given the rule that the program would be found in the last carton checked, the whole job could be done in a few minutes per room. But he knew Ho wouldn't wait out there in the sun while he looked.

And also . . . He checked his watch. Both he and Ho were running a race against the sweep of its hands. The time was twelve-seventeen.

"Not again, James!" Bob Bracciotti had protested when Marley'd told him what he and Lily were going to attempt.

"Exactly what do you see as an alternative?" Marley had asked.

"Tip the police. Let them take him. Then make a deal, let him cop a plea, whatever."

"Too risky. He might escape. He might be killed. He might refuse to deal. The law here might refuse. Making our own deal, privately, really is the only sure way."

"What if he doesn't want to deal? What if he's mad enough so he just wants to blast off yours and Lily's heads?"

"I don't figure Ho that way. He's too cool to blow his

chance. He won't simply kill us knowing that our failure to return here will bring the police down on him within the hour."

"How long?"

"Lily says it'll take twenty minutes to half an hour to drive to this place. Say half an hour. Allow the same coming back, fifteen minutes to negotiate—an hour and a quarter from the time we leave."

Marley looked up from his watch. In another twenty-eight minutes Bob would be calling Superintendent Riley. In—probably—forty-five, the police would be at the hotel. They'd be carrying not only a warrant for Ho's arrest, they'd be bringing Lily's death warrant, too. Whether Ho killed her at once, or later in the day after using her as hostage, or whether he actually released her when he left, to be hunted down in the future, she'd be condemned.

Looking through the balustrade again, Marley saw Ho giving orders to Shen. Shen handed the pistol to Ho, caught Lily's free wrist and bent it back, too. Then, forcing her ahead of himself, he followed Ho across the drive.

Ho headed toward the stairway that he'd used when coming out. Marley glanced rapidly over the crates and boxes, looking desperately for the little square diskette.

"Ho!" he shouted. "I have the program!"

Ho spun, looking up toward the central room. Maybe that meant the program *was* there. Maybe it only meant the echoes of Marley's voice didn't obscure where *he* was.

Marley stood still, far enough back in the room so that he could just see Ho and the others over the terrace railing, hoping they couldn't see him at all. From a distance, the contrast between brightness outside and relative murk within had screened him. But although he'd taken off his sunglasses to see better when he'd come in, the inside of the structure wasn't really dark; and he suspected that from close by he could be seen.

Suddenly, Ho must have seen him. He swung his pistol up. Marley ducked. Ho didn't shoot.

Marley wished he had. The gun looked like the revolver Ho had carried last night. Six shots, if he'd reloaded after Shen fired at Kip closing the gate. Possibly only four shots left. Evidently, Ho could count just as precisely: He wasn't wasting any of his bullets.

"You don't have the program, Marley," he shouted back. "You haven't been in there long enough to find it."

Marley didn't answer, but moved, crouched, to one side. Carefully, still well back in the room, he straightened again. He looked past the edge of a window.

"Where was it?" Ho demanded.

Marley prowled sideways, flashing glances back and forth between Ho and the crates.

"You don't have it." Ho snapped his head to give an order to Shen over his shoulder.

"You want to bet?" Marley shouted back.

Ho hesitated, considering, for only a second. He snapped something in Chinese to Shen. Shen shoved Lily, and all three started toward the outside stair again.

Frantically, Marley scanned side-to-side. In a single motion, he leaped to a crate, scooped three eight-by-eight flooring tiles out of it, and skimmed one of them through the window. It sliced the air in front of Ho's face, smashing against the stairway railing.

Once more, Ho spun, swinging up the pistol. Once more, Marley had ducked from sight. Ho again saved his shot. "You do that again, Marley, I'll kill her!"

"No, you won't! You're too smart, Stanley. She's your only chip. The police are on their way. You kill her, you have nothing to trade with them. All you'll have will be a murder rap. Let her go. Exchange her for the program. Take off into the woods. It's your best deal."

All the time he shouted, Marley was moving, hunched,

looking for the diskette. The area he could search was limited, though: He didn't dare come close enough to one of the window openings to be seen from below, nor go across the room so far that he couldn't pop up and check Ho.

"You don't have the program!" Ho started toward the stairway again.

"Bye-bye, Stanley; I'm taking off with it now. When you find it gone, just shout into the woods."

Marley sprang up. Ho saw him, swept up the pistol, and fired. But as Marley came into sight he'd hurled another tile spinning through the window. The missile registered in Ho's eye just as he pulled the trigger, and a reflexive jerk threw off his aim. In the split second before he could recover, Marley was gone, bounding toward the rear of the building.

Ho must not have assumed that Marley'd really left the hotel. He climbed the stairs cautiously, holding the pistol in front of himself with both hands. Shen forced Lily along, two steps behind. They came up onto the terrace near the far end of the wing. Ho spoke to Shen, who pushed Lily forward. When she was beside him, Ho shifted his aim, pointing the gun straight at her head. With another word, he started them all moving together toward the central room.

He was careful. He stayed beside the balustrade, keeping himself well away from the wall line. He walked half sideways, looking back and forth to check the openings into the main room ahead of them and those into the wing. Each move was a separate action: He'd look, decide the next step was safe, grunt an order to Shen. Shen would push Lily; they'd all go forward, and then pause again.

Shen was holding both of Lily's wrists up behind her back. He didn't force them high enough to make her bend forward. She held herself erect, her head up—almost proudly. But her jaw was clenched, and shiny lines of tears ran down her face from under her sunglasses.

They reached a wide doorway into the central room. From the terrace, Ho scanned around the inside. He spoke to Shen. Shen pushed Lily so that she crossed the threshold first. Ho moved with her, the pistol muzzle now pressed to her skull under her ear. Marley wasn't standing against the back of that wall, and there was nowhere else in the room where he might have hidden.

"Maybe your boyfriend did run out on you," he said to Lily. He stepped away from her, and let the aim of the pistol drift; but he was still on guard. He spoke to Shen once more, and when he started to walk toward the front of the room, Shen kept her moving two steps behind.

Ho went to a low stack of concrete blocks, pulled the diskette from between two of them. "A real joker," he said. He shoved it under the waistband of his jeans, under his pullover. "A real bluffer."

"He wasn't bluffing about the cops, Stanley," Lily said. "They'll be here. I wrote down about this place, and the beach."

"I'll bet you did. I'll bet you wrote down my fucking jock size, you bitch. You think it matters? You think I've got only one plan? You think I haven't got a fallback place for the pickup? You ought to know me better than that. Yeah, you're giving me a hard time. Now I've got to spend the rest of the day humping through the fucking jungle. But you're going to have to hump right along with me.

"You know, you're really doing me a favor. I mean, maybe the cops would have gotten bloodhounds or something; traced me through the woods to this place. Maybe they'd just get lucky and spot Shen and me going down to the beach. Who knows? Then what would I have done? But this way—you *are* fixing me up with a safe conduct after all. Anybody comes too close, I'll shove this gun in your eye and"—Ho raised his voice—"You hear that, ass-hole? Marley? You still in here? You try anything, she dies!"

Ho listened to the reverberations of his voice ring from the walls of the chamber and echo off through the empty rooms on either side. Silence seemed to be the only answer to it.

"Okay," he said, "let's get—"

A tile, spinning vertically, hurled down from the balcony, caught him behind his left shoulder blade. Jerking upright against the blow, gasping in pain, whirling, Ho fired one shot toward the balcony without even seeing a target. Then he spun farther around, his arm straight out and shaking with his rage, the pistol pointed at Lily's head two feet away from its end. "I'll kill her!" he screamed.

"Not yet!" Marley called back. His voice, too, bounced from wall to wall and off through the maze of empty rooms—but not enough to conceal from which room it had come.

Ho swung the pistol up, aiming at the door of that room. He snapped an order to Shen. Keeping his eyes on the doorway, darting glances from it only long enough to check his path among the crates, he began to back slowly toward the rear of the room. Shen, with Lily, moved at the same speed.

"You can't get away," Marley called. His voice came from another location, a room to the side of the first. Ho swung his aim, but Marley wasn't in view. "Go into the jungle, I'll follow you." Marley spoke slowly, at his lowest pitch, sounding like Doom. "When you come out, I'll be there."

"Yeah? And what'll you do?" There was no response. "Huh? I come out of the jungle, you come out of the jungle, I get one clear view of you, and you are dead!"

There was no reply.

"Well, you think about that, bluffer. In the meantime—"

Suddenly stepping into the doorway of the second room down the side of the balcony, Marley threw a baseball-size chunk of concrete block with the delivery of a powerhouse pitcher. It grazed Ho's forehead. He staggered, whirled, fired. But again, Marley had ducked back at the instant the missile left his hand.

Ho brought his left hand from his head, looked at the blood on it. "You fucking son of a bitch!"

"Keep cool, Stanley. This is no time to lose your head, do something rash. Now, you still think you can get away from me? That I can't break up your escape?"

Ho did seem to collect himself. He kept his eyes on the balcony, but not directed at a single room. Clearly, Marley could use the outside balcony at that level, go from room to room, appear anywhere. Ho spoke to Shen, who turned to watch the side behind Ho's back.

"What *I* can do, Marley, is kill this fucking bitch. One more time—you throw one more rock at me—I'll do it."

"And then where will you be?" Marley's voice was muffled, and it seemed to come through the second-floor windows as well as from somewhere above. He must be outside, moving to a new location. "No, Stanley, what you'd better do is leave her, take the program, and bug out. You leave her, I won't follow. That way, at least you have the program and a chance to escape. Any other way, you have nothing."

The voice had become more distant. It came from one wing of the building on the upper floor—down a corridor away from the central room.

Ho considered for a moment. "Fuck him!" he said. He jerked his head to Shen.

Pulling Lily, Shen began to move toward the open wall at the rear of the room. He had to go slowly, picking a path between the building materials while on the alert in case

Marley appeared above. Ho sidled in the same way, scanning the balcony as he did.

They crossed two-thirds of the room. *Whump!* Something sounding like a mortar shell exploded on the patio just outside the opening. Gray smoke billowed. After a moment of shock, they saw that Marley had dropped a bag of cement from the back balcony.

"Come on out, Stanley. There's a whole pile of these up here," Marley's voice taunted. "You still think you'll get away from me? Go on into the jungle. I can get closer to you. I love fighting in the jungle."

Shen looked fearfully at Ho. Lily's mask didn't change, and yet she seemed to be smiling. Ho stood very still. After a moment, he reached into his pocket. Then—very fast, eyes flashing to the balcony and down to his business—he flipped the revolver's cylinder open, snatched out three empty casings, and shoved in new bullets. So much for the idea his ammunition was limited.

Marley watched, on his knees, one eye peering carefully around the side of a door. He might have thrown something more, but didn't think he needed to. It looked as though his plan was working.

Now Ho would have to make an important decision. He had a single enemy armed only with rocks. He had two people on his side, and a pistol. He also had a prisoner to guard. Who would go after Marley? Who would carry the gun? If both men went for Marley, what would they do with Lily?

Ho went to Shen, spoke in Chinese. Looking first resigned, then resolute, Shen took the pistol Ho held out to him.

Marley smiled to himself. Although he didn't think Ho was a coward, he'd suspected the general wouldn't put his grunt on guard duty while going to engage the enemy himself. He took his sunglasses from his breast pocket, laid

them aside, put loose change from his trouser pocket beside them, checked the soles of his shoes for pebbles that
might scrape.

Ho spoke again. Shen reached into his pocket, brought
out a knife. It wasn't a switchblade, or stiletto; nothing ste-
reotypically sinister. Ho opened it; it was only an ordinary
two-and-a-half-inch-blade pocketknife. The blade would be
long enough, though. Ho grabbed Lily's hair—the men
of the association seemed to like the standard caveman
clutch for subduing women. Shen released Lily's wrist. Ho
forced Lily to her knees. He rested his fist on her shoulder,
the point of the blade touching her throat. He raised his eyes
to the balcony. Marley ducked back.

"I don't know if you can see me, Marley; but I've got a
knife against Lily's neck. You throw something at me, I may
jab her even without meaning to."

Marley didn't reply. Ho nodded at Shen. Shen started up
the nearer staircase to the upper floor.

Chapter 14

Shen went up the stairs with care, precision, even grace. Perhaps he practiced t'ai chi. He must have been over sixty, but he was lithe. Although he glanced back and forth continually, checking all around the balcony, he showed no fear or nervousness—only an intense concentration.

When he reached the upper level he looked first down the corridor to his right, then across to the one leading into the opposite wing. Marley might be at either end of the floor by now, or in any of the rooms surrounding the two-story middle chamber. He could use one outside terrace to go around the perimeter of the front of the house, enter a room, cross a corridor, go through another room to the rear terrace. Shen would have to stalk him through that labyrinth, hoping to flush him from hiding, catch a glimpse of him breaking cover, and make a lucky shot, or finally drive him into a corner. Shen looked like a man with the patience and discipline to do that job.

He was, as Marley had called him, dapper. Although sweat soaked his striped cotton sport shirt, sticking it to his back, its collar points were sharp and the breast pocket was buttoned. His pleated trousers were stained with mud, but their creases still held clean lines. Careful combing had set his thin hair in flat streaks of black and silver. This was the man who'd tailed Marley through the Combat Zone in Boston unseen although Marley knew he was being followed, and caught Marley in his own trap.

He might have figured that Marley would be gone from the rear of the house where he'd last been located, yet evidently decided he might as well start his search from there. He glided in that direction purposefully. As he moved, though, he swung, looking from side to side; and, once, he pivoted in a complete circle.

Despite the mistakes the man had made recently, he clearly knew his business. Coming to the door of one rear room, he looked through at an angle, then quickly crossed the arch to see back the other way. When he entered the room, he leaped well in over the threshold, wheeling to face anyone who might have stood against the wall.

He didn't have to take the same precaution when checking the back terrace: The rear of the room was entirely open to it. Still, he looked carefully to each side before stepping out. He saw at once the thin trail of cement that had leaked out of the bag Marley'd carried from the adjoining room. Shen glanced over the edge of the terrace, but didn't approach it closely. No railing had been installed yet on that level: The terrace was merely a shelf six feet wide.

Then he prowled along the terrace toward the corner, looking into each room he passed. He wasn't really slow, simply cautious; just the same, by the time he reached the corner, checking four rooms had taken him nearly three minutes. If Marley took care, moving without being seen, slipping back into rooms already searched, he might keep the game going indefinitely.

But, of course, that wasn't his object.

He had moved from the rear of the house as soon as Shen started up the stairway. Hiding in a front room, he'd seen the little stalking cat of a man go into the one in the rear. Now, crouching in the corridor of the wing opposite where Shen had come up, looking past a doorway and through a room, he watched him go from the rear terrace back inside.

Shen kept his knees loose, slightly bent. He placed each small foot delicately. Despite the layer of grit on the surface of the slab, he made no sound. No one who hadn't seen him enter the room would know where he was. Unless Marley could keep him in view almost constantly without being seen himself, Shen could be confident that sooner or later he'd surprise his quarry or catch him moving, exposed when he'd thought himself safe. He'd see Marley—or hear him. Marley was too big, too occidentally accustomed to forceful, direct, abrupt, blundering action, to throwing his weight around; his stealth would be like a buffalo mincing.

Stanley Ho hadn't sent Shen after Marley out of fear for himself; nor because he was pulling rank and avoiding the dirty work. He'd assigned the job to the expert.

As soon as Shen came inside the house again, Marley retreated into a room on the front side. He stood for a moment, listening. He recalculated: No, he wouldn't have been able to keep the game going indefinitely. When he heard nothing, but realized Shen must be moving, and recognized the risk in peeking to try to see the man without already knowing where he was, Marley reduced his estimate radically.

It was good he didn't have to play Shen for time: Between the two men, time would have been on the small one's side. But, of course, time was really the enemy of both. Marley'd played against it, played Shen this long, only to get a sense of the man. He'd forfeited precious minutes letting Shen hunt him; making Shen believe *he* was the hunter, when they both were hunters. In the silence of the cavernous building he'd heard the rapid ticks of his watch, felt it hammer his wrist in fifth-second beats, until he could see a way to set a trap and let Shen hunt him into it. He'd have to spring it soon: His watch said twelve thirty-nine.

Shen heard a clink, as though some piece of tile had been brushed against, knocked to the floor. He darted to the doorway, then paused. A sound made by clumsy movement was exactly what he'd been expecting to hear; but he wasn't an amateur. He knew well that tossing something away from you, clubbing your opponent when he sticks his head out to look, was a very old trick. From the doorway, Shen could look down to the floor below and see Ho and Lily. Ho must have heard the sound, too; he was staring up at the balcony. Shen caught his eye. Without putting his head through the arch, he made as though peering from side to side. Ho shook his head to show Marley wasn't in sight.

Shen came out of the room, and began to float down the corridor to his right. The sound he'd heard had been soft; it had come from this side of the central room. The first doorway he came to was on his left, leading into a room on the front side of the house. Keeping away from it, close to the right-hand wall, Shen passed by. He looked into the room as he went, seeing most of it, but didn't cross and put his head in to check the corners.

That seemed like a mistake. Surely a man with experience in Shen's profession, knowing the noise he'd heard down the corridor could have been a trick to lure him that way, shouldn't pass without checking thoroughly anyplace where his enemy might hide and come out behind him. But he went on.

Although he seemed to place each foot as carefully as a tightrope walker, his shoes did scrape the concrete floor ever so softly. The sound marked his progress while he passed the opening, and for a step or two beyond until—presumably—the wall muffled it.

Four seconds passed. Suddenly, Shen broke through the doorway, wheeling from side to side, finger tight on the trigger, ready to blast down Marley standing pressed against the inside wall, off guard because he thought his enemy had passed.

Marley wasn't standing against the corridor wall, or anywhere else in the room.

He wasn't standing on the front terrace outside the room, either. Shen could see that at once: As with the rooms in the rear, the outer wall of this one was open, intended to be mostly glass. By hunkering very low, Marley might have hidden behind the roofing tiles stacked four feet high in the corner between the central section of the building and the wing. Two steps toward the terrace allowed Shen to check that. Marley wasn't there, either.

Click! Something struck the terrace out near the front corner of the central section. The sound was light, not clatteringly obvious like a lobbed rock. Marley must have been just stupid enough to think it would be mistaken for a stepped-on pebble—if he wasn't completely stupid and believed Shen would respond to any noise without thinking what could make it. Whatever it was, it was a ruse. It had to have been a chip of something tossed from somewhere farther along the wing terrace: probably from the next room. Shen realized that however quiet he'd been when sneaking back to this room, he had given his position away to anyone nearby when he'd leaped in. But by showing he'd heard, Marley'd given away his own proximity.

With the contained stillness of a frog waiting for a fly, he listened for Marley to move, to try slipping away from where he thought he'd drawn Shen to look. Marley didn't move.

If Marley wasn't moving, he was probably hiding, back tight against the wall of the adjoining room, waiting for Shen to step out onto the terrace. If he believed Shen would be heading toward where the sound had come from, he'd expect to strike from behind. However, Shen could throw the big man by his own device by stealthily returning to the corridor and entering the room from there—behind *him*.

Oh so quietly, watching both ways—the terrace and the doorway, too—he cross-stepped back to the corridor. Certain where Marley was, he nonetheless bobbed his head out and back, out and back, quickly checking either side before leaving the room. Then he was a mist, drifting along the wall to the next doorway, seeming not to touch the ground at all. When he spun around the jamb into the opening, it was as though he had materialized instantly out of nowhere.

Marley wasn't in the room.

Shen darted across it. He had no doubt Marley'd been there—couldn't have been farther away. Marley must have moved when he did, fleeing one way or the other along the terrace. He'd have to be fleeing—there was no place on the terrace to hide. There was no place to set an ambush. Shen rushed out.

He whirled, looking to see Marley dashing through one room or another, listening for the running footsteps. Just at the upper edge of his vision he saw a shape, movement: Marley rising from a crouch on the roof, his arm swinging from back behind his head, snapping downward, something leaving his hand. Shen—understanding, beginning to dodge, his arm coming up to point the pistol—had a split second of reaction before the roofing tile Marley'd thrown struck his shoulder. Marley leaped from the roof, crashing down onto the terrace. Shen, staggered, was swinging around and up again even as Marley sprang forward from his landing crouch. Arms shooting out like catapults, Marley rammed Shen full in the chest. For two steps Shen seemed to be trying to run backward on a floor being pulled from under him. Arms spread wide, frantically circling, he seemed to be trying to fly. His hand constricted around the pistol grip firing one shot at the horizon. Then he toppled off the terrace.

As he fell, he let out a short "Ahhhh!" of dismay; and when—spread-eagled—he struck the ground two floors below, the thump was louder than the cement bag Marley'd dropped before. The sounds were unmistakable. "Shen?" Ho shouted from inside. "Shen?" There could be no doubt about what had happened. There was only one question to ask. "Shen?"

Ho allowed one more second of silence, had his answer. Yanking Lily to her feet, he released her hair, grabbed the waistband of her shorts at one hip. He jerked, trying to make her break into a run with him toward the patio. She pulled back. Whirling, he slashed, just—deliberately— missing her face as she recoiled from the blade. "Next time!" He jerked her again, and she did run with him.

Marley saw the slash from the balcony. From two-thirds down the stairway, he saw the pair run awkwardly across the patio and start uphill. From the floor of the room he watched them enter the woods. Then he started after them.

He sprinted. He'd let Ho and Lily go into the woods, out of his sight, so that he'd be out of Ho's. But he couldn't give them too much lead or he might lose them.

The forest was farther behind the hotel than it had appeared from below. By the time he reached it, Marley felt as though he was running through steam. And then, going up the steepening slope through the woods felt like trying to run in a tank of hot water. He slowed, not for relief, but to be quiet.

Ho and Lily weren't being quiet. Marley could hear them breaking through the underbrush up ahead. He climbed rapidly but silently, pushing branches away with care, slipping between stalks. In a few moments he had closed on them enough to hear their gasping. They were moving off to the left now, keeping more nearly at the same level. He veered in that direction, kept climbing until he'd crossed behind them and gained slightly higher ground.

He followed them by sound alone for two minutes, then caught up enough to have momentary glimpses of them below and just ahead. Ho still clutched Lily's waistband, half shoving, half pulling her along. Linked that way, rushing, lurching, and bumping one another, they blundered through the brush like a single rampaging animal, a runaway ox. Marley could shift and twist and use both hands to bend back branches. He wasn't silent, but they'd never hear him over their own noise.

Lily batted with both hands at foliage in her way. Ho struck out at branches with his fist, in which he held the knife. He never turned his wrist to let the blade point away from her.

Light reached the forest floor as a somber glow through layers of green and yellow leaves. Despite Ho's and Lily's crashings, a profound stillness filled the wood. A living stillness, though; not empty: a sense of awareness, of watching, waiting.

The slope they were crossing steepened sharply, bending around to the right. A little brook cut deeply into the hillside. The stream itself was only three feet wide, but the tops of its banks were six or eight apart. Ferns grew lushly on either side.

"Down there," Ho ordered, shoving Lily. He released his grip on her as she slid down the bank. She sank at once onto her hands and knees in the water, her shoulders heaving with her panting. Ho let himself down sideways into the cut. He stood, swaying with his own heavy breathing. His eye level was just above the ferns. After a moment of catching his breath, he scanned around over the ferns and beyond them. He moved his head slowly, methodically; but his eyes darted: a man in control of himself, not panicked

by being in the jungle, yet aware a predator might pounce
from any side. He saw nothing, no movement.

Marley peered down the stream at Ho and Lily from between and under the screen of fronds. He lay on his side,
propped on one forearm, just eight yards up the hill. He
kept his own deep breathing slow and silent.

"Cool off," Ho said. He crouched and—between wary
glances at Lily and all around—splashed water up onto his
face. Lily rolled to her side and lay curled on a little shelf in
the stream.

Ho stood again. Always watching, he slipped his left arm
out of his sweater, then the right. Another careful scan,
then—all at once—he had the sweater over his head and
off. He checked to be certain the diskette was secure under
his waistband. Then he crouched again, splashed and
rubbed cool water over his bare torso. The man was fleshy,
his navel indented as though a finger had poked into his
buttery belly. But the soft bulges in his chest and arms
weren't only fat. He looked like a scaled-down sumo
wrestler. Like one of Gideon's good warriors, he lifted
cupped-palmfuls of water and drank while constantly on
guard.

Soaking in a hot tub of his own sweat, Marley envied
him. With his mouth dry as flannel, he watched Ho drink.

Ho wiped water over his face again, then rose. He se-
cured the diskette inside the top of his jeans, tied the
sweater around his waist.

"Okay, bitch. Listen." He raised his head, raised his
voice slightly. "And you listen, too, Marley. I know you're
there, someplace. You hear this." He paused for a moment, almost as if expecting an answer. Somewhere up the
hill a bird screeched.

He looked down at Lily again. She had pushed herself up
on one arm. Pale ivory against the vivid foliage, her
clothing wet and semitransparent, she looked like a naiad.

"Sit up," Ho ordered. He unbuckled his belt, pulled it free from his jeans, tossed it to her. "Put this around your neck. Put the end through the buckle, pull it around your neck."

Staring at him, Lily slowly complied. Ho leaned, grabbed the end of the belt. Straightening, he had Lily on a leash. He gave a little tug. Choking, Lily grabbed at the collar.

Ho gave slack enough for her to get her fingers under the loop. "You can keep your hand there so I don't tighten up too much and choke you by *accident*. But you try to get away . . . And if you try to fight me, Lily"—Ho lifted his chin—"Marley, *you* try jumping me"—back to Lily—"I'll scar you—I'll cut your nose off. I'll jab your eye out. That's what I'll do. And that'll just be a start. If they catch me—Marley, if you bring the cops down on me—I'll see to it, Lily: I'll tell our people what to do when they come for you. They'll carve on you and send you back and see how your lover-boy likes you with no face."

As always, Ho spoke in a voice like polished wood. Lily looked up at him with her face as hard and unrevealing as her dark glasses.

"Move," Ho said with a jerk of his head.

Marley let them get a little farther away from him before rising and slipping down the bank into the stream. He took one moment to drink as Ho had done, and to lie in the water and roll once to soak his clothes. He checked his watch. The time was twelve forty-six. The police had been called. Then he began following them again.

The woods were thick enough so he could follow closely without being seen. Since he knew where Ho and Lily were, while Ho didn't know *his* position, Marley could even stay close enough to catch glimpses of them. But the foliage wasn't so dense that he could close in, suddenly be there as Ho pushed away a branch, and strike.

He did increase his pace. Ho wasn't running now. Holding the end of his belt, walking at Lily's side and half a step behind her, he let Lily move at her own speed. He kept them going at the same level across the hillside. Over the course of five minutes—without haste, without giving himself away—Marley was able to panther his way past them. He would, he decided, simply have to stay ahead and hope for an opportunity to present itself. Surely he'd come to something—another stream bordered by dense ferns, a thicket—where he could crouch in ambush.

Ho directed Lily to angle slightly downhill. Marley moved in an arc to match their new vector. The slope flattened. Flatter ground should be wetter: Surely the vegetation would be thicker. Marley moved more quickly to put himself closer to the line Ho and Lily were taking. If he could find one good, thick bush to hide behind . . .

Suddenly, he found himself coming out of the woods onto a road. On the other side of it stretched open pasture—cleared fields like those around the hotel. Ho and Lily were close behind him. Marley spun back, dashing into the woods again and hitting the dirt. Ho brought Lily down to the road.

Ho halted. "Give me your glasses," he snapped, the fist holding the knife pressed to his forehead in an attempt to shade his eyes. Lily hesitated, and Ho jerked the belt. "Give!"

Lily took off her glasses, handed them over. He put them on. She shielded her own eyes with a palm.

"Okay," Ho said, "let's go."

They started along the road. They had come out of the woods within a few feet of where Marley had been. Now they passed within three yards of where he lay, and there was never any way he could reach them without being seen.

Lying there, watching them walk away from him, Marley tried to form a new plan. The narrow road ran nearly level around the slope. It disappeared back into what obviously was a deep ravine—probably a watercourse—between this

arm of the mountain and the next. The road must be an
extension of the one that went past the hotel; but here it
wasn't asphalted. Rutted, stony, too rough to be a traf-
ficked throughway, it likely led into the ravine and stopped.

Where could Ho be going to? He hadn't come onto it by
accident—surprised to find it there, as Marley had been.

Unless Ho was to be lifted from the island by a helicop-
ter—which seemed doubtful: the machine would be too
easily tracked—he had to go down to the shore. From
glancing over a map of the island, Marley remembered that
most of the east coast met the sea in cliffs. He remembered
vaguely that there were a few narrow and virtually inac-
cessible beaches. Evidently, Ho knew a way down to one of
them.

Rising carefully, stealing forward to the edge of the road,
Marley waited until Ho and Lily were out of sight around
the bend. He came out onto the road, himself, to survey
the landscape.

As it curved, the road passed into the trees again,
through a finger of forest that pointed for a short distance
down the hillside and into the ravine. Beyond it, the broad
slopes of the mountain were open—north and south, and
eastward all the way down to the sea. There were outcrop-
pings of bushes, here and there a lone tree: but—except in
the ravine itself—no real cover. With his eyes he followed
the line of the ravine. That line was clear: The cut must be
deep. He couldn't see its bottom. He could tell by the con-
tours of the slopes on either side that the streambed mean-
dered somewhat, but fell in a generally direct line almost to
its mouth. There, it seemed to turn first left, then right
sharply—as though the northerly slope was a left hand
clasped around the fist of the southerly one. That might
mean the stream had found a way to reach the sea between
two sections of cliff instead of falling over one.

Shading his eyes with both hands against the glare, Marley looked more carefully across the farther slope. A threadlike scar wound back and forth, north and south, moderating the steeper places, but generally following the eastward line of the ravine.

One of the southward sweeps took the path over a ridge and out of sight. In that direction, another mile away, Marley could see another ridge. Beyond that—a blue-gray, shimmering shape—yet another. The island was made of mountains thrusting from the sea. Naturally, every coast was cut into successions of ridges by watercourses. Perhaps the next one—to which the path seemed to lead—was the one that Ho would take descending to the shore.

Looking farther down the slope, Marley saw that the path returned, following the nearer ravine once more and going down into the ravine near the bottom.

So, there did seem to be a way to the shore along the nearer ravine. There might, equally, be a way along the next one—to a different beach, with a headland of cliffs between the two of them. Which was Ho going toward?

Marley could find out, of course, by watching from his present vantage. By the time Ho and Lily had disappeared over the ridge, and then come back into sight—or didn't— they'd have half an hour's lead on him. He'd never catch them. Or Marley could follow them. But out on those open slopes, he couldn't see Ho without being seen. He couldn't follow closely without endangering Lily. If he couldn't catch up, take Ho by surprise, what was the point of following at all?

Marley made the only possible decision. He loped along the dirt road until it entered the forest, then cut downhill and through the woods to the ravine. Now he would be ahead of Ho and Lily—exactly the position he wanted. *If* he'd chosen the correct path.

For a few seconds, he climbed down the side of the ravine holding on to tree trunks, finding footholds behind roots and small bushes. Then there weren't any more of those. Whenever the rains came, a torrent must rage between the ridges, scouring the ravine's walls and tearing out vegetation that had dared to take root too low. Some few shrubs had dug in firmly enough at the edge of that death zone to have held for several seasons and have hope for more.

Gripping one, Marley tested his footing on the bare slope. Dry and crumbly, the soil broke away under his weight. Taking a deep breath of resolution, he released his hold and let himself slide sideways, half erect, the eight or ten feet to the bottom.

The floor of the ravine was dry, stony, nearly barren. While sunlight beat directly down into it, the thick foliage on either side above screened it from the fields. Marley would be able to make his way down the streambed without worrying whether he'd be seen. What worried him was whether he'd ever get out again.

He started walking.

As he went, the sides of the ravine rose ever higher above him. They'll come down again, he told himself. From the road, he'd seen that the land rolled up and down within the general plane of its slope toward the sea.

The pitch of the sides steepened. He hesitated. Climbing up back there where he'd come down would be difficult. Here, it would be impossible. Yes, the sides would come down again—but when? How far? If he'd made the wrong decision, if Ho and Lily went south to the next ravine, he'd be too far away ever to catch up with them by the time he could get out of this one.

But if he went back, he'd be where he was before—which was nowhere.

I'll go on another five minutes, he decided. Maybe the slope will have changed by then, and I'll be able to climb up and look around.

Within two hundred yards, the sides of the ravine did change—they became steeper yet. The one on his right had been flayed to a skeletal outcropping of solid rock, and the stream—deflected by that—had cut around and deeply into the opposite bank. The floor dropped abruptly over what—were there any water—would be a steep cataract.

Marley paused again, looking ahead, looking back. To go forward meant clambering down over those rocks—to reach what? To go back meant ten minutes walking uphill in the sun to reach where he'd been when he started. He felt a sense heavy as the heat that whatever he did would be wrong, and a desire of almost overwhelming power to be out of that oven in the earth as quickly as possible no matter what that meant. He sighed and turned downhill again.

He had to climb down carefully, stretching a leg to locate and test one tiny ridge in the water-polished rock, then another, finding those that would give him footholds. And he had to try to move without touching the rocks for more than an instant at a time with his hands—or, worse—the more sensitive skin of his forearms. Under hours of tropical sunlight, the stones had reached the proverbial egg-frying temperature. Unless he could find a hold on one that had been shadowed by another, they seared him almost beyond his will to endure. He wrapped his handkerchief to glove one hand. That made the descent possible, although more than a few seconds' contact with a rock was painful even through the cloth around his hand, or that of his trousers.

Seared when he touched the rocks, he was roasted even when he didn't. Sweat burned his eyes. And without dark glasses, he felt the light reflecting from the tan and sparkling rocks like a knife slicing between his eyelids.

He squinted against that light, his lids almost completely closed; yet brightness forced its way through the slits and filled his head with a pounding pressure. Inside his head and outside: Everything everywhere was becoming a single brightness.

Staggering, almost falling, Marley lurched to one side of the ravine, where a jut of the outcropping cast a two-foot-deep cave of shadow. He tumbled forward into it, against the wall; sank to his knees, put his forehead down to the ground.

After some time—probably a few minutes, although for all he could tell it might have been hours—the ringing in his ears subsided, and the brightness condensed and went outside his head again. He wiped his dripping face. Thank God, at least he was still sweating. If he was dry, he'd be as good as dead.

He'd made it to the apex of the bend. He could see that after another dozen feet, he'd be able to stay in shadow by hugging this side. He forced himself upright again and went on.

Reaching that shade, he rested once more. How long had he been in the ravine? About twenty minutes. He stared down at his watch for a moment in wonder—partly that he'd lasted that long, partly that the time hadn't really been twenty years. How far had Ho and Lily gone in twenty minutes? Was he still ahead of them, or had they passed? Or had they . . . He didn't want to think about them having gone south across the field.

And during this time the police would have arrived at the hotel. Would they take time to try to track Ho, Lily, and Marley, or would they call in patrol boats to guard the beaches? An airplane to fly low over these slopes? Marley feared the police finding Ho almost as much as he, himself, feared losing him.

No point in speculating, just go on, he ordered. And he didn't have to decide which way to go anymore: There could be no return over that cataract of fire.

Moving was easier, quicker in the shadow of the bend;

and in another five minutes he found the grade of the streambed shallowing again. The great rocks became boulders, then stones mostly buried in sand. Up above, the top of the ravine wall was lowering on the right side. About thirty yards ahead, where the cut bent left once more, the edge of the field showed only a dozen feet or so above the floor.

The edge of the field *showed*. Bushes dotted the edge, but the goat-grazed grass of the pasture stretched between them. Marley made for that place feeling the relief of a convict seeing a break in the prison walls. The wall wasn't vertical—probably about sixty degrees: too steep to walk up, but it wouldn't have to be *scaled*. Now, if he could only kick holes deep enough in the rotten soil to hold his weight until he could reach a bush . . .

He kicked into the earth wall on his right, all too easily making a six-inch-deep hole at knee level. He put his toe into it, tried his weight. It seemed to hold him. He stepped up, his hands sliding up the bank searching for something to grip. His left found a half-exposed rock. Distributing his weight, he raised his other leg and began to kick another hole. He felt himself sinking, tried desperately to grab something, and then the stuck-together sand under his foot disintegrated and he slid almost ceremoniously down to the bottom.

Marley went two yards farther down the ravine, looking for a better place. He tried again, did get a second foothold, put weight on it, slid down once more.

Hopeless. The bank could not be climbed—not in that section, at least. And—soft as it was—it was an anvil for the sun, which beat on him like a white-hot hammer with the rhythm of his own driving pulse. How much longer could he go on before keeling over from heat exhaustion? Not long, not long enough. He would have to go on staggering down the ravine looking futilely for another place to climb, hoping at last merely to live long enough to find his way out the bottom. He wouldn't be able to see where Ho and Lily were, to know they were going off in another direction entirely. A part of him was beginning not to care. A part of him was beginning to imagine another cascade ahead, one impossibly steeper than the last, to imagine he was trapped in that slit in the earth and would never escape.

CHAPTER 15

Marley pushed himself upright. He found a pebble, put it in his mouth, wishing he'd remembered that mouth-wetting trick sooner. Then—since he couldn't fly—he started walking down the streambed again.

Three minutes later he came to a place where the bank on his right had fallen. Flooded, the stream must have found a weaker area in the side of the field and taken a bite. Although the soil was even looser, Marley was able easily to climb up the shallower incline. "Always darkest just before the dawn," he thought; and then of course— Yankee that he was—reminded himself not to count on it.

He paused just as his head reached the level of the field. Ho and Lily were on the path that went along this ravine.

At that moment, they were a couple of hundred yards uphill and heading away from him, following one of the switchbacks; but the winding path would bring them back near the edge of the ravine, perhaps fifty yards below his position.

There was still no way he could attack. He'd have to drop back down to the streambed again. But at least he'd chosen the right route. By lying in the cut with his head just below the field, he could look up from time to time and watch their progress. And—pure bliss—he could enjoy a blessed touch of the breeze wafting up the slope. That kiss of coolness and the triumph of having taken the right track brought new strength. He waited until Ho and Lily had passed him and were on the stretch of path that would lead them back to the ravine's edge. Then he slid down to the floor again.

He lay flat against the right-hand wall. He had no way of reaching Ho and Lily; he'd have to move down the ravine with them. It seemed he might better escape being seen by remaining just behind them.

A few minutes later, Lily's and Ho's heads came into sight. Ho was walking behind her, still leashing her with his belt around her neck. Marley let them go on until the edge of the bank blocked them again, then crept along the bottom of the ravine after them.

They didn't speak, and their footsteps were seldom audible. Only from an occasional scuff or grunt could Marley place them. He moved quietly, too, trying to match his speed to theirs. If he went too fast, he might suddenly come into Ho's sight. If he fell too far behind, and then encountered difficulty like another rocky, steep place, he might lose them.

Suddenly, after about five minutes, he heard Lily speak. "I got to have a rest, Stanley."

"Just keep moving."

"If I don't sit down for a minute, I'm going to pass out. I'm not faking. There's some shade ahead. I got to sit down."

"Okay, we'll take a break."

Ahead, near the edge of the bank, Marley saw a single,

scraggly tree. It must be growing just to one side of the path. In a moment, Lily and Ho appeared next to it. Marley could see them only from the waist up. He froze, hoping they wouldn't look back and see him. Then they sat. Ho—keeping Lily to his left—disappeared entirely. Lily's head still was visible.

"Can I take this off my neck?"

"No."

"It's killing me, Stanley. It chokes me, and the heat . . . If you want to kill me, Stanley, just kill me! Just do it! If you're not going to kill me now, I got to get some air!"

"Jeez, I'm sorry you're not comfortable, Lily. I really wish you were comfortable, you know? Okay. You take the belt off your neck, and you put it around your leg. Do it slowly."

Marley could see Lily loosen the loop and lift it over her head.

"Aren't you going to say thanks, Lily?"

"You're really getting a cheap thrill out of holding me with that thing, aren't you, Stanley?"

"Yes, I am. I am."

Lily bent forward, evidently slipping the belt loop around an ankle. She straightened again, and scooted back enough to lean against the tree trunk.

Marley began to prowl along the bottom of the ravine. Nearly straight down from the tree a large chunk of rock— an outcropping four feet high—jutted from the bank about halfway up. From the floor of the ravine, Marley could just reach the bottom of the outcrop. With a foot planted on its top, he'd be able to leap up to the field. His task would be to climb up the bank—gripping the rock—high enough to set that foot on that top.

"We can take five minutes," Ho announced.

"You got an appointment?"

"Yeah," he replied curtly.

Lily tipped her head back against the trunk.

Sod held the surface layer of soil, but erosion had undercut it. Although below the undercut the bank angled outward into the ravine, the top of the rock actually was set in from the edge of the field by over a foot. Marley studied the configuration, imagining how he'd have to move—risking falling backward as he leaped up, put his palms onto the grass, and vaulted over the obstacle. He estimated he could make the maneuver. And the plus side was that the overhang would screen him as he neared the top.

Inspecting the bank carefully, he found a fist-size stone half protruding at just below knee level. Slowly, he scratched loose the soil around it and worked it free. The hole made an excellent place for his foot. He tried it cautiously. First a slight pressure, then more. It held.

He studied the side of the outcrop, spotted an indentation that would give a grip for one hand. Taking a quiet, deep breath, he thrust himself upward, reaching, seizing that fingerhold.

His forearm brushed the bank beside the rock as he reached, and a pebble and a few tiny clods of earth broke loose and cascaded.

Marley froze, lying tight against the bank, trying to press himself into the angle with the rock. Was he a child trying to hide by holding its hands over its eyes? He tried to think whether the rock and overhang would shield him from view from above. Maybe, at a certain angle. Clinging there, he waited nearly a minute. Nothing happened. Ho didn't shout.

Well, the sound hadn't been loud. After another moment, Marley carefully lifted his head and peered around the rock. Ho still wasn't in sight, but by leaning out, he could just see Lily. She was lifting her hair, turning her head slowly from side to side as though to cool her neck. For one instant she caught Marley's eye. She showed no surprise at seeing him—evidently she had heard the noise—and turned away again.

Marley breathed. Lying against the pitch of the bank, he dug with his fingers to make his next stepping place. From it, he'd be able to thrust himself high enough to do the rest of his climbing—only another two steps—on the rock. Trying for silence, he dug by half inches; and as he loosened the soil, he broke the clods in his hand and let them slide down in tiny pieces.

"How could you have an appointment, Stanley? How could you fix a time for somebody to meet you down there on that beach? You didn't even know you'd have to go there."

"I told you I had a fallback. I always have a fallback."

Ho's voice was muffled, Lily's loud and distinct. Marley realized that she was talking for his benefit. To get him information? Or to cover the sound of his climbing?

"Yeah, you are a pretty smart guy, Stanley." Lily's tone was of rueful admiration. "How'd you set it up this time? I don't see how you could've."

Ho didn't reply, and she prompted, "Tell me. I mean, you only had like a couple minutes on the phone last night. What could you set up?" Now she sounded genuinely curious, even full of wonder at Ho's skill. "Come on, tell me. How could you have an exact time for somebody to pick you up here?"

"It doesn't have to be an exact time. The boat's coming past the other beach—the hotel beach—about two o'clock. That's about right now. That was the earliest they figured they could make it. If we aren't there, they're just going to cruise the coast very slowly—like they're fishing. They come by here—down there, where we're going. If they don't see us, they keep cruising, time it, and come back in an hour. But if we keep moving, we'll be there on the first pass. So, put your collar on like a good little doggie, and let's go."

"You said five minutes. It hasn't been five minutes. I have to rest, Stanley, or you'll have to carry me."

"Two more. You got two more minutes."

Toe in the hole he'd made, Marley shoved upward, grabbing for another handhold. He caught a ridge in the rock. He saw an indentation, brought his left foot over and against it. Then slowly he brought over the right leg, slipping it under the other. With his right arm he pressed against the bank, trying to hold himself up from it; but there was no way he could prevent his leg from scraping the soil as he moved it.

"What's that?" Ho said.

"What?"

"I heard something, down there."

"Oh, yeah, Stanley. It's James."

Even clinging to a burning rock in hundred-degree heat, Marley felt as though a bucket of icy water had been poured down his back. Fingers like claws around ridges in the rock, toes jammed against its rough surface, face pressed into his elbows, he clung to the outcropping. He lay against the earthen bank, trying to compress himself into the corner between it and the rock.

"Don't you see him?" Lily asked. Ho must have risen and been peering down into the ravine. "He's right down there, Stanley. And he's got six cops with him."

"Don't you wish. I thought maybe he would be there."

From the way Lily had faced when speaking to him, Ho must have been sitting just downhill of her. He must have come from that position to look over the edge. The overhang must be screening Marley.

"I've been expecting him to show up someplace," Ho went on. "But maybe he went back to get the cops. Anyway, he couldn't climb up even if he was down in there.

But we aren't waiting around to find out." His voice became more muffled. He must have stepped back again. "Put the belt back around your neck."

The overhang must have concealed the full bulk of the rock outcropping. Ho hadn't seen Marley, hadn't looked carefully, because he didn't realize there was anyplace where Marley might be hiding. He was—in theory—still vulnerable to surprise.

But Marley couldn't move. He knew that any shift would scrape the bank or rock. While he might previously have hoped to catch Ho off guard, now the man was alerted. And he must be on his feet, and close to Lily. Marley's moment had passed.

"Stanley, give me a break!"

"Give you a break? I'll give you a break, Lily. Sure. When we get down to the beach, I'll give you a break. What do you want? Your arm or your leg. Come on!"

"Wait, Stanley!"

Wait! Marley was clinging to that rock by his finger- and toenails, controlling his breathing, fearful that the slightest movement would reveal him to Ho, trying desperately to hold on and keep himself hidden until Ho and Lily were out of hearing; and Lily asks Ho to *wait!*

"Give me a chance! I know what I did was bad, but think of all the good things I've done for you. I'm on my knees. I'm begging you!"

Marley was dumbfounded. Lily begging? Begging *Ho?* Had the prospect of being dragged away again when rescue seemed so close unnerved her completely? Could she really think Ho would relent? Could *she* be so frightened, lose control— "Oh, please, Stanley! Please!" She broke into sobs.

Of course not. She didn't understand Marley's predicament. She was trying to buy him time to make his attack.

For an instant he almost tried it. Flinging away all attempt at stealth, scrambling up the rock, throwing himself over the projecting sod, he would charge like a raging lion at Ho—who, by then, would have seized Lily and be holding the point of his knife to her jugular.

"Please, Stanley. I've done good things for you."

"Not lately. Come off it, Lily. You know this won't work. You know there are rules. You break the rules, you pay for it. Put on the collar."

"Stanley—"

"Put on the collar!"

Put on the collar, Marley echoed. Move! Get him away from here. Under the strain Marley's muscles were beginning to quiver. He feared losing his grip—even if one toe slipped he'd send an avalanche of soil and pebbles roaring down and crashing to the floor of the ravine.

"Okay, bitch. Let's go."

"Oh, Stanley!" A moment later Marley heard her cry, "Oh, Stanley, not so fast," from a little distance. If she couldn't keep Ho within Marley's reach she would signal that they'd moved.

Marley slid down the bank, and then began to creep carefully along it again. There'd be another chance. There had to be. A woman as gutsy as Lily had to have one.

The streambed began to drop more steeply. Water racing with force increased by the slope had left less sand on it. Soon the entire floor of the ravine was made of bare boulders. Marley had to clamber over them, careful not to twist an ankle. Like the ones he'd crossed before, these reflected heat and brightness, so he was grilled from above and below. At least this time he could move upright without having to touch the rocks with his hands.

Thirty yards ahead the ravine curved sharply to the left, the right-hand bank turning to appear as a wall before him. The ravine must be making its final one-hundred-eighty-degree bend to reach the sea. As he approached, he could make out the line of the path descending across it. Ho and Lily should appear at any moment. Marley crossed to the left side, lay against the bank in a place where he could just see the upper end of the path, and waited.

They did appear, Lily first, walking with both hands up to her neck to keep the belt from tightening and choking her. Ho followed, at the length of the strap. He had tied his sweater around his head so that it hung to shade his neck. Wearing that headdress but naked to the waist, heavy, swarthy, he looked like some barbarian pirate. He should have been carrying a cutlass or scimitar instead of the little pocketknife.

Marley crept along the north bank, keeping them just in sight as well as he could while watching his footing. He reached a point where he had to pause and wait until their path carried them around the bend. Then he hurried across the streambed and followed on that side. By that time they must have been two minutes ahead of him. As he moved along the right-hand bank again, he kept scanning it, hoping he would find a place where he could climb up to the path and move more quickly. The ravine floor was becoming an increasingly difficult tumble of huge boulders.

As Lily and Ho rounded the hill, the view of the sea opened before them. From a narrow V it spread to an infinite width of white-fringed pale blue water and milky sky. The hill shaded the cocoa-colored beach—barely twenty feet wide—that stretched half a mile or more along the coast. A steady, light breeze blew in from the water. Way out, several miles away, was the dark shape of some ship; and closer—perhaps three hundred yards—a small powerboat was idling down the coast trolling fishing lines.

"Yeah!" Ho exclaimed. He waved his free arm over his head. "Go on! Keep moving!"

The path descended rapidly, cutting around across the abrupt rise of the hill away from the mouth of the ravine and avoiding the stream of rocks carried out and strewn across the beach from it.

"Keep moving!" Ho ordered again as they reached the sand. "We got to go out where they can see us." He gestured for Lily to proceed toward the water's edge. She hesitated, and he pointed the knife at her, shaking his fist. "Make my day, Lily. Try to fight me."

Ho moved up beside her, then took the lead as they crossed the beach. There wasn't any surf. Ho took them both to where the lacy lines of foam rushed up around their ankles. Again he waved, pulling the sweater from his head and flagging that back and forth at arm's length.

The people in the boat must have seen them. The boat began to come about.

"They see us!" Ho shouted. "They're coming. I made it. I fucked 'em all! I fucked Marley, and you . . ." He turned to Lily. "I *will* fuck you, Lily! Oh, yeah, I'm going to have some real fun with you!"

"Please, Stanley!" Palms up in supplication, Lily reached out toward Ho. Suddenly grabbing the belt in both hands, she jerked it downward out of his grip. Instantly, she wheeled, running back across the beach toward the path and the ravine.

"Bitch!" Ho was two steps behind her.

Lily sprinted, speeding faster than the white spume racing up the packed sand from the sea. Her legs flashed. Ho couldn't match her stride for stride, but his were longer. He lunged, grabbing for her, missing by inches. Out at sea, the boat suddenly showed white teeth.

Lily's hair was whipping out behind her. Lunging again, Ho brushed it with his fingertips. Gasping, they both were leaning forward, driving through the softer sand. Lily staggered, almost falling forward. Ho reached, trying to grab her waistband, just missed. She veered, keeping on the beach instead of scrambling up to the path that paralleled it on the hillside. She was aiming toward the boulders at the mouth of the ravine. Her breath sounded in her throat in little screams. Ho's was nearly a bellowing. And the boat's engine now could be heard as a distant angry thunder.

Lily might have thought if she reached the rocks she could dodge, put obstacles between her and Ho. She had no chance of doing that. He was too close—right behind her: one step, half a step, reaching, touching her, almost close enough to grab—right there!

Marley was there. Suddenly appearing, he leaped down from the path, crashing into Ho, knocking them both sprawling sideward onto the sand.

Marley landed on top. For an instant, Ho's right arm was pinned under him. He tried to free it, to bring the knife up and around, but Marley clamped his wrist and held it down. "Drop it!" he shouted. Right hand grabbing the back of Ho's head, he twisted, forcing the man's face down into the sand. "Drop the knife!"

Ho squirmed, straining, trying to free himself. He writhed, his legs scissoring, kicking. Hunching forward, Marley put his weight on Ho's upper body, and bore with all his strength on the man's head. Ho opened his fist and the knife fell from it. Instantly, Lily sprang forward, snatched up the weapon, and leaped back again.

Still pressing Ho's face down, Marley jerked the wrist he held, forcing it behind Ho's back. Suddenly he twisted away, coming up on one knee. With grips on wrist and hair, he forced Ho around and up, half sitting. "Get the program," he shouted.

Again, Lily darted in, snatching the diskette from under

Ho's waistband. Marley shoved, sending Ho sprawling, and leaped to his feet. He darted a glance toward the boat. Its bow wave had vanished. It seemed to be slowed to idling. A man at one side was watching through binoculars.

"You want to fight some more, Stanley?" Marley shouted.

Ho had pulled himself up to a sitting position. He was snorting, spitting, brushing sand from his face. He looked up at Marley looming over him, and shook his head.

"You want to try to get away?"

Again, Ho shook his head.

"You're finished?"

"Yeah, I'm finished."

"Yes, you are. Your friends out there can see that. Do you see them? They're just sitting there. They know that by the time they could get here, I'll have broken your neck. Lily and I will be back up in the ravine; and who knows how close the police may be behind us. Right?"

Ho looked out at the boat, which seemed merely to be holding position.

"Okay," Marley said. "Now, I've got a deal for you, Stanley. I'm going to let you go. I'm going to let you swim out there to them. All you have to do is agree to amnesty for Lily. Just exactly the way she said before—just exactly in those words. No retribution, Stanley: You agree to that—give your word, or whatever it is, on behalf of your association—you're a free man."

Sitting, knees bent, hands between them on the sand, Ho stared sideways up at Marley. "No," he said.

For an instant, Marley stared back, astonished.

"The program," Ho said. "You give me the program, I'll take your deal. Otherwise, no."

"You're bluffing."

"Try me."

"You're crazy."

"No, I'm not. I told you, Marley: There's nothing the cops can do to me that'll be worse than what'll happen to me if I give up that program to save myself."

"If I leave you here, your buddies'll come in for you. They'll find out you haven't got it."

"They'll know I tried. But whatever gets decided about me, there isn't going to be any question about Lily. If she's smart, she'll take that knife and slit her own throat right now." Ho turned to look up at her. "You know that, Lily, don't you?"

"I think he's bluffing," Marley said. "Come on, Lily, we'll leave him."

"James, he's not—" She stood shaking her head, her hand out toward Marley, the diskette in it.

"Give me that," Marley commanded, taking it from her abruptly as though afraid she'd hand it over to Ho. "Come on!" He took her arm, turned her, and began moving them away from Ho.

They'd gone a dozen feet when they heard the rumble of the boat's engine. Turning, they saw Ho stand. He walked down to the water, waving his arms back and forth, crossing one another in front of his face, and the engine was cut again.

The boat wallowed, rocking in place. Ho walked forward, farther into the water to where the wavelets rushed up to his knees. He splashed himself, washing away the sand sticking to his body and face. Then he sat down. He crossed his legs, folded his hands in his lap, allowing the cooling water to sweep over his legs and up to his waist as he stared out to sea.

"James, he's not—"

"Be quiet!"

Lily looked stricken.

Marley called out, "We're going, Stanley. It's your last chance."

Ho never turned. The powerboat's rocking was barely perceptible. The other ship, out near the horizon, might have been painted on the flat blue of the sea. A line of foam surged up the beach and retreated, and another succeeded it, but nothing changed.

Marley stared at Ho for a long moment, then walked across the beach toward him. Lily followed.

Ho waited until Marley and Lily were standing knee-deep in the water beside him before turning his head just enough to look up at them.

"So?"

"If I let you take this diskette and let you go, you agree to amnesty for Lily?" Marley spoke as though the words were brass on his tongue.

"That's right."

"Okay, you bastard, then say it."

"If you give me that thing, I agree to total amnesty for Lily. No harm to come to her, or hers, never."

"He's supposed to say it in Chinese?" Marley snapped at Lily.

"Yes. Just to make sure."

"Okay, say it."

Ho spoke in Chinese. Lily nodded.

"All right, Stanley, you win this much. Here you are." Ho began reaching upward, but before his arm was extended Marley snarled, "Take it and get out of my sight!" and flung the diskette contemptuously down beside Ho's leg. The surf carried it a yard up the beach before Ho snatched it out of the water.

For an instant, fury flashed across Ho's face; but then he seemed to control it and decide that equanimity in contrast to Marley's anger would make his triumph more complete.

He wiped the plastic once with his hand, then nodded. "It's done, then," he said. "But since it's done, I'll tell you,

Marley, she isn't worth it. She's a two-faced bitch. She sold Detweiller, she's sold me, she's sold her people—she sells herself! She'll sell anybody, do anything, if she thinks it'll—"

Marley had leaned forward. He held up one admonishing finger. "I made a resolution about punching people, Stanley. Don't make me break it." Then, wheeling around, he took Lily's arm and started them walking away.

CHAPTER 16

Marley tried to remember being hot. He'd returned to Boston just at the start of a nor'easter. The airport closed behind him within half an hour. Gale-force winds drove blinding snow. Traffic crawled. Two inches were piled on the roads by the time he'd turned off the interstate onto the secondary route to Carlisle. His car's heater seemed to be winning the battle to save his nose and feet from frostbite against the stored-up cold of the garage, but then he had to get out and help push a car that had skidded and stuck in his way.

Joanna had a huge fire blazing in the woodstove. Marley'd warmed his hands at it, and feeling was beginning to return to his feet. The heat on his sunburned face was actually painful. But although she'd turned up the thermostat for the oil heat, too, he felt a chill on whatever side of himself he wasn't toasting. He tried to remember what the steambath of the jungle, the furnace of that ravine, had felt like.

He'd taken his scotch straight. He held it in both hands, warming it so it would the better warm him. Having finished telling her all that had happened on the island, he stared at the fire, thinking about the impossibility that he could ever have imagined himself *too* hot. And thinking about other possibilities he could all too easily imagine.

When he'd arrived, Joanna'd greeted him with an almost overpowering hug. As he'd told his tale, she'd exclaimed again and again things like, "Oh, God!" and "You could have been *killed*!" and—with wide-eyed wonder and admiration—"How *could* you? How could you be *so brave*?" She was wearing those tight jeans, and ankle warmers, and a bulky dark purple sweater, and she looked both cold-night-by-the-fire cozy and smart. She had always seemed to Marley like amber, polished and charged. Now her gleam wasn't hard, but the energy she radiated was stronger than ever.

Of course, sexual desire reflexively follows escape from danger. And there was all that unrequited lust that Lily had deliberately aroused. But he shouldn't let either of those lead him to lascivious thoughts about Joanna. That wouldn't be right.

"Russ does think he can recover the program?" she asked, apparently wanting further reassurance.

"Yes. He thinks it'll be hard because he'll leave out steps thinking he's already done them; but in time . . ."

"He said a month or two?"

"He's going to work hard. He's strongly motivated. I think he really was—*is*—pretty burned out. But right now, with the combination of guilt and gratitude and anger he's feeling he seems to be fired up again.

"Of course, it'll be a big help that he doesn't have to actually reinvent the program."

"*That's* an understatement, James." Joanna regarded Marley speculatively. "Would you have given that man the diskette anyway—to save that girl—if you hadn't known you could destroy the program by getting salt water in the disk?"

Marley shrugged.

Joanna shook her head. In a tone half admiring, half exasperated she said, "Of course you would have." Then, "But how could you know he wouldn't realize what you'd done?"

"I couldn't. When I saw him sitting in the water there, I thought of the trick. And I remembered that he'd splashed water—fresh water, from a brook—on himself while he had the diskette stuck down in his waistband: So, perhaps he didn't realize the disk inside the plastic case could be affected. Of course, *water* wouldn't hurt it. It was the salt. But it didn't matter. The deal I offered was to give him the *diskette*. I didn't promise him the *program*."

"You Yankees are shrewder than *anybody*."

"Merely precise."

"Whatever you call it, it's terrific. *You* are terrific. You foiled the villains, saved the program, saved the girl . . ." Joanna paused, her eyes shifting away from Marley to the fire. "Reunited the lovers so they can live happily ever after . . ." The flame in her eyes didn't seem to be reflection.

"Yes."

Then she looked away from the stove. She let her head tip slightly to one side, and her face seemed to soften. "That's nice," she said.

"Yes. I think so."

"He really loves her?"

"Oh, absolutely. In a way—I told you what he said—in a way I'd never quite imagined."

"Do you think she really loves him? She's not just after his money?"

"Yes. I think so." Marley smiled, quickly, ruefully. "Both. I think she loves him for himself, and also she wants to be rich. I think she's a betrayer and she's also tremendously loyal. I think she's selfish and she'll also sacrifice herself for others."

"You like her."

"Yes. Very much. I told her I don't think I'll ever trust her. But I like her. I guess I decided that since both sides of her are real, I shouldn't act toward her on only the basis of the bad one."

"That sounds like Russ."

"I hope you're right."

"My, you seem to have mellowed, James."

"Perhaps I have. I do think I'm not quite so certain that things are either right or wrong, always, under all circumstances." Marley was leaning forward toward the stove, elbows on his knees. He'd turned his head to speak to Joanna. He stayed that way, looking at her steadily.

"Well," she said. Sitting back against the arm of the couch she clinked the ice in her glass, sipped, looked over the rim at him. "The weather report says we may get two feet of snow. You won't be able to get home to Vermont."

"Looks that way," he replied.

"And nobody will go to work tomorrow."

"Roads will be impassable."

"And the kids aren't due back home for two more days."

Marley nodded solemnly, as though noting and filing the information.

Joanna sipped the last of her drink. Marley drained his. She stretched, reaching high first with one arm, then the other, twisting. "Well, then, James," she said, "are you ready for bed?"